Praise fo

'Very topical, terrifying, superb concept for a crime novel.'

Stav Sherez

'A darkly twisted crime novel set in a future world that seems to grow closer every day. Fantastically imaginative and gripping.'

Angela Clarke

'An ingenious and highly plausible look at crime in a future with 100% surveillance.'

Claire McGowan

'Compelling, relevant and chilling. Is this where we're heading?'

Abi Silver

'A techno-thriller with a fantastic premise.'

AK Benedict (City MA)

Jem Tugwell is a crime fiction author with a Crime Writing MA from City University. *Proximity* is his thrilling debut novel, inspired by the fascinating possibilities of technology, AI and the law of unintended consequences. In a past life, Jem had a successful career in investment management, and he now lives in Surrey with his wife. He has two great children and a dog. Outside of his family and writing, Jem's loves are snowboarding, old cars and bikes.

 www.jemtugwell.com

 jem@jemtugwell.com

 @JemTugwell

Proximity

Jem Tugwell

SERPENTINE

BOOKS

First published in Great Britain by Serpentine Books
This edition published in 2019 by
Serpentine Books Limited

www.serpentinebooks.com
info@serpentinebooks.com

A CIP catalogue record for this book is available from the
British Library.

PB ISBN 978 19 1602 230 0
EBOOK ISBN 978 19 1602 231 7

Printed and bound in Great Britain by Clays Ltd,
Elcograf S.p.A.

For Mum and Dad, who never got to see this book, and Rax without whom nothing is possible.

1

Thief

For the first time in ten years, the real me walked free. I savoured every beat of excitement that pulsed through me. All those failures, but now it was working. I let the corners of my mouth drag up an unfamiliar smile. *They* couldn't see me, and what was left of the police force wouldn't even know where to begin.

The smell of cut grass hung in the air and blended with the occasional tantalising floral notes of her perfume. It drew me along; my mind full of the things I would do to her. She was heading home through the quiet streets of Datchet, crossing in all her usual places, but simply following her signal would have been too sterile. The hi-tech soles of her shoes gave a bounce to her stride and set her hair swishing. I wanted to reach out and stroke it.

I craved the proximity.

A car turned into the road, and I ducked behind a tree even though I was hidden from *them*. I waited, but as the self-drive car slid silently past me, I saw that the only person in it had the seat reclined, with their head lolling, mouth open, fast asleep.

The minor delay waiting for the car added to my ache. I had planned to give her a few minutes to settle once she got home, but I couldn't wait. I quickened my pace and closed the gap. I became her shadow, but she didn't feel my darkness behind her.

Karina touched her front door, and it unlocked. I scanned the street but saw only rows of closed doors and wispy trees. I slipped my mask on and stroked her shoulder.

She gasped and span around. I raised my hand and sprayed the liquid into her face. Karina screamed, and her hands clawed at her eyes to stop them burning. I shoved her back into the house and closed the door behind me.

She was mine now. My possession.

2

DI Clive Lussac

The rotating blade snagged, blood spurted, and a finger hit the floor. I paused the video stream I was watching, dragged my feet off the desk, and tipped forward so that my rigid chair dropped back onto all four legs. I yawned and stretched the sluggishness out of my limbs. Today was another day at the office with nothing much to do, so I was half-heartedly trying to get through my backlog of compulsory episodes of *Safety First*. This episode showed how dangerous the old versions of tools used to be. I sighed. These were all the same ones I remembered from my childhood. Not like the ultra-safe new tools, packed with safety sensors and checks that made them nearly impossible to start.

I pressed *'Play'* again and winced. The editors had chosen all the worst examples of people chopping bits off themselves, getting stuff in their eyes, and choking on sawdust. It reminded me of my metalwork teacher swearing at me as I dripped blood onto the floor after yet another cut. I held my hands up towards the screen and wiggled my fingers to show that the old tools hadn't stolen anything that should still be attached.

The show ended with the usual 'we're safer now' messages and statistics on how much money the hospitals saved because they didn't have to treat 'self-inflicted' lifestyle injuries.

I couldn't face another pious episode, so leaving my chair behind, I sauntered down the empty corridor to the office's snack area. The exuberantly muraled vending machine stretched across one wall. As I approached, my embedded iMe device connected with the machine and its synthesised human voice said: 'How can I serve you, Clive?'

I crossed my fingers behind my back. 'Give me some chocolate – a Mars bar.' I spoke slowly and clearly to aid the voice recognition.

'Sorry, Clive, but you still have an Excess Consumption Order and your iMe reports: high blood sugar level. You are already at 59% of your restricted daily calorie allowance and 60% of your saturated fat allowance,' it stated and then added in an upbeat tone. 'Please make another selection.'

I uncrossed my fingers – it never worked, but I had to try. 'Give me a coffee then.'

'Sorry, Clive, but your iMe reports: slightly raised pulse and blood pressure, and high caffeine levels. Please make another selection.'

I banged the glass, 'Just give me the drink, machine.' The *only* reason I had a raised pulse and blood pressure was because these damn things wouldn't do what I wanted.

'Sorry, Clive, but your anger and violence towards me have been marked on your personnel file. I can provide you with water. Please take two glasses as your iMe reports: slightly dehydrated.'

'OK, OK. Give me the bloody water then.' I picked up one cup and took a reluctant sip. I left the other cup in the serving hatch as a show of dissent and unfurled a one-finger salute.

I trudged back along the corridor. My churning resentment of the machines weighed me down. I glanced out at the vivid April morning, but the sun, bright enough to make me squint, cast deep shadows inside me.

***

'Get what you wanted from the machines, sir?' asked DC Zoe Jordan.

She'd been my partner for two weeks. The latest in a long line of officers forced to rotate through the Proximity Crime Unit. Her hair was a shade darker brown than her eyes and seemed wilfully stubborn. She pushed a piece behind her ear, but it flounced back to its original position, like a sulky teenager dropping into a chair.

'Of course not,' I grunted as I slumped into a chair.

Looking at her, I was painfully aware of every one of the twenty-five years between us and every wrinkle on my face. Our clothes summed the pair of us up perfectly: my black trousers were slightly grubby, creased and worn; her colourful suit gleamed new with an elegant, crisp collar.

'And I've told you before, Zoe – Clive or Boss. There's only two of us.'

'Sure… Boss,' she said.

Her carefree smile brightened the room around her, especially when she flashed her teeth. Like with everyone under thirty, they were glaringly white. I felt all gaunt and washed-out next to her, just like when I stood under the harsh, over-bright lights above my sink.

'You enjoying PCU so far, Zoe?'

Her curt nod seemed to say yes, but her compressed smile disagreed.

'It wasn't always *this* bad.' My hand traced the office. While the Cyber Crime department lorded it up in the glamorous New Scotland Yard offices, we were always on the move. Always to somewhere smaller and cheaper. Currently, PCU existed on the ground floor of an architectural experiment in concrete on a shabby corner of the Slough Industrial Estate.

'So, what was it like?'

'Frantic. We did everything before they got named Proximity Crimes: theft, assault, muggings, murder – the lot. Used to be loads of us. Now…' My voice trailed away as I remembered the faces of colleagues long gone. Of the fifty or so desks in the PCU office, only four were ever occupied. Even the cleaners barely bothered anymore, and a film of dust covered the unused desks.

'It's not as nice as my old office at Cyber,' she said, as though forcing herself to find a negative.

Outside, the high wall had been built too close to the windows. It blocked most of the natural light, so the buzzing fluorescent tubes were on all day. The longest side of the office housed the main display wall. Left alone, its flickering glow bounced across our desks as it paraded an endless stream of scrolling health and safety warnings. I groaned as the instructions on how to avoid back damage when tying your shoelaces were replaced by an animated film explaining the mandatory use of the handrail on the stairs.

'Now people put up with their three months here while dreaming of going back to Cyber or Anti-Terrorism. No one stays.' My voice echoed in the empty space.

She nodded. Then stopped herself. 'Why's that, Boss?'

'You know why. You've only just got here, and you already know PCU's Four-Step Modern Police Procedure: receive a report; drag it into the Monitor software; wait to be given a list of the people who were there; then send the list to Uniform to arrest them.' I sighed my regret, conscious of how much my job had changed.

'But weren't you the first person to get iMe used in policing?'

'Don't rub it in. I only wanted to be able to prove who was at the crime scene. I didn't mean to get all of my mates sacked.' Part of me still believed my decision was right. Bringing iMe into policing had helped people, saved people even, but I hadn't thought through the consequences. It had ruined my dream job.

'But everyone's healthier and safer now. It's a good thing.' She looked away from my shaking head. 'There's a software upgrade soon. Sounds great: security updates, extra allergy checks and more heart monitoring.'

'Yeah, fantastic.'

'You want anything from the machines before it starts?'

'No thanks. I can't take another domestic with an appliance.' I paused. 'Unless you want to use some of your allowance to get me a Mars bar?'

'What? Of course not.' She glowered at me. 'I'll get some water for both of us.'

I fiddled around on my HUD while she was gone. The HUD, more formally called a Head-Up Display, was the only good feature of iMe. It made it look like there was a screen a metre from your eyes. With voice control or a virtual keyboard, it was easy to use and securely integrated calls, mail, banking, browsing and apps. You had everything you could ever need. Anywhere, anytime.

I pinched my fingers in front of me to pick up a message icon from my HUD screen and threw it towards my face. On the screen, the icon grew and morphed into the actual text. I skimmed over it, but it was another reminder about the upgrade.

A few minutes later Zoe came back with two bio-plastic cups of water that she placed on either side of the chipped veneer desk. 'It'll start in a second,' she said, and found a chair. I preferred to stand.

The upgrade began with a slight heat in the back of my neck, then a growing high-frequency vibration. My ears filled with static that I endured for the next thirty seconds. I had my hand on the back of my neck, and my head tipped to one side. People said I looked like a cross between a meerkat and a puzzled dog. Zoe upgraded with the tranquillity and elegance of a meditating Buddhist monk.

I scowled as the iMe logo and slogan appeared on my HUD screen: *Enabling a better you*.

3

Thief

The faint hum of all the hidden electronics couldn't drown out Karina's crying. The metal walls and painted white floor of the room shone with newness. I'd chosen the finish to be easy to wipe clean and sterilise. A wall of prison bars split the space in two, I clanged its door open and stepped in the cage.

'Why?' she sobbed, 'why me?' She pressed herself further into the corner and brought her knees up to her chest to form a defensive barrier.

With her head down and her chin on her chest, it left me staring at her almost vertical centre parting. Her bobbed hair dropped forward like two auburn curtains, hiding her face. I could feel the sweat under my mask, and I ran my hand through my hair. It felt lank and greasy.

'Does it matter why?'

'What? Let me go. I... I won't tell anyone.' She looked up and stared straight at me – little specks of gold and blue visible amongst the pale green of her eyes. She was a pretty thing, even in the baggy T-shirt and shorts I had given her for the night-time and the dry, little patterns of fear left by her tears and mascara. 'They'll find me anyway.'

I could feel her spirit. It would take time to break her.

'I can't let you go – you're mine now.' Then, as much to myself as her, 'I'm committed.'

Her eyes dropped, and the room seemed darker. She muttered another 'Why me?'

'That's the wrong question.'

Her head came up a bit. I could almost hear her thinking, but it only resulted in another 'Why?'

'You're better than that, Karina. I'll give you a hint…
How long have you been here?'

She tried to work it out, and then her eyes flashed with
comprehension and hope as she nodded her head. 'The
police must see where I am. They'll come straight here and
rescue me. They'll get you.'

'There you go. Right thought process – wrong
conclusion.' My head shook in contradiction. 'Your
boyfriend's been home all night. He'll be worried about
you. He'll have called you, got no answer, and then paid
for a trace. Your signal should have brought them straight
here.'

The hope drained from her face as she thought it
through. 'They should have found me by now.'

'Exactly.' I looked deep into her eyes. 'It's just you and
me.'

As I turned the lights off, I heard Karina gasp at the
sudden blackness of the room. 'Why are you doing this?'

'The far more interesting question is *how*.'

4

DI Clive Lussac

My life looped around again as another lonely night rolled into a tedious day. PCU's workload didn't stretch one person, let alone two. As Zoe knew what to do, I left her to it and drifted.

Shit. Mary. We'd been rocky for ages, and it never helped when she said I didn't listen to her. I hadn't ever consciously not listened, my mind simply drifted off, and I stopped hearing her.

But the truth lay under the *'iMe Status'* button on my HUD. I clicked it and a small figure, my Buddy, ran along the bottom of my screen trailing a banner saying *'Active Excess Consumption Order. No deviations to Model allowed'.* Buddy shook his head and gave me a double thumbs-down.

Mary's eyes, the angle of her hips and her arms across her chest had screamed that getting my second Excess Consumption Order and being marched off to another Risk Awareness Training course instead of taking her to dinner on her birthday was the end of my marriage. Separate flats and separate lives.

I opened the report of my deviations to the Model Citizen. Each coloured bar in the report showed my performance against a category defined in the Model and was meant to be solid, conformant green: exercise, sleep, drugs, blood pressure, fat, calories, etc. You were allowed a small amber tip where you were outside the Model, but still inside your Freedom Units allowance. The allowance gave the pretence of free will and choice and let you decide where you yielded to temptation. At least today, my report didn't flash red all over like an overly-decorated house at Christmas. Buddy looked a little happier now.

I smiled. The idiots in the Ministry of Well-being and Health hadn't thought through the name Freedom Units. Everyone called them FUs and every time I used the acronym, I was thinking, *Fuck You, Well-being and Health.* I was defiant – but losing the battle.

An Incident flashed up on my HUD, and I looked up when Zoe didn't deal with it. She wasn't at her desk, and I hadn't even noticed.

Having no choice, I did some work.

It was a simple domestic violence case. Uniform had attended a flat where a woman had been assaulted, and they needed confirmation that her husband was with her at the time. The Incident contained links to both people, as well as the location and the date and time of the assault. I picked up the whole Incident with my pinched fingers and dropped it into the Monitor window on my HUD. I selected the period thirty minutes before the time of the assault and pressed *'Search'*. This time, Buddy trailed out a banner that said *'Searching'*. After a couple of seconds, he packed the banner away, threw the search results onto my HUD screen and scampered off.

The results opened and showed two dots overlaid on a floor plan of the flat: The woman's dot was in the lounge, her husband's in the kitchen. The husband's dot moved around the kitchen as I fast-forwarded. The dot for the woman stayed still, then she moved to the kitchen and stopped in the doorway. After about twenty seconds, the man's dot rushed to the woman's, they circled a few times and the man's dot left. The woman's dot didn't move again.

Proof enough for a conviction. I sent the history trace back to Uniform and leaned back.

Modern policing – no thought needed.

5

DC Zoe Jordan

I missed Cyber. Two years on the front line of policing replaced by this compulsory rotation. It was bad enough that I had to come to PCU at all, but three months with next to no work and a grumpy boss would be a real test of my endurance.

I got back to my desk. Passing the time would be easier if I could find a personal connection to Clive, so I tried to get the conversation going again, but the words crossed to the other side and wilted. We were separated by age and outlook more than the furniture. My side of the desk was sunny, but his was in dark shade.

I tried again. 'What made you join the police, Boss?'

'God, that was a long time ago.' He looked up at me.

I smiled, encouraging him to continue.

'I'm a bit embarrassed to say.' Clive clasped his hands and circled his thumbs, trying to hide behind the action.

'Go on.' I flashed another smile and paused to nudge him on.

'Well, er, I guess I wanted to catch crooks and stop murders.'

'You have.'

'Maybe, but there's a downside.'

'How do you mean?'

He shrugged, 'I know it's wrong, but I kind of miss them.'

'You can't mean that?' Shock loosened my jaw, and my mouth flopped open. It took a few seconds to recover. 'That would mean someone innocent has died.' *How can he even think that way?*

'Yes, I know. But I miss… the challenge, solving the puzzle. You know, to feel useful.'

My forehead furrowed. Simple to solve crimes were a good thing. Why would you want it to be hard? 'You want people to die, so you feel *useful?*'

'Obviously not.' I had backed him into a corner. 'There's *nothing* to do.'

'So, apply to Cyber.'

I thought I could see his eyes water, so I looked away. In the fading light outside the grimy window, I could still make out the outlines of the graffiti on the wall.

'They said I was too out of touch,' he whispered, then louder, he added, 'I can't take every aspect of my life being micro-managed.'

'But that's nothing to do with work. That's to make your life healthier.'

He seemed to want to go back to the gluttonous, lazy chaos of before iMe. Why couldn't he embrace the positives? Didn't he want to live longer?

I tried to hide the hardness of my expression, and the words 'suck it up' almost escaped, but I put a brake on my mouth before my thoughts came out. 'Don't forget all the good you've done, Boss.'

'Yes, I guess, but I need to use my brain again before I can't remember what day it is.'

***

As the motion-detectors of the outlying office lights clicked off, we huddled in the small island of light over our desks, and the sea of darkness pressed in around us. It was nearly six, and then I could go home. Clive looked like he was drilling down, deeper and darker. Each unhealthy thought feeding the next. I could almost feel the cloud over him. Why couldn't he see that not having much work was a good thing? It meant that people were safe.

The bing of the new report arriving interrupted me. I picked it up and read it.

'No way!' I said.

Clive ignored me.

'Boss. Boss?'

He shook himself loose and came back up. 'What?'

'I've got a Missing Person report.'

'What? That's impossible.'

6

DI Clive Lussac

I stared at Zoe. 'We haven't had anyone missing since the beginning. Ten years now.'

'That's what I thought... but I've got someone called Karina Morgan reported missing. I can't see her signal.'

'It's a mistake, she'll have a signal,' I said. 'Run the signal trace again.'

'I've already run the trace three times – all with the same result.'

My shoulders dropped in disappointment. Surely Zoe could handle something as simple as this?

'Let me look,' I said. 'Throw your HUD at the display wall.'

She bunched her fingers together to 'grab' her screen and used a flick of her wrist to throw it at the display wall nearest us.

The scrolling health and safety warnings on the wall stopped. I sneered at the frozen message about wearing anti-cut gloves when chopping vegetables. According to the Ministry of Well-being and Health, *'One Risk is a Risk Too Many'.*

The wall blinked and showed a duplicate of Zoe's HUD. I lumbered up with all the grace of an arthritic bear and walked past Zoe's side of the desk to the wall.

'Give me control, Zoe.'

I watched the cursor on the wall as she moved her hands in front of her face and selected an item from the menu. 'Ready,' she said.

I pinched the Missing Person report on the wall with my fingers and dragged it to the Monitor window. I looked at Zoe and made an exaggerated show of dropping the report, so she could see how to do it properly. As we were looking at Zoe's HUD, her Buddy rolled out the *'Searching'* banner. I waited, but her Buddy removed the banner and unrolled a new one that I had never seen before – *'Error: No Signal'*. Zoe's Buddy gave a disappointed shrug and ran off.

Weird. I picked up and dropped the report again, and again, repeating the search, trying to make it work. Each time Zoe's Buddy rolled out the error banner.

'This makes no sense. Can you check with support?'

Zoe gave me an *I told you so* look, said, 'Call iMe Tech Support,' and touched her jaw. I heard the call ring through the speaker in the wall.

'Tech Support, this is Rob,' the voice said.

'Hi, Rob, this is DC Zoe Jordan at PCU. I got a Missing Person report on Karina Morgan, and I'm getting a No Signal error when I search.'

'Hi, Zoe. I saw the No Signal alert. We're checking, but we think it's a bug in the signal database not returning the data.'

'So, nothing to worry about?'

'No, Karina will be wherever she normally is. She must have signal data, you know that.'

'Sure, we'll park it then. Thanks, Rob.'

'Later,' Rob said, and the call dropped.

'It's nothing,' I said, and headed back to my desk.

Before I made it, I heard an incoming call. 'PCU,' Zoe said.

Her HUD was still mirrored onto the wall, so I could hear the panicked voice.

'Hello. I reported my girlfriend missing, and nothing's happened. She's still not back. I can't find her.' He spoke so fast his words ran together. 'You need to help me.'

7

Thief

I had chosen a classic for today's look, and the little black dress waited on the hanger for Karina's body.

She turned her head to me, but I saw only half of the Karina from last night, as if she had a dimmer switch and it was turned down. 'Why are you doing this?'

I settled on the bed next to her and took her hand.

'Why? Honestly, Karina, that again?' I sighed. 'If I explain why I stole you, you're not going to say, "OK, I understand, crack on", are you?'

Squeezing her hand, I stood. 'I've got to go to work now, but I'll be back later for more games.'

She flinched and looked worried, almost as if being alone here was worse than being with me.

'Your clothes are there. Food's in the cupboard – easy to open stuff to get you through the day.' I slid my hand to the shackle on her wrist and made a small 'O' with my fingers, using it to follow the heavy chain from her wrist, to the large eyelet set into the wall. I could have gone for a light carbon fibre rope, but there was something more dramatic in the weight and bulk of the chain, something more gothic. Best of all, it rattled as my hand passed over it. From the wall, the chain dropped straight to the floor where it pooled like a fat, sleeping snake, its tail secured to the floor. 'There's enough chain for you to get to the toilet, shower, and the food.'

She grunted and pulled on the chain, 'Let me fucking *go.*'

'Feel free to try to escape, but I've been planning this a long time. You can make all the noise you want, but no one will hear you.'

In my reflection in the wall, I looked calm and in control, but I was buzzing inside. *Finally, finally.*

Maybe my psychiatrist, Dr Owen, hadn't lied after all. 'If you can't control your own life, find things you can control,' he had said. Deep down, I knew that Karina wasn't what he meant, but then again, he'd never given any specific advice. He was full of vague generalisations and clichés that didn't mean anything, so this was his fault.

'Shower and get changed.' I patted the towel and underwear to make it clear. 'Don't make me cross with you.'

Karina stood frozen – a small statue of terror.

I stood and went back outside of the bars, then turned the key to lock the cage door. I removed the key, slipped my finger through its handle and swung it around my finger. I left the room, shutting the outer door with a dull thud and turning the wheel after me. Bolts on the sides and top slid across the opening to nestle into their matching clamps. I turned to the monitor, lifted my mask with relief, watching her for a while, and then pressed the intercom.

'That dress suits you.'

Karina's head jerked from side to side, her eyes searching the walls of the room. 'You're sick. Are you watching me shower and on the toilet?'

'Trust me, I've no interest in you using the toilet.' I watched her for a moment. 'Bye, Karina.'

Her eyes hunted for the cameras.

***

When I got home from work, I enjoyed some playtime with Karina and put her to bed. Afterwards, I replayed her day. I skipped through the boring bits – her life flashed by in jerky, thirty times normal speed.

Watching live was better, even when she was sleeping. She knew about the cameras, but she wouldn't know if I was here.

'Karina,' I said, finger on the intercom. 'Karina.'

I waited as the sleepy figure stirred, and I brought the lights up gradually. She looked pretty in the white nightie I'd given her. The floaty material's sheen brightened under the lights, and I could see the little pink bow in the centre of her chest.

'There's something I want you to do for me,' I said.

8

DI Clive Lussac

Karina being missing with no signal was obviously some sort of technical fault, but Zoe and I settled into the car. 'Let's go,' I said. It would be a fool's errand, but better than sitting alone in my flat.

Zoe said, 'Car... Destination... Karina Morgan's home.' The car confirmed the address and the screen between us redrew to show us a house in Datchet.

I passed the journey staring out of the window, watching the dark evening chase the last patch of bright sky away. I huffed breath onto the car's window, creating a small condensation circle. I drew a sad face in it. iMe would fix the bug, and I could go home.

'What are you thinking, Boss?' Zoe asked.

'It's going to be a waste of time. iMe coverage has been 100% for years now. There's no way she can be missing.'

'Her boyfriend sounded upset, and she isn't at home. So, where is she?'

I studied the photo of Karina from her Ministry of Well-being and Health profile – sparkling grass-green eyes, auburn hair and an expression that hinted at mischief and fun. 'She'll be out enjoying herself and her boyfriend's upset.'

'But why no signal?'

Zoe sounded shocked, and a little rattled, so I tried for a supportive smile. She must have been about fourteen when iMe was made mandatory and defined how she behaved. I shuddered; the implant process had been bad enough for me, let alone a kid.

'Don't know. Dead or alive, you still have a signal. They know where everyone is. You can't be *missing*.'

'What are we going to do?'

I watched the constant clasping of her hands. She had no pre-iMe adult experience to fall back on, and I wondered if the threat of a problem with the system was getting to her.

'Don't worry. While iMe resolves the issue, we'll rely on old procedures and start by talking to the boyfriend. We'll ask about Karina's life, routine and where she works.'

I turned back to the window and saw rivulets of water running from the bottom of the mouth I had drawn in the condensation.

***

If I had written a list of the unlikely boyfriends for Karina, Dave would have been at the top. Six feet two inches but beanpole thin, he had loops of skin hanging under his earlobes from stretchers he no longer wore. I couldn't be bothered to count all his piercings or the multitude of tattoos.

Dave looked really agitated, so I let Zoe start the questioning. I paced around the room, looking for anything out of the ordinary. It had the usual projection wall, but its sleek frame-less sheen looked strange against the plastic floral wall wrap. Fashion went in cycles I knew, but I didn't get this look. My grandma's old wallpaper was similar, and we had papered over that for her.

Dave looked up to address the building's control system. 'House... Blinds... Night-time,' he said, and the glass of the room's windows blackened, hiding the small patch of grass outside, and a cityscape of St Paul's Cathedral at night faded in.

'What does Karina do?' she asked.

'She designs Sentiments... in Windsor.'

I nodded. Lots of people used them on their iMe, but my Sentiments were permanently disabled. Why would you want to share a little graphical character that automatically showed your current mood? Feelings were too personal to make public.

'You've got to find her,' Dave added. 'She can't be missing.'

'Don't worry, Dave, we will,' Zoe said brightly, trying to show him some hope. 'So why didn't she work from home?'

'She used to, but the isolation got to her, and she likes to people watch. She gets inspiration from seeing people's faces and body language. She says it helps her Sentiments look more real.'

'And Karina always came home at the same time?'

'Yeah, usually home by six, unless she has a networking event... where is she?' Dave said, sounding close to tears.

Dave pushed his palms over his eyes and pushed his fingers into the hair over his forehead. He circled his hands a couple of times before removing them. I wondered if this was to hide the tears or if he couldn't cope with the uncertainty. Karina's location should have been a couple of clicks on his HUD away.

'What sort of networking event?' I asked.

'They're arranged every month by the iMe company for people who design things for them. You know, technical briefings, new versions, that sort of shit.'

'Was there an event tonight? Could she be at iMe?'

'No.'

'So, she should've been at home?'

'Yes, but she wasn't here when I got back from work.' Dave wiped his eyes with the back of a hand again.

'You work?' I couldn't help myself.

Dave stared, clearly pissed off, but used to the conclusions people of my age jumped to based on his appearance. 'Yeah, why wouldn't I?'

'Somewhere local? A warehouse?'

'No, I work in London,' he said, 'I'm a senior partner at InfoTech Marketing. We do all the big media streaming firms.' Now his eyes challenged me, and I shelved some of my preconceptions.

Zoe cut in to smooth things along, and Dave talked her through the details of Karina's workplace, commute and schedule. 'No sign of damage or a struggle?'

'Nothing. I phoned her friends, her work – nothing. I paid for a signal trace but only got an empty report. I shouted at iMe and then called you. What's going on?'

'It's a simple technical issue. Nothing to worry about.'

'Yeah, that's what they said. But if her signal's gone, how's she going to get home? I mean, she won't be able to pay for anything or even get a cab.'

'She must have a signal, mustn't she?' I said, trying to keep the *dur, stupid* undertone out of my voice. 'iMe think it's the reporting of her tracking signal that's got an issue. Her iMe's close proximity functions will still work. She'll still be able to use TouchToPay,' I said this with certainty based on no knowledge whatsoever. 'Don't worry, we'll find her. She can't have got far.'

As we headed out of the house, Zoe paused by the front door, and rubbed at some discoloured specks on the wall.

'Why can't cleaners use sprays properly?' she said.

9

DI Clive Lussac

On the journey back, it struck me that in the old days I would have been researching Dave and Karina and not staring out of the window. Better late than never, I flicked through the images Dave had sent of his girlfriend. She was more beautiful than in her government profile photos. I still couldn't put her together with Dave, but she obviously saw something in him. Perhaps it was like art: where someone's brilliant is another person's rubbish that a child could have painted. If Dave could be with Karina, then I had some hope for my barren love life.

The ringtone buzzed in my ear, and I checked the caller ID on my HUD: DCS Bhatt. The ringtone continued. I couldn't ignore my boss, so I touched my jaw to answer the call. With a physical phone, I could have held it away from my ear to lessen the impact of the verbal stream of disapproval coming at me, but when it's in your head, you have to take it at full volume.

'Yes, ma'am,' was all I could manage. 'Right away,' and the call ended.

'We're in the shit, Zoe. Bhatt wants us now.'

***

Bhatt made us wait outside for a few minutes after I knocked. Was she busy, or was this delay to emphasise her annoyance at something we had done? Either way, when we shuffled in, we were two nervous school kids before the head teacher.

'Sit,' Bhatt said, without looking up. We did as we were told and waited. Instead of speaking, she stood, still not looking at us, and crossed to a small wash area in the corner of her office. She put her hands into the clear tubes. Soapy water swirled up, covering her hands before being sucked away. The noisy blast of drying air ruffled her sleeves.

Back in her desk chair, she re-straightened the cuffs of her immaculate white blouse. Bhatt and I went back a long way, and I'd never seen her without her black hair held back in a tidy ponytail. In an unguarded moment, waiting in the rain in some stakeout or other years ago, she'd told me that it was because she was Indian and female fighting her way up in the police. She said she couldn't afford to show anything that senior ranks might misconstrue as feminine 'weakness'. She was a supportive, good boss, but God help you if you cocked up.

'Tell me you've solved it, Clive,' she said, as always not interested in skirting around the subject. 'Tell me you've found Karina Morgan.'

'You're taking it seriously?'

Bhatt stared at me, eyebrows raised. Inviting me to dig myself further into a hole.

'But, ma'am, it's a technical–'

Bhatt's finger went up to silence me. 'I'll pretend that you didn't say that. Have you found Karina Morgan?'

'Um, no. Sorry.'

'Sorry isn't good enough on this.'

'It's a missing person,' said Zoe, trying to come to my defence.

Bhatt glared at her until Zoe dropped her eyes to the carpet. 'DC Jordan, this is the first time we've worked together, so I will make some allowances, but don't interrupt me again unless it's to tell me you've found her.'

'Yes, ma'am.'

'Clive, where have you got to?' Bhatt said.

My mind turned at the speed of a drill with a flat battery. 'Well,' I said, trying to buy some thinking time. 'There are no tracks and no signal.'

Bhatt looked furious. 'That's it. That's all you've got?'

'But… it shouldn't happen.' I faltered, and Zoe protected me by throwing a graph onto Bhatt's display wall. It was simple, showing signal strength on the left side, and time along the bottom. My eyes followed the green line showing Karina's signal strength was at a solid 100% for most of the day. Then, at 17:37, her signal crashed vertically down to 0%, where it stayed.

'We went to Karina's home and interviewed her boyfriend,' Zoe said. 'He said that he didn't see any mess or sign of a struggle at all.'

'Do you believe him?' Bhatt asked.

'He seemed to be telling the truth. He appeared concerned about Karina, but it could be an act,' Zoe offered.

I said, 'But if Dave's done something to Karina, how could he hide her signal? He's in marketing – he's not technical enough.'

'What else could it be?' Bhatt said.

Zoe shrugged. 'iMe Tech Support says they haven't found a bug… but there must be one. Otherwise we'd have a signal.'

I didn't get it either. 'Zoe's right. We're being told there is no problem, but we don't know where Karina is. So, by definition, that's a problem.' I churned the dilemma around. 'We've always been assured that a technical fault is impossible,' I said. 'It would undermine the whole integrity of the system.'

'But it's more likely than someone working out how to hide Karina's signal,' Zoe said. 'It's iMe we're talking about, all that encryption and technology. It's so secure, where would you start?'

Bhatt held one finger up to show she wanted some thinking time. We waited. Zoe's eyes were back looking at the grey carpet. I joined her and saw a multitude of small spots and marks that showed the carpet's age and told of a hard life.

'So, you agree that we have two scenarios: one is an unexpected technical fault, which is unlikely; the second, even more unlikely, is that Karina really is missing, and someone has hacked the system.' Bhatt seemed pleased that she had led us to a conclusion.

'Yes,' was my only embarrassing contribution.

'And neither scenario is good. In fact, both scenarios are a potential disaster. When the press finds out, there'll be a huge storm. People panicking about their money and security.' Bhatt's tone changed, emphasising every word to make sure we got the message. 'It's already political, so I need you two,' she paused to stare at us, 'to solve it quickly. Do I make myself clear?'

'Yes, ma'am,' Zoe and I said in unison.

'We need to keep it quiet, so don't talk about this to anyone other than me, OK?'

Another stereo, 'Yes, ma'am.'

'I'll get you in to see Art Walker tomorrow morning.'

'Wow, the head of iMe?' Zoe said.

'Yes,' Bhatt glared at Zoe for daring to say something unprompted. 'Art will know what's really going on. You need to get him to tell you if it's a technical fault or not, without being fobbed off with the corporate, *there's no problem* line.'

'You called him Art,' I said. 'You know him personally?'

Bhatt looked like it was the most natural thing to know one of the most powerful men in the country and call him by his first name. 'Oh, we've met a few times.'

'And you can get us space in his diary at short notice?'

She smiled. Of course she could.

'So, what now?' I said.

'Last time I looked, Clive, you were meant to be a detective inspector. Go and do your job.'

10

Thief

'I'm sorry, Karina, things aren't working out between us.'

'Why?'

Her favourite word again.

She had tried so hard, been so positive and upbeat. Everything I'd asked of her, she'd done. She'd worn what I'd given her, played every game and obeyed my every command.

'You've been great, but I need something else.'

'But I've done everything you asked.' She was getting anxious. 'You know… *everything.*'

Everything had been good. 'I know.'

I thought this level of control would be enough for me. Sadly, for Karina, getting what I wanted wasn't the same as getting what I needed. It was too easy, and she was too perfect. It didn't address the real issue.

'And we've been good together,' she said.

She had played the role of captive well, but she must have rationalised that conflict and argument wouldn't help. She smiled and feigned enjoyment. She was good, convincing almost, but it was just Stockholm syndrome. Any psychological alliance she showed me was a survival strategy. She was doing what she needed to get through each day.

'I know. I'm going to have to let you go.'

She smiled and then frowned, trying to work out what I meant. 'Really? Let me go?' She ended with a smile.

'I've loved having you here, but I need the space.'

'You said that you couldn't let me go… couldn't take the risk.'

'I know, but I've been thinking about that. You've no idea where you are and haven't seen my face.'

'That's true, I haven't,' she said, willing her enthusiasm to sway the argument. 'Anyway, I don't know anything.'

'I'm planning to leave you in Windsor Great Park. You promise that you won't tell the police about me?'

'I won't tell. Please let me go.' Her eyes pleaded with me like a dog begging for food.

'OK. We both need to move on,' I said.

She beamed and looked around the metal room and the cage. I don't think she ever expected to leave. She collapsed back onto the bed and sobbed as the relief and hope came welling up.

She thought she had a future.

11

DI Clive Lussac

Bhatt hadn't been able to get us an appointment in Art Walker's diary before late afternoon the next day and, even then, we had been made to wait twenty-five minutes in reception. I was fidgety and frustrated. Every step away from the front desk towards Art's office made my mood worse, as my rubber-soled shoes squeaked like I was being shadowed by a vocal mouse. I could sense the assistant's annoyance. Zoe dropped a pace behind me so that I wouldn't see her fighting to control her laughter.

'Please wait in Mr Walker's office,' the assistant said. 'He will be with you presently.'

Thankfully the carpet of the office muffled the mouse sounds, and I walked into the centre of the room. The hush was broken only by the click of the door closing.

'Interesting room.' Zoe circled, taking it all in, crushing the thick carpets. A new side table, still with its label boasting that it was made from recycled veneer, was placed by the door. Art had dedicated one whole wall to a disturbing display of photos of himself. The room's confusion of styles was crowned by a six-foot marble water feature that gargled in the corner, gold cherubs spouting jets into the air.

Zoe's hair was its normal wild self, but she hadn't conformed with my order yesterday to 'be smart'. The black skirt, cut below the knee, was formal, but her vibrant green shirt was so bright. It wasn't appropriate, but it was too late now. My 'smart' suit was overdue a trip to the

31

cleaners, and the backs of my trousers looked like a bad case of crow's feet wrinkles.

'I was expecting hi-tech gadgets and modern furniture. Not... this,' I said.

'I know, right?'

I touched one of the high-backed chairs that were facing the desk. The burgundy leather looked a little distressed but was wonderfully soft and supple. 'They're made to look old.' I loved the smell – it reminded me of a new car from years ago, before everything went faux.

Zoe rubbed her hand on the arm of the other chair. 'Wow, super soft. They must have cost loads.'

'It's not like iMe can't afford it,' I said, my anger returning. 'Art making us wait like this is emphasising his importance and that we're only the police. He's saying we don't matter to him.'

'He's basically in charge of everything, Boss, so you can't be surprised if he's a bit late. And the meeting was arranged at the last minute.'

'If he thinks he's above the law just because—' The door opening broke my rant before it really got started.

The man was instantly recognisable, even if he did look about five inches shorter than he did on the TV. Although his hair was short, black and clean, something in his manner made me think of slick hair oil.

'Art Walker, sorry to keep you.' He sauntered to his desk. Definitely not apologetic. His immaculate suit was complemented by a sombre tie and a sly smile. 'I was with the prime minister.'

I introduced Zoe and myself. Second nature made me hunt through my pockets and dig out an old business card that was as crumpled as my suit. I held it out towards Art, but he smirked and left my hand dangling. Shaking his head, he said, 'Exchange contact details.' His ID flashed up on my HUD.

I dropped the card on his desk. 'I believe Chief Superintendent Bhatt called you yesterday.'

Art fussed with the adjustments on his techno-chair as we slipped into the high-backed ones. He must have set his chair high because he was able to look down his nose at me. 'Nisha did call me. She said something important had come up. That's why I agreed to squeeze you in.'

'We're here to ask about Ms Karina Morgan. She's missing.'

Art rubbed his hand over his mouth and chin. 'Why would an old case be important now?'

'No, this is current. She went missing yesterday.'

Art stared above our heads at the wall covered by his photos. 'That's simply not possible.'

I looked at Zoe. 'Karina Morgan, female, mid-twenties. She works as a Sentiment designer. Her boyfriend reported her missing when he got home after work yesterday,' she said.

'You should track her. My staff can help you if it's too difficult.' He started to rise as if to leave.

Did this guy think we hadn't tracked her? 'Obviously, we've done that.' A little sarcasm in my voice. 'That's why we need to talk to you.'

'Why?' He lowered himself back down again.

Zoe glanced at her notebook. 'Her signal tracks lead to her home. She did her usual commute: train then walk then home. Same route every day. Her signal stopped at 17:37 at her home, but she wasn't there. We have no idea where she is.'

'Stopped, as in went red?' Art asked.

'No, her body would have been at her house. The signal just dropped to 0%,' I said.

'That's not possible.' Art gave a dismissive flick of his arm. 'The signal can't drop. Tech Support would have known.'

'Zoe talked to Tech Support. They got a No Signal alert, but they couldn't contact Ms Morgan and said that nobody else was at her house.'

Zoe nodded. 'Her vital signs were all normal to the end of the signal. Pulse and breathing spiked a bit high, but she showed no alcohol or drugs. No risks taken.'

'As I said, it's not possible.' Art smiled again but with a reptilian coldness in his eyes. 'The tracking signal doesn't fail.'

What's he hiding? 'You're saying you've never had a problem? All tech has glitches now and then.'

The smile stayed fixed, but he bristled against the questioning. *I bet he doesn't get challenged very often.* 'We had a few issues in the early days. But not now.'

'Really, what about two years ago? You know, version eleven – the hot spot version.' I rubbed my neck at the memory – it had taken weeks for the burn to heal.

'We fixed that inside a day.' His smile was gone, leaving a cold glare from his eyes. 'Our processes and people have changed since then. Everything's tightly controlled now.'

'How?'

'Our test procedures were found to be deficient, so we changed things. Emma is much more rigorous. Very different, very thorough.'

'Emma who?' I said.

'Emma Bailey. She's our test manager.'

I typed the name into the notes section on my HUD for us to follow up on later. A quick scribble in my old notebook would have been much less intrusive than my fingers waving in the air tapping invisible keys on my virtual keyboard, but I had tried to move with the times. Just a little anyway, and it meant that the note auto-synchronised to Zoe.

'But you still have programmers – they must make coding errors.'

'If they do make mistakes, Emma catches them.'

'So how can we have a missing person?'

'Isn't that your job to find out?'

'Yes, but the system has to work for us to do that.'

His face started to flush. 'It does work.' He paused, trying to control his voice. 'It's made life better.'

It sounded like the beginning of one of his corporate speeches, but before he could get going, Zoe said, 'I love the convenience.'

Art smiled at her. 'Me too.'

I snorted. 'It's not perfect. Your form of convenience is really control, and if I'm controlled, then I've lost my personal freedom.'

'Ah, you're a libertarian.' He dragged his eyes from Zoe and back to me. 'Did the obese celebrate the freedom to eat themselves to death? Did the drinkers appreciate their livers failing? I don't think so.' He switched to his sincere CEO face to deliver the familiar message. 'It was our responsibility to eradicate those problems. People weren't going to change themselves, but defining and controlling their behaviour against the Model Citizen through iMe has been extremely effective.'

Yeah, yeah, yeah. This was always the argument: the state knows what's best for you. You had to conform to the Model Citizen or pay the price. I hated the constant comparison to the set of perfect behaviours defined by the Model. How can eating chocolate be defined as a high-risk activity?

'Enabling a better you,' I muttered the iMe slogan.

Art nodded sincerely. 'Exactly. People need help. And look at the health benefits.'

iMe wasn't helping my mental health. 'We're not here for a lecture,' I scowled at Zoe. She had taken us away from the real topic. I wondered if that was what Art intended.

I paused, trying to regroup. 'So, you're saying that it's impossible not to be tracked. What about a soldier? You wouldn't want an enemy tracking our soldiers, would you?'

'That's not the same as your civilian Sentiment designer.'

'So, there is a way?'

'Not for a civilian. Not for your person.'

'But it can be done? For someone who's not a civilian. How does it work?'

He paused, considering. 'Confidentially, for people of strategic importance, their tracks can be concealed from the public.'

'How?'

'That's classified.'

'But there is a method for soldiers?' His obstructiveness was pissing me off, and I wanted a reaction. 'And for celebs who pay enough?'

Art stared at me, his frown pushing the ends of his eyebrows down, trying to intimidate. 'Don't push your luck, Inspector. You already know that I'm not without influence with your superiors.'

I could do without another bollocking from Bhatt. 'I'm only repeating a rumour. I was only asking if it were possible that my missing person's tracks could be hidden.'

He stood and waved a dismissive arm at the door. 'I've wasted enough time on this. I have another meeting.'

I wasn't getting anywhere with the confrontational approach, so I tried a gentler line. 'We need help here – since iMe, we've never had a person we couldn't track.'

Art's eyebrows straightened, and his face softened a fraction. 'You can send a formal request for an encrypted signal check. Just to remove any doubt. I'll approve it.'

'What's an encrypted signal check?'

'Just send it to Tech Support. You won't be authorised to see any detail. You'll get a simple yes or no. But it won't help you.'

***

Back in the car, Zoe and I faced each other over the tabletop screen. 'Let's send that encrypted signal request now,' I said.

'Do you know what it is?' She threw her HUD screen at the screen so that I could see what she was doing.

'No idea. But there's obviously some way a person can hide their tracks. Or at least some way that the system can hide them from us.'

'So how do I send it?'

'Just try sending a standard message and put "encrypted signal" all over it. Say it's authorised by Art.'

She moved things around on the screen, dragging and dropping Karina Morgan's details, the location and times into a message. She pressed *'Send'* and the message window collapsed into an icon of an old postal envelope. Zoe's Buddy ran onto the screen, grabbed the envelope, folded it into a paper aeroplane, launched it across the screen and unfurled the *'Message Sent'* banner.

'We'll head back to the office while we wait for a response.' Travelling while facing the rear of the car calmed me, but I needed to turn to face the front for voice commands to work reliably. 'Car... Destination... Office.'

'Destination... Office,' the car repeated and slotted us into the traffic.

I turned back to Zoe, who was flicking through reports on the screen.

'You seemed to like him, Zoe.' I was still irritated by her vocalising her love of the system in the meeting.

'Not really, but I do like iMe.'

'Clearly, and he liked you.'

'No, he didn't.'

'Yes, he did. What was that he said as we were leaving?' I attempted an Art Walker impression. 'I'll certainly be happy to answer any of *your* questions, DC Jordan.'

'He was a bit of a creep.' She glared at me. 'You trying to get at me, Boss? If you've a problem, then come out with it.'

She was right, Art's refusal to help had wound me up, and I was projecting my anger onto her. 'Sorry, no. Just the bit about liking the system took us off the point of the meeting. It broke the flow.'

'Fair enough. But iMe is good.'

'How can it not get to you? Can't eat this, can't do that.'

'It makes life simple. You can't get tempted.'

'Simple and dull.' I let out a long sigh. I could feel the weight of the case on me and spent some minutes watching the roads and wallowing in the familiar and strangely addictive sensation.

A binging sound broke me free. 'Well?'

Zoe looked up from the screen. 'There are no encrypted signal tracks.'

'He did say it wouldn't show anything. Do you trust Art?'

Zoe considered it. 'He's a bit slippery.'

'I thought he was avoiding the questions.'

'So, what now? How do we find her?'

I was so used to relying on the system that my mind was empty of ideas.

I didn't need iMe to 'enable a better me'. I needed the old me.

12

Thief

When I returned, Karina looked much brighter. She had washed her face and brushed the shine back into her hair. She almost hopped with the excitement of a child promised a trip to the beach.

'I have to worry about logistics,' I said. 'I have to get you out of here and to the park without being tracked and without you being seen.'

'Yes, yes.'

'I need you to drink this.'

She hesitated, looking with suspicion at the glass tumbler full of cloudy liquid.

'Be a good girl, Karina. Don't make me change my mind. It will make you sleep, and it will make all of the other things I have to do so much easier.'

She drank it all, grimacing at the taste, then placed the glass back on the little tray and wiped her mouth. She looked at me with expectation. 'I can't wait to get home and sleep in my own bed again.'

'Best you lie down.'

***

I started getting everything ready; going through my plan in my head, but *who next* kept coming into my mind, jamming my thoughts. Perhaps the reason Karina couldn't satisfy me was that she was kind of a victim, like me. We were both controlled.

I busied myself with the task at hand. I had to get Karina out and to the Great Park without problems. I had a long list of things I needed, so I headed to the garage.

I need someone else. But who? I needed to go pro-active, to retaliate.

I let my mind run free, giving an idea the space to grow. *Of course, that smarmy bastard.*

Dr Owen would be proud of me. He had always gone on about life's *journey* and *personal growth*. Now, like a good little patient, I was learning from my mistake with Karina. My next one was smug, powerful, and connected. He was part of the *cause*.

I dumped the things I'd collected in my bag. *Don't get ahead of yourself.* I still had Karina to evict. I had no choice, she would be in the way, and I wanted to give *him* my full attention. It would be more difficult to get him than Karina. He was more public and visible, but my mind was logical, and I liked to work things out. Where there's a will, there's a way. I definitely had the will.

***

The strip lighting's cold white light reflected off the brushed metal surfaces. I'd chosen my protective coveralls because they had a flap covering the zip and the seams were fully taped: '*an impenetrable barrier against all manner of liquids*' was the manufacturer's claim. I needed that to be true, but I could feel a lot of sweat building inside the suit, sticking my T-shirt to my back.

When I planned this it had seemed simple, but doing it was much, much harder. It was making me sick and dizzy. My mouth filled with excess saliva and I fought the gag reflex. I lost and bent over, dry-heaving three, four, five times. Each one was accompanied by a strange half-retch, half-burp noise. I closed my eyes and tried to slow my breathing and the feeling passed. Being sick would give me something else to clean up.

The metal surgical tray held the empty packaging from five central line catheters I had already put in place. I picked the last unused one up, popped it open, and placed the packaging tube back on the tray, making sure that it was perfectly parallel and aligned with the others. *Last one.*

I checked the tap was closed and touched Karina's carotid artery.

13

DI Clive Lussac

I had wrestled with the problem all night and felt a little light-headed from the lack of real sleep. If it was a technical fault that iMe couldn't find, why hadn't Karina come home? She couldn't have got out of the UK to iMe-free Europe without a lot of checks and security. Plenty of posturing civil liberty campaigners had sworn to leave the UK if iMe came in, but they never did. Was it possible that Karina's signal was being hidden? So, who had the knowledge to do it and what had they done with Karina?

I shrugged on my ancient Spirit of the Honey Badger T-shirt that was becoming more hole than shirt. Stepping into a pair of faded red joggers, I hopped a couple of steps as I pulled them up and headed to the kitchen. Finally, I had a case to challenge me, and it felt good to have to think. I was looking forward to work for a change, and there was no better way to start an exciting day than with a fat-boy full-English breakfast: sausage, bacon, eggs, the works.

Not that I would get it.

People chose all sorts of voices for their machines: actors, singers, cartoon characters. Mine were Doctor Who Daleks: *'the emotionless master race bent on domination, utterly without pity, compassion or remorse'*. They personified my on-going battle against the world. When government policy was implemented through unthinking rules and technology, when my fridge was the guardian of the food in *my* house, then my machines were Daleks.

The merciless fridge crushed today's fragile hope.

For the fifth time, its stilted, electronic voice said, 'I cannot release the items you have requested, Clive.'

'I need a good breakfast today.' I was begging now, and I had no business begging my fridge for a sausage. It wasn't good for my self-worth.

'You have four days left on your Excess Consumption Order. You are on a restricted diet.'

I could see the food through the fridge's transparent front, all the separate loaded compartments. Everything I wanted was in there. The articulated arm moved inside the fridge and selected a food container.

'Don't give me that bird food again,' I pleaded. I'd seen a news article a few days ago about a man who had been arrested for attacking his fridge with an old axe. I knew how he felt, but my axe had been handed-in during a Dangerous Tools Amnesty.

'Low-sugar granola is not bird food, Clive. I have added some dried strawberries as your iMe shows a slightly low potassium level.'

'Fantastic,' I said, but the irony was wasted on the fridge.

'Enjoy your meal,' it said.

I hoped it didn't understand sarcasm either.

***

We needed to get a better understanding of how the system worked, so Zoe and I were back at the iMe offices. I hoped we would have more luck than with Art. As we entered the office, the two people we were there to see were already waiting.

I wore different shoes to avoid the 'mouse squeaks' in the iMe office corridors. My only suit was on duty again, but instead of yesterday's white shirt, I had gone pink with a loud tie. My nose crinkled at the smell. I'd tried to mask its musty odour with a good spray of deodorant, and maybe I'd overdone it. Zoe's stylish white top made the contrast between us too much to bear. *I must get my suit cleaned.*

The two people stood up, and the names Manu Ameobi and Emma Bailey came up on my HUD. Manu Ameobi was a striking figure. Not unusually tall, maybe six-foot one, but he had the wide, muscled shoulders and slim waist of a swimmer. His skin was dark as ebony, and this set off his shining, broad smile. He held himself with a warm self-confidence that wasn't close to arrogance.

Emma Bailey was nearly invisible beside him. She stood maybe five foot six and had a birdlike quality to her movements: small and fast. She was stick-thin, and her muscles and veins stood proud of her tight, ghostly-pale skin. Emma looked like she needed some vitamin D.

'You're the technical architect and test manager for iMe, is that correct?' I said as we took our places at the meeting table.

They nodded.

'What does that mean?'

Manu leant forward, and Emma leant back. The volunteer and his evasive shadow.

'I'm the technical architect,' Manu said. 'That means that I have the overall responsibility for how the system works and how the different parts fit together. Technology needs a designer, in the same way that a building needs a structural design.'

Manu stopped and waited for Emma.

'I'm the test manager,' she said. I had to strain to hear her. 'What Manu designs, the programmers have to write. I make sure that their code works as intended.' She paused to check that we were keeping up. 'To do that, I design and run tests that prove iMe functions properly.'

I pointed at Manu. 'So, you design iMe.' My finger swung towards Emma. 'And you check that it works.'

Manu and Emma exchanged a quick glance, eyebrows raised. 'Grossly oversimplified, but yes,' Manu said.

They may have been acting as if I was a slow child, but I was pleased I could follow a technical conversation at all. 'How do you test it?'

'I think of all the ways that iMe is used. Then I create scenarios to simulate that usage. Then I prove that iMe works in each scenario,' Emma said.

She spoke slowly and carefully, like she was trying to force understanding into me, but I was frowning in confusion. I understood the meaning of each word, but not the whole sentence.

She gave a tiny shake of her head in annoyance. 'A simple example would be a front door lock,' Emma said. 'We have all of the legal locks in our testing area. I program the door lock, so iMe thinks it's my house, and test that the lock opens when I touch the door. Follow so far?'

I nodded.

'Then, as a second test, I program the lock, so it isn't my door, then test that the lock doesn't open.'

'OK, and you do that for every possible usage? Kids, adults, everyone in the country?'

'Yes.'

'That must take a lot of time.'

'It does, but it's the only way we can catch any mistakes the programmers make before we release an upgrade to the system.'

'But how can you test every scenario with millions of people using it?'

She was calm, but a little defensive, as if I was questioning her ability. 'The millions of people all use the system in the same way, so that simplifies it. We're constantly adding new tests.'

'Also, the programmers can't write code for every possible eventuality. There are too many,' Manu added. 'They can write "*if* A *then* do B". In Emma's lock example: "*if* the person is authorised for the door *then* open it", but there is always a catch-all piece of code that says, "and *if* something happens that we didn't think of *then* generate an alert".' He paused to let us catch up with what he was saying.

'So that way you don't have to write code for every single possibility,' Zoe said, grasping the concept way before me, 'and you don't have to test for every possibility to ensure that iMe works.'

'Exactly,' Emma said.

Manu nodded his appreciation of Zoe getting the point so quickly. I was still replaying it in my head so that I understood. He said, 'And if we get an alert, then I modify the design and we add code and tests to make sure that we cover that new situation.'

'Are you saying that iMe can't go wrong?' I asked, a little confused.

'Effectively,' Manu said. 'The tests prove iMe works as we expect, and the alert means that an unexpected situation is handled in a controlled way.'

'And if it breaks, you know about it. That's what you are saying?' I was trying to simplify it.

'Yes.'

'Then you knew Karina Morgan's signal failed?'

Manu and Emma shared a sheepish glance.

'Yes,' Emma said. 'Her signal disappearing generated an alert. We're looking but can't find a logical reason yet.'

'Did you tell Art Walker when you first got the alert?'

Emma nodded.

I looked at Zoe, and she flashed me a look that she was thinking the same thing. We were getting the runaround. They said they had extensive tests, and iMe worked in those situations, but they were also saying that if anything happened that they didn't expect, the system said 'oops' and generated an alert.

Shit, do they program the self-drive cars the same way? Is there a bit of code in a car that says, 'unexpected situation' and lets you die horribly? No wonder the cars went so slowly.

'OK, let's step back. How does iMe work?' I said.

Manu sighed. It must have been the millionth time he'd answered this. 'The iMe is embedded into your neck. It generates a signal for your location and monitors things like your heart rate, blood sugar, caffeine, and calorie intake. All that data is collected and measured against the Model Citizen standard by the Ministry of Well-being and Health.'

'Everyone knows that. I meant *how* does it do it?' I said.

'Well, there are lots of sensors embedded in you. They're in both your body and brain. That's how the measurements are made and why you can hear your music in your head, make calls by talking, and see data on your HUD.'

'Everyone knows that as well. We're not foreigners. What makes it *secure*?' Zoe said.

'I can't give you the details. That's classified information, but basically, all the data and transmissions are encrypted and linked to your DNA to make them unique.'

All this technology talk was making me thirsty. 'Could I have some water?'

Emma reached behind her and passed me a glass and a cold bottle of still water. She glanced at Zoe in a silent question, but she shook her head.

I poured the water, drained the glass and refilled it. 'Why have I got a missing person?'

Manu and Emma paused for a moment, and then Emma said, 'We've been discussing this, and we think that the reporting software is simply not finding the data. The programmers haven't found the cause yet.'

I groaned inside at more stonewalling. Time to address the other possibility.

'Could someone mask or suppress the iMe signal?'

They both laughed at my apparent stupidity.

'No, you would need to know how we encode the DNA,' Manu said. 'You would need the military strength encryption algorithm we use and so many other things. You would also need a huge amount of time.'

'Can't I put something over it? Like in a sci-fi film?' I'd seen a film with people sitting with aluminium foil over their heads to block a signal. They smiled like they pitied my naivety.

'That wouldn't work. You can't simply block the signal. We have invested years and millions of pounds into this technology. That's why it still works deep underground. The signal always has multiple routes, and there are so many receivers.'

'Could a receiver fail?'

'One could, but there are multiple receivers for every area. There's built-in redundancy to guarantee 100% coverage.'

'How could suppression work at all?'

'I suppose, theoretically, it would have to block all of the different transmission routes, but the signal goes through metal, concrete, everything. Blocking it would be exceptionally hard. It's meant to be. That's all I can think of.'

'Yes, that's the only way,' agreed Emma.

I tapped my finger on the desk for a minute, thinking about it. 'Then it can't be done by some simple criminal or a civilian. It would have to be someone with a huge amount of money to invest in working out how to get around it. Right?'

'Right,' Emma said.

'Or the system is broken.'

Emma reddened, and her posture became rigid. With great care and politeness, she said, 'The system is extensively tested all of the time. I ensure that everything works in line with Manu's designs or what Art wants. Nothing is left to chance.'

'What Art wants? I didn't know he chose the functionality.'

'Art has some personal requirements that the system has to provide.'

14

Thief

The bench I had chosen was surrounded by shrubs. Tonight, London was separated from the stars and moon by thick, dark clouds. I was sitting in deep shadow, wearing monochrome clothes: black shoes, black trousers, black jacket. I hoped that I would be like a black hole in the darkness. Even my woolly hat was black, and I kept fiddling with the front of it. It was the only nervous tic visible as I waited.

When I started investigating, I found that Alan had made it easy for me to take him. His liking for the female interns in his department was the polar opposite of his wife's appreciation of them. I had dreaded the busy family home in Hampstead, full of kids and dogs, but Alan had been evicted to a tiny two-bedroom new build house in Hounslow. Dark and empty, the house was waiting for him to get home. So was I.

He always used a car or the tube, depending on his mood and the time of day. I didn't need to worry. Either way, he would end up at home, so I decided to sit on the bench. I could see his front door from here.

The temperature was dropping, the daytime's 18 degrees was now a chilly and damp 10, but I was prepared. I'd dressed warmly and only my toes, in their light, soundless shoes, complained at the inactivity.

I tensed as each set of car lights drove along the road or as each person walked by. I couldn't risk using my HUD to track him in case someone saw the back-lit glow from my eye. The HUD didn't work with your eyes closed; otherwise you'd never get any sleep. I had to be patient and wait. To pass the time, I played a game of guessing how many cars or people would pass before he arrived.

He was the twenty-seventh pedestrian, and I recognised his walk before I could make out the details of his face in the sodium yellow streetlights.

Showtime.

***

Alan wasn't scanning for threats as he sauntered home. I ghosted in behind him, maybe twenty metres back, and followed. He either didn't notice or didn't care because he didn't turn to check who was behind him.

iMe made everybody feel more secure – people committing a Proximity crime always got caught. You were free from the risk of gangs, muggings, theft or violence. You were safe – unless I wanted you.

As he got closer to home, I closed the gap. He turned off the pavement and onto a concrete path that led through what the sales brochure for the house would have called a front garden. In reality, it was a few square meters of straggly grass, some thriving weeds and a recycling centre. His hand touched his front door to unlock it, and he pushed it open. The time he took to stamp and wipe his shoes on the thin door mat gave me the opportunity I needed. 'Alan,' I said, right behind him now.

'Jesus,' he shouted and jumped in shock, half cowering, half falling into the lounge that was also his entrance hall. 'What the fuck?'

I followed him in, shut the door and found the light switch. 'Did I startle you?'

'You... what the fuck are you doing here?'

'That's not a very gracious welcome. Your hosting skills have diminished.'

52

He kept his curtains closed in the daytime, so I had all the privacy I needed. I snapped my hand back and smashed a straight right into his nose.

He staggered backwards, the light reflecting in the soft sheen of fear on Alan's bald head. Even though he was five-foot-eleven, he was soft and weak. His power wasn't physical, but came from his political position. He pushed people around with words and threats. I watched his weak punch sail over my shoulder, hit him again, and he collapsed into the armchair and held his nose.

'You're fucking crazy!' He moaned, and took his hands from his nose, looking at the smear of blood.

I took the opportunity to smack another punch into his face. As he was sitting, I had to adjust for the height difference, and it resulted in a weird half-stoop kind of a blow. Despite being far from full power, it was plenty for Alan.

'Stop, stop!' His hands were back on his nose, and red trickled between his fingers. He rocked back and forward, sobbing, lost in his pain.

What a baby. I slipped off my small backpack and placed it on the floor. I pulled the tape from my pocket and knelt to one side of his feet. He was still blubbing and snivelling, but I didn't want to risk a kick in the face. Once I had trussed his ankles together with the tape, I stood back and looked at him.

'You really are a pitiful heap of shit.'

He smirked at me. 'You won't get away with this.' He was relying on iMe proving I was here.

'You think I would do this if I could get caught?'

'But…'

I could see him trying to work out if I was bluffing. I moved behind him, grabbed his hands and taped his wrists together to secure him.

'I'll make you pay for this.'

He must have decided that I was insane and would be caught, but I stabbed the syringe into his neck and depressed the plunger.

15

DC Zoe Jordan

Clive and I had been talking for hours. iMe's broken; no, it's being suppressed; no, it's broken. We kept jumping back to the same place, just like one of my precious, antique vinyl records when there was fluff under the needle.

'Can you believe those two yesterday? They knew all about Karina's signal failing,' Clive said, one foot banging his annoyance into the wall.

The case was just too surreal to be true. iMe didn't have bugs. Or did it?

He returned to his side of the desk and dropped into his chair with a funny 'argh' noise, like he had landed in the most comfortable chair in the world. My mum couldn't sit down these days without sighing either. 'I bet Art knew all about it when he saw us.'

'There's no way the signal could be suppressed, right?'

None of my police training had covered this situation. Why would it when day one had been iMe tracking and how to find anyone, anytime? I needed Clive to take charge and show me what to do.

'No, I don't think so. I think there's a bug and iMe are hiding it.'

I worried that he was going to go back into one of his frequent dark moods, but he jumped up and started circling the PCU desks again. Most of the time he was silent, lost in his thoughts, with the occasional mutter.

Clive finished his tenth lap of our desk and stopped right behind me. If I had one of Cyber's office chairs, I could have swivelled to see him, but I had to twist my body around on this cheap, rigid thing.

'We can't wait for iMe. Let's do a proper old-school investigation,' he said with an enthusiasm that surprised me. This wasn't the usual, dark depressive, but maybe a flash of the old Clive.

'What does that even mean, Boss?' When he was *old*-school, I was a teenager *at*-school.

'They spent a fortune on CCTV – coverage everywhere. We should check who was at Karina's house. Start with her getting home that night and then go forward and backwards to see if anyone was waiting for her or called after she got home. See if her boyfriend came home early.'

'Sure, can do.'

'Shit.' He seemed to deflate like a balloon as if all the fight leaked out of him. 'I bet they've neglected the cameras.'

The first call I made was a dead end, and I could see Clive's frustration. By the tenth, he stormed out of the room. I watched him go. I didn't want to fail.

I still had a few names on my list who said they would find me the right person and call me back. I scrolled up and down the list, hovering over each of the names, willing them to call.

I tried to wait.

I searched for an available car and told it to be at the front door. I needed to make things happen.

***

Windsor and Maidenhead Borough Council projected a corporate image of the castle and parks, but their office's boring old brick facade had nothing regal or elegant about it.

A sullen, pale man lolled at reception stroking his stringy beard and staring at the ceiling. He had the spaced-out look of a virtual reality gamer who didn't like his actual reality.

I pushed the flashing, red, urgent version of my PCU badge at his HUD and he jumped, full of anxiety. 'DC Zoe Jordan,' I said. 'I'm going to see John Robinson.'

'I don't know where he is...'

'I don't need you.' I moved towards the corridor behind him.

'You can't go—'

I held my hand out to silence him and smiled. 'I can.' The man was too used to fighting virtual dragons to be any match for me in real life. It was game over for him before it even started.

After jogging down some dim corridors, I found the office with John Robinson's signal in it. I banged the door open without knocking and went into a small space. It held a metal desk, two plastic chairs and a startled man who didn't look like he was on the up in the council. His skin sagged in layers around his neck and jowls, and his musty, old tweed jacket was now much too big for him. He was one of the No-Tucks – people who were much fatter before iMe managed away their weight, but couldn't afford the cosmetic surgery to remove their excess skin.

I pushed my badge at him and got the same reaction as I had at reception.

'Ah... DC Jordan...'

'Mr Robinson, you didn't call back.'

'Well... no...' He looked around for an excuse, but all I could see was draft health and safety stuff. The one he was writing said something about the dates for training on the council's new dress code to ensure standardisation across all gender categories. 'I was going to, but I've been busy...'

'Nothing is more important than this.' I leant on his desk to emphasise the point and was rewarded by a wall of lentil breath that was so bad I could taste it.

'You were enquiring about CCTV footage?'

'Yes, specifically Holmlea Walk in Datchet on the evening of the 23rd April. I saw the cameras when I was there. I need it *now*.'

'Oh, I'm sorry... but I don't think I can help you.'

'Has the footage been overwritten?'

'No. But you must understand, DC Jordan... The council's under tremendous pressure to deliver services across the whole of Windsor and Maidenhead, and CCTV was tremendously expensive.'

'You said *was* expensive.' I knew what was coming.

'With the introduction of iMe, the CCTV became redundant. With the cost of the equipment, all the maintenance and cleaning the cameras – well, the council couldn't justify the cost.'

'You shut the system down.' *Another dead end.*

'Yes.'

'And left all the cameras up as a deterrent and to save the cost of taking them all down.'

'Yes, you have grasped the situation quickly.'

'Not really, it's a story I've heard a lot today.'

***

By the end of the morning, I was ticked off and back at my desk in PCU. I'd been to all the councils and outsourced security companies. I didn't just try Karina's home, but also her work, the train stations and the route of her walk. To be thorough, and hopefully impress Clive, I also checked the homes of Manu Ameobi, Emma Bailey and Art Walker. Nothing. All those cameras and not one of them worked.

Clive came in and slumped into his chair. His earlier spark was gone. I think he had avoided coming back earlier to spare himself the disappointment. 'Been researching Art. Anything on Karina?'

'Nothing, Boss.'

'Shit.'

'I also tried the iMe people's homes: Art, Manu and Emma. Same story.'

He seemed underwhelmed. I didn't get a 'good job, Zoe.' Instead he shrank further into his chair.

'I need a drink,' he said. 'Pub lunch?'

***

I stood at the bar with Clive and looked around the pub. The high ceilings and large windows gave it a lovely bright and airy feel. The wooden tables with places set for food with chequered linen and electronic menus made up about 75% of the space. The rest was a 'snug' of comfy chairs, sofas and display walls.

'What do you fancy?' he said.

'I don't drink.' My health preferences were set to no alcohol, no caffeine and low-sugar, and that cut out loads of the bar's drinks and juices. I scanned the filtered list of drinks left on my HUD. 'Just still water, please.'

'Still water and a pint,' Clive said to the barman.

'I'm sorry, sir, but you know I can't give you beer while you're on duty and you have an Excess Consumption Order. I can only serve you water or a zero calorie decaf drink,' the barman replied.

'Medical advice used to be that booze was good for stress relief,' Clive tried.

'No way that's true, old man.' The barman softened his tone. 'I can send you some whale song music if you're stressed.'

Clive looked at me like he was trapped in some kind of parallel universe.

'Fuck, what sort of pub serves whale music instead of beer?'

**

We took two armchairs, sitting opposite each other with a round table and our iced water between us. Clive picked up his menu.

'Everything good is greyed out,' he moaned.

I picked up mine. As it was a weekday, all the red meat options were unavailable. 'Salads look tasty.'

He swiped left and groaned. 'Maybe for you. I don't mind a chicken Caesar salad but my version's got the cheese, dressing and croutons crossed out. It's basically grilled chicken on plain lettuce. Food's so boring.'

I zoned out his complaints as I got a personal mail notification in my ear and brought it up on my HUD. The mail was from Mum, with next week's menu choices. 'If you find food boring, you should use the RBR collaboration site like we do.'

'What's that?'

'It's like a dating site for food but based on the menus from the Roux/Blumenthal/Ramsay kitchen. You put in your age, gender, and preferences. Then you select what foods you like and dislike, ideal preparation times, and technical ability level. You have to sign the disclaimer to let them see your health records so that they can plan for any allergies, restrictions on diet and calorie targets.'

'And then what?'

'You get a weekly choice of ten menus, and you choose the seven you want. It's so easy. It only gives menus that you like and with the correct portion sizes.'

'Do they send you a chef to cook it?'

'Of course not. The raw ingredients get ordered and delivered automatically, then your fridge dispenses the ingredients and pushes the cooking instructions to your HUD when it's time to cook.'

'Great,' he said, disinterested.

'Choosing what to eat is always the hardest part of food shopping, and RBR minimises all of the wasted food that used to go past its sell-by date and get thrown away.'

'Maybe I'll take a look,' Clive said.

I was only trying to be helpful, but he couldn't be arsed to improve his health.

He looked at the menu again. 'Chicken and lettuce it is, I suppose.' He clicked to order and put his menu down.

I chose a nice mixed salad.

'This place used to be a proper pub. Booze and sports on TV,' he said.

'You can still get both here.'

'I can't get booze.'

'Well no, not today. When does the order end?'

'Two more days.'

'That's not long. Why ask for a beer today?'

'You've got to try.'

'Really?' I rolled my eyes. 'Well, there's still sport.' I nodded at one of the large screens around the pub showing the highlights of some football match. I hadn't connected to the audio stream, so the players chased the white ball around the screen in silence.

'That's not football. Not like when I was a kid. I gave up watching when it went fully non-contact.'

'I never followed it.'

'To be fair, with all the diving the game was non-contact for years before tackling was banned for being too dangerous.'

Next to me, a large man in builder's clothes groaned, and I looked up. He was gesticulating at the TV, and I wondered what could be so annoying. 'Put the fucking game back on,' he shouted.

'Boss.' I grabbed at Clive's sleeve so he could see the screen. 'Look.'

The newsreader looked shocked. I couldn't hear what she was saying, but the banner underneath her on the screen said, *Junior Technology Minister Alan Kane Missing*.

16

DI Clive Lussac

'How did the press find out first?' I asked.

Bhatt sighed. 'He was meant to be the chair for a briefing multicast. When he didn't show up, one of the journalists paid iMe for a signal trace.'

Bhatt seemed about to launch into a tirade about journalists, but she forced herself to stop, and her office went still and calm. I thought Zoe and I had got through unscathed, but it proved to be a false hope.

'Clive, find him, or there'll be real trouble. Career ending trouble.' Bhatt started again.

'Yes, ma'am.'

'I've had calls from the chief constable's office *and* the prime minister's office.' She was repeating herself. 'I'm at risk. They said *my* position was dependent on a successful conclusion to this. That means both of *your* positions are as well.'

For the first time since I had known her, Bhatt looked worried. She started pacing and stopped to wash her hands for at least the fifth time.

'The press are whipping up a real panic. They're spinning it like it's the end of the world. The end of iMe. It's just as well they don't know about Karina.'

I didn't know what to say. I hoped to find safety in silence.

'I have a press conference in an hour, and I have nothing new to tell them. I'm going to get annihilated. You need to give me *something*, Clive. And quickly.'

I searched the carpet for some familiar stains, hoping it would hide me somehow.

'Clive,' she snapped. 'Haven't you got anything to say? No help or information?'

'To be fair, ma'am, we've only just been given the Alan Kane case. We've run the tracks and Kane's signal stops after he got home.'

'I know that, but it doesn't help me.' She shook her head in frustration.

'Can we have more staff on the case to help?'

She went back to her desk, still rubbing her hands, as if she would gain some comfort from the action. 'I'm working on it.'

'But–'

'I said I'm working on it.' She shut me down with a swipe of her finger. 'What's your next step?'

'We're going to Kane's house.'

'Go,' she said. 'Call me to tell me what you find. Give me something to tell the press conference.'

We left the office and headed for the car. Bhatt was only thinking about Alan Kane now.

I couldn't let them forget Karina.

***

'Do you think that Alan and Karina knew each other?' Zoe said when we were comfy in the car.

'I like your thought process, Zoe.' We hadn't had time to look for a connection between the cases. 'Do you mean as lovers?'

Karina was pretty, and the news was full of Alan's previous form with Esme, the intern. It would also give Dave a motive. 'Check for links between them.'

Zoe noted it but said, 'That's not what I meant. I meant a background check on both of them as individuals. Something or someone in their pasts.'

'Good thinking, add that to our list.'

Unlike the journey to Karina's home to talk to Dave, I used this car journey to do some research.

Alan Kane was one of the civil servants on the iMe pilot program, but still couldn't resist temptation. Three years ago, the papers were full of calls for his resignation, and his wife telling of betrayal and infidelity. How could someone who knows the technology, take an intern to their hotel bed at the party conference and not think about their signal tracks? One tabloid had the trace from iMe and showed some images of Kane and Esme's separate green signal dots enter the hotel bedroom. The dots came together and spent the night and morning moving around the bed. A TV show ran a mock investigation into why iMe wasn't accurate enough to tell who was on top. Kane's affair and divorce made a splash in the press, but the career dive made much bigger waves.

Recently he had been on the comeback trail and back in the news.

Now he was missing.

***

I selected a few menu items on my HUD and then double clicked on the search warrant. Alan's front door unlocked.

The house was a soulless, sterile place. Alan had no pictures or personal items here; just drab rented furniture to match the bleak rented house. I tried not to see the similarities with my own flat.

It was like Alan had moved in with a suitcase of clothes and hadn't committed to life here. More likely, he was hoping the house would be a temporary base while he worked on alternatives. Who was he dreaming of though: wife and family, or Esme? Probably both.

We checked through the house, and its small size meant that we were done almost before we started. Each room was the same bland box. He had made no attempt to leave a personal footprint anywhere.

'We've got two signals we can't see now. What's happening to iMe?' Zoe grumbled. She had asked so many times, and each time her hands clasped and unclasped.

I shrugged. 'Try not to worry. Focus on the here and now.'

She wore grey today and looked diminished by the gloomy colour, like it had seeped into her skin. She scanned the room. 'No sign of a struggle – just like Karina,' she concluded.

'Not quite. There's something not right in here. Look again. Think about what you can see. Ask yourself what doesn't look right or seems out of place.'

'What? I can't see anything.'

'Stand by the front door and tell me again about the last few minutes of the signal. Overlay the signal with what you can see here.'

Zoe's hands typed on her HUD, and as she watched the signal trace again, I could see colour changes flashing in her eye, like being outside a dark room with a display wall playing a film.

'Well, he came home and opened the door, stepped in and wiped his feet,' she frowned, 'then the signal goes jerky. Maybe he tripped and stumbled back into this room.'

'Stop,' I interrupted. 'There was a spray pattern on the wall in Karina's entrance hall. I didn't think it was anything at the time.'

We scoured the walls around Alan's front door but found no trace of a similar spray.

'Send a forensic drone to check the spray residue on Karina's wall, and get one to scan this house as well.'

'Sure, Boss.'

'Carry on replaying the trace, Zoe.'

'Alan turned around and went to that chair for a minute, then his signal stopped.' She looked at the armchair: a nondescript thing, bought by the landlord, not for comfort or style, but for the price and all its compulsory health and safety stickers.

Zoe brightened. 'The chair's been moved from its usual place – the feet don't match the indents in the carpet.'

'And?'

'This section of carpet has been vacuumed. You can see the marks still. If you were cleaning, then why only do this little bit?'

'To hide something or to clean something up. Look carefully at the carpet between the chair and the door.'

'Is that a faint drag mark to the door that the cleaning didn't remove?'

17

DI Clive Lussac

The only redeeming feature of the PCU office was that we could treat it as our own. We had cleared an area around a display wall and started throwing images at it. The boundary of the space was made of unused desks, shoved into a rough semicircle. It gave us room to walk and think, and the edges of the desks made convenient ad hoc seats.

The display wall showed the main page of our case file. Under the heading *'Missing'*, we had images of Karina and Alan. The emptiness of the rest of the case file shouted our lack of progress. Under the *'Possible Suspects'* heading, only Art Walker, Manu Ameobi and Emma Bailey stared back at us. Pushed out to one side to reflect our uncertainty, an image of Karina's boyfriend, Dave, made an appearance. I drew a question mark on Dave, grinning childishly as I placed it so that it looked like it hung from one of his dangling earlobes.

Zoe tutted and shook her head.

I stood back to look at the wall, taking in the sparseness of our efforts. 'We haven't got any real suspects.'

'Who should we add?' Zoe asked as she stepped forward and moved the question mark I had drawn away from Dave's ear. I resisted the urge to move it back.

'Alan's wife and Esme, I guess, even though they probably couldn't suppress Alan's signal.'

'OK.' Zoe's hand moved in front of her. She swiped right to create a new page on the wall, and, one finger extended, wrote in mid-air. Her notes automatically mirrored on the wall.

'And, we can't rule out iMe staff. Get a list of who works there. We'll use it as a long-list and then narrow it down.'

'Who else?'

'Another possibility is anyone with enough money and time, but that's too long a list to be useful without a lead.'

'Yep.' She added more notes.

'And check out any "I'll bring the system down" type threats against iMe. Kane was linked to iMe and his going missing could be political rather than personal.'

'Yep,' she said again, her hand still out in front of her.

'One person missing could be a bug, but two feels more contrived. The marks on Kane's carpet looked like someone dragged him out.'

iMe were looking into the 'error' option, so we needed to investigate the criminal possibility. I paced the corral of desks, dragging my finger across the dusty desktops, hoping for inspiration, but getting nowhere. My heart started beating a little quicker. In the old days, I would have been full of bravado and determination to find the victims and catch the villains. Now, I felt guilty about the excitement the challenge of the case brought.

A call from Mary cut through my thoughts. 'Clive, we've finally got the house valuation, and I sent you the divorce demand earlier.'

I hadn't even looked at the demand. I knew denial wasn't really going to get me anywhere, but the demand felt so final. I headed for the far end of the office so that Zoe couldn't hear.

'Clive, are you listening?'

'Sure, I need to action the divorce demand.'

'Please do it now. Dragging it out will only make it more painful for us both.'

'I'm sorry it went wrong,' I said, regret in my voice.

Mary was quiet for a moment, and her sadness resonated as she said, 'Don't start, Clive. All your second chances sucked me dry.'

I knew she was right.

'Bye, Mary.' I hung up and opened the demand.

I skimmed through the first few pages of legal terms and conditions until I could see the list of her grounds for divorce. It was a long list, including my repeated deviation from Model Citizen, untidiness, mood swings, not listening, incompatible menu choices, inability to adapt or to change. It went on and on.

I clicked *'Acknowledge'* and saw a page for me to enter my counter-grounds. It invited me to *'Click all the things that apply'* but all I could really put a tick against was *'Micromanagement'* and *'Bossy'*.

I clicked *'Next'*, and my HUD showed the financials page. As we had no kids or pets, we qualified for the auto-settle quickie divorce. Our only asset was the house, and its value showed at the top of the page. Underneath was the government's 15% buy-back fee for the house. I winced at the amount, but it was cheaper and quicker than lawyers.

I clicked *'Apportion Blame'* and waited. The settlement page appeared. The result was 90% to 10% in Mary's favour. My continual deviation from the Model was the main reason for the score. It was hard to disagree with the truth.

Was this really the end of my marriage? Was an empty flat my future?

I moved my hand past the *'Click to Accept'* button and pressed *'Save for Later'*.

***

Eventually, I joined Zoe in the research, and we stayed until 11:30pm. I checked the backgrounds of Karina and Alan and searched for any links between them. Zoe was looking at iMe and the history of the staff. I stretched and yawned, too tired to continue. 'Let's call it a night, Zoe. What have you got?'

She looked exhausted as she rubbed at her eyes. 'I've got some more iMe staff for our possible suspects list.'

I looked at the images Zoe threw at the wall. She attached a name, age and job description to the bottom of each. She touched and moved them around, grouping the people by their job descriptions.

'Anything else?'

'Be patient, Boss, there's only me and I cancelled my friends to stay here.'

'OK, sorry.' I wasn't sure if she was complaining about missing her evening out or the lack of help.

'But there is something…' She teased me by not finishing.

'Which is?'

'While I was researching the staff of iMe, I took a look at the history of the company. You know that all the recent press about iMe is linked to Art. The story is written like he was the brains behind it. Like the whole thing was his idea.'

'So?'

'Ever heard of Esteban Jimenez?'

The name trawled up a hazy memory, but I couldn't place it. 'Um, I think so.'

'Well, his name came up on a pre-iMe old news item, so I did some digging. It seems like he was in at the start of iMe. He was Art's business partner.'

'Wait, maybe...' I squinted, trying to sharpen the image, 'Oh, yeah, I remember. What happened to him?'

'The reports I found hinted that he and Art had a bust-up about iMe being taken over and used by the government. He left or got kicked out – it's not clear. The rumour is that he went off-grid.'

'Off-grid? What does that mean?'

'Apparently, he found a way to step outside the system when he wanted.'

'Really?' *The central premise of iMe is that it's meant to be impossible.* I would love to be able to choose to go off-grid when I fancied a drink or chocolate.

'That's what an old magazine said. But it isn't that simple now. Without iMe there is no money, so he must still be connected somehow.'

To get all iMe's convenience of health, security, and not needing keys or passwords, the government managed your life. No way to have one without the other.

'And?'

'There are large holes in his signal history. In fact, the history trace is more gaps than signal. Look.' She found the history data and threw it on the wall as a new page. 'This is the last twelve months.' The wall showed a horizontal white line for periods of no signal, with sporadic green spikes. It looked like a heart monitor flat-lining, spiking as the defibrillator tried to restart a heart. 'Each green spike is where he has a signal and is connected, and then it's off again. I think he can turn it on when he needs it.'

That sounds perfect to me. Maybe this was perfect for the case as well – the breakthrough we needed. 'Maybe he can make others go off-grid as well.'

Zoe nodded, swiped left on the wall to get back our case overview and threw a photo of Esteban onto the wall.

'We'll go and see him right after the morning briefing with Bhatt.'

I moved Esteban's picture under the *'Possible Suspects'* heading, right next to Art Walker.

18

DI Clive Lussac

Zoe and I were back at PCU for the 6am briefing with Bhatt. Zoe's hair looked like it resented having been dried in a hurry, and the lack of sleep was encouraging all my negativity. I could feel a band of tingling pressure starting at my temples and spreading across my forehead, like the inside of my brain was touching my skull.

'Can you bring the case up, Zoe?' I said.

She nodded and duplicated our case wall onto Bhatt's office wall.

Thankfully, we had much more to show her than before.

'We're looking for links between Alan Kane and Karina Morgan, and also for other possible suspects,' I said. 'Zoe?'

'So far the only link between Alan and Karina is membership of the same gym. Alan stopped going three years ago, but Karina's membership is still active, and she goes regularly. Her medical and health records show she's in line with the Model Citizen exercise directive.' Zoe threw a report of Karina's deviations to Model onto the wall.

God, she is a good girl. Green bars everywhere on the report. Only the fat and calorie sections had a small amber tip showing that she was within her FU allowance.

'She spent most of her FUs on crisps.'

Bhatt frowned in disapproval. 'Don't call them that. Did they go to the gym together?'

'Sorry, ma'am... Alan Kane's gym membership lapsed when he got divorced. He and Karina were never in the

74

gym at the same time, and there is no data showing any physical proximity.'

'Right, keep looking for links. What else?'

Zoe swiped the wall back to show the case overview with its pictures of Karina, Alan and the possible suspects. 'Esteban Jimenez,' Zoe said.

'Now there's a name I haven't heard in a long time. One of iMe's two founding fathers.'

I was surprised again that Bhatt had information that would help us and hadn't mentioned it. 'You know him? Until yesterday, we thought iMe was all Art.'

'iMe *is* all Art,' Bhatt said.

'But not originally?'

'No. What's he up to now?'

'Show that trace you had yesterday, Zoe.'

Zoe tapped Esteban's image on the wall, touched her fingertips together then and spread them. The image expanded to match her finger movements and opened a full page on Esteban. She had a lot more data on him now and talked Bhatt through the graph of the sporadic signal over the years.

'It's not conclusive yet,' I said. 'Show the overlays.'

Zoe moved her hands and Bhatt, and I watched the wall as it followed Zoe's actions. She selected Kane and Karina, Esteban, Art and the other iMe staff. The wall redrew again to show a series of dates along the top, with each of the names she had selected down the left side. Each person had a signal line running horizontally across the page. Karina's line was green until the 23rd of April before it ended. Alan Kane's was similar but went further until he disappeared.

'You can see Karina, and Alan's signals just stopped,' I said. 'All the iMe staff have signals for the whole period.' I pointed at the solid straight lines. Esteban's signal line had big gaps in it during both disappearances. 'You can see that Esteban doesn't have a signal.'

'So, we don't know where he was?' Bhatt asked.

'Zoe and I are going to try and find him straight after this, ma'am. Zoe found an old contact entry.'

'Good, he seems to know how to cheat the system he designed.'

'Can you put up the next one, Zoe?'

The wall redrew again, this time showing a map of Berkshire. Two green dots pulsed a slow and steady beat.

'This is the night Karina went missing from her home in Datchet – a minute before her signal went.'

Zoe's hand followed my commentary and hovered over the first dot. Karina's name popped up next to it.

'The other dot is Emma Bailey. At this scale, the map shows her at home in Egham.'

I nodded, and Zoe spread her fingers to zoom the map out, so we could see West London and out as far as Swindon. Now we had green dots for everyone on our possible suspects list. No one's signal was anywhere near Karina's home. Everyone had an alibi.

Everyone except Esteban.

'Given that everyone else has a signal that proves they weren't near Karina or Alan, then it must be Esteban,' Bhatt said, excited that we had a breakthrough.

'It looks that way,' I said. 'But there's a complication.'

Zoe did another finger dance in front of her face, and the wall displayed another map.

'This one is from immediately before Alan Kane's signal stopped.'

Kane's signal showed on the map of Hounslow.

'Again, no one is near Kane's home in Hounslow. Still no signal for Esteban.'

'So? What's the complication?' Bhatt said, a tint of exasperation in her voice.

I pointed at Art's signal. It showed that he was in his Mayfair flat. 'This looks like Art is at home alone, having a quiet night in, but...' Despite Bhatt's impatience, I couldn't resist a little dramatic pause. I nodded at Zoe to do the reveal.

'When I checked the detail of Art's signal, it showed as encrypted.'

Bhatt nodded in understanding. *Christ, she knows.*

'You knew about encrypted signals and didn't tell us? It would have been useful.'

She held that annoying finger up again to stop me. 'Careful, Clive. Of course I knew. You know the other departments I run.'

'But these people could be being taken by someone with an encrypted signal.'

Bhatt gave a derisive snort. 'You need an authority signed by the home secretary to encrypt your signal. It's not going to be someone that trusted. It can't be Art.'

'But we don't know where he was. The signal data we have only tells us where he was before the encryption.' The next bit made me mad. 'And apparently, only he can approve a signal trace on someone encrypted.'

***

After the briefing, I was still trying to understand why Bhatt hadn't told us about encrypted signals. We were back at our case wall. DS Martin Adams and Freya Murray were the only serving PCU officers left other than Zoe and myself. Adams had a bad back and was off sick, and Murray had been loaned to Cyber. I knew Cyber was the key department now, but Bhatt's refusal to give us Murray back made things harder. *Is she protecting Art somehow?* It made no sense to dump it all on Zoe and me, but Bhatt said she had no choice. Last week's cyber-attack had raised the terror threat to *imminent,* and it was always the prime minister's priority. All available resources were committed elsewhere.

'We need to find Esteban. What was that contact you found, Zoe?'

'It's from an ancient WhatsApp account.'

'Christ, can we still use that?' No one had used WhatsApp or Facebook or any of the old social media sites for years. Too much catfishing, too many trolls, too many encrypted messages between terrorists. They had all been replaced by the little blue TrueMe app which was always on the iMe screen and guaranteed the identity of the person you were talking to. Schools took kids to the Museum of Technology to learn about the demise of the old unregulated social media sites and to laugh at all the old 'smart' phones.

'There's a way to use it. I know someone in the police cyber-crime labs. They're sending me a special version of the app we can use on iMe.'

***

The wait for the app was frustrating, but after an hour, Zoe had a version of WhatsApp on her HUD. She threw her display onto the wall so I could see as well. The app looked a bit like a cut-down version of the old WhatsApp screen with a blank discussion area on the right, and room for chats down the left-hand side. Only one name showed: Esteban Jimenez. I wasn't sure that we could really contact him this way. If we couldn't, we would have to go to all the places his signal had shown up. They were scattered around the south of England and it would take a lot of time to go to all of them. I hoped the app would shortcut the search.

'Tell him we need to see him straight away,' I said to Zoe.

She tapped his name on the screen and said: 'Mr Jimenez, this is DI Clive Lussac from PCU. We urgently need to talk to you. Please can you contact me immediately.' The words were converted to text and appeared in the app window as she spoke. Except my name, which showed as Clive Lissa. Voice recognition always got it wrong. Zoe corrected it and raised her eyebrows to check the message was OK to go. I nodded, and she pressed send.

We both watched the app and hoped. It had been hacked together in a rush and provided no feedback on whether the message had been delivered or read.

We both gasped when the words *Talk or Meet?* appeared in response to our message.

'Tell him, meet,' I said, and we waited again.

Our eyes were locked on our HUDs, oblivious to the rest of the world.

'Come at 10am,' came the reply, followed by the location details for a lay-by on a road near Salisbury. He must have known exactly where we were, as the meeting time was perfect if we left in the next ten minutes.

Zoe went off to use the toilet while I connected with an available police car and told it to pick us up.

Minutes later she burst back into the room with enough momentum to thump the door into the wall. The handle sent a few pink flecks of plaster floating onto the floor.

I span to face her, startled by the noise.

'Karina's signal's back on,' she panted.

19

DI Clive Lussac

'How do you know her signal's back, Zoe?' I asked.

'I got iMe Tech Support to monitor it and tell me if it came back on.'

'That's great.' I was impressed with Zoe, but why hadn't I thought of that? 'Where is she?'

'I literally just got the alert. I'll check now.'

'Share your HUD,' I told her, feeling the relief. *We've found her – no, iMe found her.*

My screen blanked and showed Zoe's HUD. Out of the corner of my eye, I could see her hands moving around. I focused on the screen as menus and search boxes came up, like I was watching someone else playing a computer game. I held my breath as the HUD drew a map of Windsor Great Park. In the centre, a dot showed us Karina's location.

'Fuck.' I staggered back and grabbed for a desk to stop me falling. *'Fuck.'*

Karina's signal glowed a sickening red.

Red and green were the colours of people's tracking signals. Green for go and red for stop, like the traffic lights. Someone had stopped Karina.

'Check the history,' I said.

Zoe threw a graph on her HUD. Karina's flat 'No Signal' line drew along from the left and then jumped vertically as the signal strength returned to 100% and settled there. A red, unwavering line.

Zoe gasped, and I stared.

Of course, people still died unnaturally. There was the occasional, simple to solve, domestic or gang killing. Most were early checkouts: desperate, messy suicides, or euthanised OAPs in their care home beds. Now I was getting divorced from Mary, would I end up some old, lonely man and go the same way?

I shook the thought aside. Nothing we found about Karina hinted she was suicidal, or even depressed. This didn't feel like a suicide. We had a murder to solve.

'We need to get to Karina. Use that app to postpone Esteban.'

'Sure, Boss.'

Because forensics were automated, and we always knew who was present at the time of death, we had nothing to do at a crime scene. Mostly we didn't bother to go and simply waited for the report. This was different. This felt like the old days.

I went to the cupboards at the back of the office to hunt for my crime scene bag.

I had a vague recollection of putting it in a cardboard box when we last moved offices. I searched and couldn't find it. I stood and looked around. Mary always joked that I did 'man' looking. She was right, so I went back through the cupboards more carefully this time. At the bottom of the first one, behind a box, I saw the dusty corner of a bag. I reached in and dragged it out. My old bag looked sad and neglected. I opened it up, but all it contained were old silicone gloves that had fused together into a gooey mess.

'Esteban replied, Boss.'

'What did he say?'

'He said he can see her red signal.'

'He seems to know everything. We'll get to him later.' We could reuse the car I had arranged for the trip to Esteban.

'Let's get to Karina.'

***

In the car, we watched the preliminary drone camera footage from Karina's location in the Great Park. The high elevation images showed the tops of the trees, the glittering lake and the Totem Pole in the distance. The car slowed, signalled to the on-coming traffic to stop, and turned right into Wick Road. The local Uniform had one car parked on the left, and our car reversed us into the only other space. We got out, and I flexed the grumbling muscles around my knee, trying to shift a nagging ache. It was another bright spring morning, but in the shade of the tall oaks on both sides of the road, I shivered.

'In there, sir.' The PC who had been on guard pointed the way. 'The forensic scan is nearly done, and we've enforced a no-fly zone for press drones.'

I nodded my thanks as we set off past a group of onlookers and their dogs. A collie shook, splattering the mud and water from the lake over their owner's legs. The small metal gate resisted on its rusting hinges as we went into the park and past the two green and white posts with the by-laws telling you what you could and couldn't do on the king's land. My mind jumped off at a tangent as I wondered if they had written a 'no dead bodies' rule.

Most of this part of Windsor Great Park was grass areas punctuated by individual tall trees, and the dappled sunshine moved with the trees' branches. Nice place for a walk, but I could see little shelter for a body.

The exception was the clump of dense green ahead of us, which provided a natural screen to hide an electricity sub-station from the road. On the park side, the sub-station hid behind a wooden fence, grey and green with age and mildew.

We ducked under a canopy of branches. In the open, the air was clean and fresh, but here, where Karina's body lay on a bed of russet leaves left over from the autumn, it was damp with the smell of earth.

We needed to wait a few metres back until the forensic scan finished. The large drone we had seen the images from rested quietly on the grass. A matte black thug of a thing, it squatted on five long, crane-like legs. Its circular body was nearly a metre across and about 500mm deep. Evenly spaced around the edge, six propellers faced the sky. The loading hatch in the top of the drone was open, waiting for the return of its micro-drones.

Zoe fidgeted as she waited, her feet rustling the leaves.

'Karina looks peaceful,' she said.

It looked like the leaves had been kicked into a mound. A low organic altar for Karina's body to rest on. Her hands were folded onto her lap, and she held a single, yellow daffodil that matched the print on the cotton of her dress.

'Is this where the signal came back on?' I wanted to double check.

'Yep. She didn't move after it restarted.'

Karina looked peaceful, except for the six micro-drones buzzing around her like angry wasps. Their flight pattern looked random, but their imaging cameras would provide a perfect 3D model of the scene that we could 'walk' around and examine later.

The drones all stopped moving at the same time, hovered, then headed off to map the surrounding area. Their departure meant that the preliminary forensic report was ready. When it messaged in, I brought it up on my HUD, then threw it at Zoe's. The first line told us what we feared.

'Case Classification: Murder.'

I read on.

'Cause of Death: Exsanguination – body drained of blood.'

I flicked through the images in the report, looking at small puncture marks in each major vein and artery. The innocent little holes didn't look like fatal wounds, but from the cause of death, each must have dangled a cannula and tubes to let her heart pump out her blood. I hoped Karina wasn't conscious when it started.

Zoe's face had washed-out to a pale grey-white. Despite the coolness of the shade, sweat shone on her brow.

'You OK, Zoe?' I asked.

'Yep.' The croaky sound said she wasn't. 'She can't be dead.'

Her denial was understandable. This was the first murder in ten years with no proximity data from iMe at the time of death or immediately prior to it. I tried to stay calm. I tried to think like the policeman I used to be. I couldn't stop the frisson of excitement flowing through me.

'Whoever put her here didn't just dump the body. They took some care,' I said, hoping to find something to comfort Zoe.

'Like they put her gently to bed, then arranged her.'

Karina wore the same haircut from the photo Dave had given us – a bob, the tips cut towards her chin, and the fringe brushed over her right eye.

'The floral dress and tights look like the same ones Dave said she wore when she went missing,' Zoe said.

'Yes, but they're too clean to have been worn every day.' The hem of the dress was neat and straight, halfway up her thighs. The material was smooth and certainly didn't have the creases from days of use.

'There's something on her neck.' I bent forward to look closer. Karina's pale blue skin had two marks running along the top and bottom like two parallel tracks. Not strangulation marks, but maybe the slight indentations left by a tight strap or collar.

The slight breeze stirred the branches, and the canopy swayed above us, moving the light across Karina's face like a floating shroud. The tranquillity of the scene moved me, compounding the shock and revulsion of a violent and bloody death. How could someone who had cared enough to arrange Karina in this spot also been able to kill her?

***

Eventually, the ambulance arrived to remove Karina, and the peace of her resting place was destroyed as her body was rolled and then bagged.

I needed some space, so I backed out from under the bushes, stretching in a spot of warming sunshine. I lifted my head to the light, hoping it would help shift the despondency spreading through me. *Poor Karina.*

There were no iMe signals of anyone bringing her body here and the Uniforms had interviewed all the walkers in the park. Nothing.

How can a body get itself here? Who'd brought her?

One murder and one missing politician.

We had failed Karina. We had to find Alan before he was killed.

20

DI Clive Lussac

Bhatt was waiting for us when we got back to our office. The last of the daylight was disappearing, and the gloom matched all our moods. Zoe and I walked Bhatt through the drone footage and forensic model. Other than Karina's body, we couldn't find anything. No prints or forensic trace of another person. The iMe signal data was notable by its absence.

Outside the office, the rain started to hammer down – noisy, dancing splashes on the aluminium windowsills. The darkness of the evening pressed into the office. I had let Karina down.

'We have to face it. Someone knows how to hack the iMe system,' I said. 'How else can someone carry Karina's body to the park without us seeing their signal?'

Zoe was still pale, and the cold white glow of light from the crime wall on her face wasn't helping. 'Esteban,' she said. 'He has big gaps in his signal.'

'He's our only real lead at the moment,' I agreed. 'And he knows we postponed our meeting and probably where we went.'

'Have you any new evidence to link Karina and Alan together?' asked Bhatt.

'No. There's only the old gym membership.'

'What about links between Esteban and Karina or Alan?'

'Nothing.' I couldn't hide our lack of progress.

'You have no other leads?'

'Not really. In theory, it could be anyone. It's like an old case, and we have no physical evidence.' I stopped speaking and waited. Bhatt was thinking.

She looked up. 'If Alan Kane dies, the shit will really hit the fan.'

Somebody killing a junior minister would be huge. People were used to living in safety, and any threat could undermine the whole system. 'There would be chaos.'

'That would be an understatement.' Bhatt went to sit down but saw the layer of dust, so moved to a desk that a bum had wiped clean before. 'We rely on iMe tracking so completely, our security, our money… our policing.'

I'd never seen Bhatt so vulnerable and concerned before.

'It's more worrying if the two cases are separate.'

'Why, Boss?' asked Zoe, forcing her hands apart.

'Because if a different person abducted Alan Kane, then we have two people who can hide their signals.'

'Oh.'

'Exactly. But it feels too unlikely.'

'You need to see Esteban,' said Bhatt. She had been quiet, and it worried me. She didn't normally hold back.

'We're seeing him in the morning,' I said. 'He sent a location to meet while we were out.'

Bhatt was still for a moment, then she spoke slowly and quietly. Such a contrast to her normal full volume commands that it was all the more chilling. 'The prime minister called me. She wants Alan Kane back.'

***

I had a red light.

It came on when I woke up, but I had ignored it. The solid light had started blinking and now was replaced by an animated red figure running along the bottom of my

HUD. My Buddy ran to the right-hand side of the screen and rolled out the alert message as he ran back to the left: *'Your voluntary exercise session is overdue'*. He stopped, waved, ran to the right and pulled out the message again. And again, and again. The little bugger never tired. It was distracting, and from painful experience, I knew that if I ignored it much longer, the incessant 'bong' would start in my ear, and that didn't ever stop. iMe never *forced* you to do anything, of course. It was always your choice, but iMe moaned so much and so consistently that you either surrendered and did it 'voluntarily' or went mad.

My gym kit was on the floor where I had dumped it after my last session when I had almost collapsed, panting and sweaty, vowing to do more exercise so it wouldn't hurt so much. If I'd put my kit in the clothes processor then, I could have pulled on nicely cleaned and ironed clothes. Instead, I sniffed dubiously at my socks, shrugged and pulled on my crisp and smelly kit.

As with all newish homes, my treadmill was built into the floor and would only allow aerobic pulse rates, unlike the hardcore professional Anaerobic+ bikes. I stood on the treadmill, and it started moving. My little red tormentor was now my green training Buddy, and I could see him, my heart rate and ECG heart readout on my HUD. As the speed of the treadmill rose, so did my pulse. My little Buddy ran happily and effortlessly with me, *encouraging* me with inane superlatives. Apparently, I was 'super awesome', I was 'the man', I was 'powering through'.

I screamed at him. 'Why can't you shut up and let me suffer?'

***

The exercise made me hungry, but with one day left on my Excess Consumption Order, my fridge delivered another bird food breakfast. Even so, I was looking forward to the day. I booked a police car for the trip to see Esteban and it arrived exactly on time at 8am. I got in and set up Zoe's address as a way-point so I could pick her up.

Now I was in the car, I felt tired and lethargic. Unfocused, just letting the roads slide past in a blur. In films and books, the characters' brains always seemed to be working at full speed. They were heroes – active, coming up with ideas. My brain didn't feel like that today. Instead, it was as quiet and empty as an airport at night. Of course, my brain could work. It used to be good, but it was as if I was in standby mode with a little red dot showing power was there, but nothing was working. It was like I was waiting for something.

The night's rain had passed and despite the bright morning sun, the roads were still wet. The car's tyres hissed and splashed on the roads as we drove. 'Destination in five minutes,' the car said.

I messaged Zoe, but all she sent back was an ambiguous 'Nearly ready.'

Is that a unit of time?

***

A set of ornate metal gates started to purr open as we approached them. The car slowed, crunched over the gravel and pulled up outside a smart, old house. High hedging separated the house from its neighbours and provided a green security veil. I got out of the car when Zoe didn't appear straight away. Sniffing some blossom in the air, I approached the glossy black front door.

It opened, revealing an older version of Zoe; maybe late forties, but I was in dangerous territory trying to guess a woman's age. She had Zoe's olive skin, but it showed signs of having been lived in. A good life. A happy life, I thought, judging from the laughter lines around her eyes. She smiled now, white teeth gleaming against her lipstick. Her beauty struck me, and I caught a hint of her delight in life. It reminded me of Mary before she froze me out.

'You must be Zoe's boss,' she said. 'She's having a bad hair day. She'll only be a sec.'

'And you must be Zoe's sister,' I said, cringing at the lame and cheesy line, but it was the best I had on the spur of the moment. I had expected Zoe to get straight in the car, not for me to need to look my best. I did my crumpled jacket up to hide the spot of yoghurt on my tie.

Over the years Zoe's mum must have heard better lines, but her smile remained. 'That's very sweet of you, but I'm Sophia, Zoe's mother.'

Her eyes held me a moment, and I lost confidence. I dropped my gaze, and then I panicked, worried in case she thought I was checking her out. I was, but I didn't want to be *that* obvious. I made a clumsy attempt to make it look like I was admiring the house. 'Nice place.'

I worried that I would see a frown of disapproval when I looked back at her, but she wore an amused smile, like she was wondering how bad I was going to make it for myself.

A noise behind her saved me from any more embarrassment. Sophia turned as Zoe appeared and pecked her on the check. 'Later, Mum.' Whatever Zoe had tried with her hair seemed to have worked, as it was now under temporary control. She must have got her hair from her father, as Sophia's was black, straight and perfect.

As the car pulled away, my rear-facing seat allowed me a view of Sophia, still framed by the front door.

'What are you smirking at, Boss?' Zoe asked.

I was thinking about Sophia, but I couldn't tell Zoe that. Another reason why I didn't use Sentiments: my thoughts would be far too transparent. What would it have chosen? A happy puppy? I would have died. 'Nothing,' I said, but Zoe crossed her arms in disbelief.

She was still staring at me when she shook her head and tutted. *Really?* No way.' she said.

'What is it?'

'Nothing, just Mum,' she snapped, trying to shut the conversation down.

A few minutes passed in an uncomfortable silence. Every so often her eye changed colour as she read something on her HUD, and her hands typed out the response. Her frown deepened, and I checked her Sentiment. *Shit, she's angry.* I decided to keep the silence going until her Sentiment changed from the red-faced figure with arms crossed and a tapping foot.

'No,' Zoe blurted out. 'That's too weird.'

I wasn't sure that she meant to say it out loud. Her Sentiment still tapped its foot, but I ventured a tentative 'You OK?'

I looked out of the window to avoid the daggers her eyes threw at me.

After more angry messages, Zoe sighed. 'Right… er, I can't believe I have to ask this, but my mum wants to know if you're married.'

Does Sophia like me? Why else would she ask the question?

Legally I was still married as I had pressed '*Save for Later*' on my divorce demand, but I ventured a tentative 'no'. I was grinning like an idiot, but Zoe wasn't in any mood to return my smile. I shut it down as she typed a short response.

It would have taken me weeks to get around to vocalising a personal question. Some people came straight out with this stuff. I envied them their 'nothing ventured, nothing gained' approach to relationships.

Zoe and I had stayed firmly away from family and personal stuff in our conversations. We kept a mutual, unspoken agreement to keep it all about work, so I knew nothing about her life.

'Don't you both live with your dad?'

'No, he moved out when I was a kid.'

'I'm sorry. Do you still see him?'

'Occasionally…'

I thought she was going to say something else, but she must have got another message because she shook her head again and said, 'Never or not now… married, I mean.'

'Not now.' I repeated the small lie. Mary and I hadn't lived together for months, so I didn't feel married. I needed to press that button.

After more typing and another head shake, she said, 'Apparently I need details.'

'Life's like a bicycle ride,' I said.

'What?'

'Sometimes you pedal, sometimes you freewheel. I pedalled hard to win Mary – my wife.'

'That makes no sense.'

'She was pretty, and I was clumsy.' I sighed, reflecting on where it had all gone wrong. 'Little by little I slowed and stopped pedalling with Mary. I was always at work and she blamed me.'

Zoe left a silence for me to carry on.

'I think Mary stopped pedalling for me as well. At some point, we veered off in different directions.' I stared out the window. 'Now I'm alone.'

***

Our car skirted Salisbury and after a few miles pulled into a lay-by, we got out, and I breathed in the brisk, fresh air – clean county air that the city didn't understand. I stood and turned into the wind, feeling the life of it, letting it buffet me. We were on the top of a hill; crop fields a patchwork of greens and yellows around us.

In the distance, I could hear a mechanical wail. If I didn't know better, I would have said it was a high-powered petrol engine being pushed hard. The pitch of the noise dipped for a fraction and then wailed again. It was close now. I hadn't seen a petrol car for years. The pollution tax was massive, and a permit was nearly impossible, but a big, red shape was approaching us. *It can't be*. But this was real. The car stopped next to us. A shock of noise and heat. A prancing horse on the bonnet with the word Ferrari underneath. The window purred down.

21

DI Clive Lussac

'Inspector Lussac?' the driver said. I nodded, and he smiled. 'I'm Esteban Jimenez.' He spoke with a soft Spanish accent, the split of the syllables and emphasis both in different places to how I had been saying his name. His was more melodic than my flatter accent. He pronounced his name as Es-TE-bahhn, not EsteBAN. The J in his surname was more of an H sound – Himenez – at least I got that bit right.

Even stationary, the car seemed angry and impatient. Zoe took a few paces back from it. She looked like she was staring down a wild animal. Esteban turned the engine off and got out. The growl was replaced by gentle pings and ticks as the metal started to cool.

The car was fantastic, like the types of car I had on my wall as a kid. The sun caught the paint, highlighting the metallic flecks. It shimmered. All I could do was stare at it.

'People say you live off-grid, but you're not exactly hiding away in that,' I said, indicating the Ferrari.

Esteban gave a self-deprecating shrug. 'Well. I don't live in stealth mode all of the time.'

I tore myself away from the car and looked down at Esteban. He was Zoe's height and wore a black shirt with white flashing on the shoulders.

Zoe gave up waiting for an introduction. 'I'm DC Zoe Jordan.'

Esteban shook her hand. 'Zoe. Nice to meet you.'

'We need to talk to you,' I said.

'I know, but not here.' Esteban moved to the boot of the car and opened it. It swung up and open silently.

I could feel my hair being tossed and knotted by the wind. Zoe had given up on hers, and it flapped around like a flag. Esteban's shirt collar took occasional flight in the wind, allowing a glimpse of the stiff hi-tech looking neck collar he wore.

'Please,' he said, indicating that we come to him. 'I want to help.'

I paused. I didn't get the sense that he was our killer, so I headed to the car. Zoe followed.

The boot of the car was empty except for a box holding two collars similar to his. They were about 50mm thick, with padded top edges to protect the wearer, and appeared to be crafted out of some sort of brushed metal. Esteban lifted one out. It looked light in his hands. He stepped behind Zoe and lifted her hair away from her neck, before spending some time putting the collar on her, spinning the knurled metal thumb-wheels to adjust the fit.

'Shit,' she said, distressed hand movements flashing around her head. 'My iMe's lost signal. Shit, shit.'

'Please don't worry,' Esteban said. 'It's only temporary.'

'But, but… I can't get my HUD to work.' Her arm movements got more frantic like she was swatting at imaginary flies.

Esteban came behind me, and I ducked down so that he could reach. The collar was heavier than I thought. He clicked it closed, and I could feel movements that made it wrap around my neck. Not so tight that it suffocated me; more like a tie that was slightly too tight. Esteban fiddled some more, the collar started to get warm, and then my HUD had a blank screen with the message: *Unknown Error: Please report to Tech Support*.

Even though most of my life was pre-iMe, this still felt unnatural. For the first time in over a decade, I wasn't being watched. Did a collar like this make those marks on Karina's neck?

I stepped up close to Zoe and whispered, 'I know you're used to having a signal, but go with the flow here. We need to make progress in the case, and we can overpower him if it gets messy.'

As I stepped back, she nodded, still hopping from foot to foot in agitation, unsettled by the disconnect.

'iMe working as described,' I said. 'An unexpected situation handled with an error.'

Zoe stopped moving. 'Just like Manu said.'

Esteban closed the boot and opened the car door. He touched a button on the front seat, and it purred forward to allow access to a small back seat. 'I'm sorry, Zoe, but the inspector looks too tall to fit.'

'I don't know.' She took a step away.

Esteban smiled and walked over to our car. 'It's safer than this heap of shit.'

He put his hand on the top of the door and pushed the self-driving car. It rocked alarmingly. 'These are too high. The weight's in all the wrong places.' He pushed on the door, and the plastic flexed easily. 'Built as cheaply as possible. They have no strength and no crash protection.'

He walked back to Zoe and took her by the elbow. 'This is made of expensive and immensely strong composite materials. It's built to go 250mph, so at the speeds we travel at, it's not stressed at all.' He threw a dismissive nod back at our car, 'That's always at the limit of its engineering… dangerous piece of crap.'

'They don't crash, and your car puts everyone at risk for your selfish pleasure. And it runs on petrol – it's dangerous.'

'Zoe, please trust me.'

With obvious reluctance, Zoe got in. I settled into the sumptuous interior in the front passenger seat. It was almost sensual, and I couldn't resist running my hand over the shiny carbon fibre and soft cream leather. The detailing, with intricate red stitching, was perfect.

Esteban got in and smiled at Zoe. 'OK?'

She shook her head and said, 'Still no signal.'

He pressed a big red button on the steering wheel, and the engine shouted into life, then settled into a crackly burble. 'You're going to *drive*?' Zoe sounded terrified.

'Too right,' Esteban smoothed the sides of his short moustache and pulled his hand down to flick the end of his goatee. 'All seat belts on?' We started moving, and Esteban floored the throttle, pushing me back hard into my seat. The rear of the car wiggled as the tyres struggled to find grip, stones kicking up, thumping into our car.

The digital readout on the car's dash blurred as the speedo tried to keep up with the car. In only a couple of seconds we were doing 90mph. More than twice the speed limit. 'Esteban…' I tried.

'Not now. I need to concentrate.'

He looked at one with the car, calm and serene as it went around a sweeping bend at 120mph like it was on rails. On the straight, Esteban continued, 'It's why we have self-drive cars now. People were too lazy to drive properly. You must concentrate and be aware to drive, but everyone wants to be somewhere else, talking to someone else.'

I was expecting my iMe to flash all sorts of warnings onto my HUD: excess speed warning, extreme danger, excess G-force warning, but it stayed with *'No Signal'*. The risk levels would probably use five years' worth of FU's in this one trip. I was pinned to my seat as we went around another corner.

I glanced at Zoe to check she wasn't too scared. The worry in her eyes conflicted with the huge smile of excitement she wore. She was gripping the seat hard. I could see that her fear was still there, but she was enjoying it.

When I looked back at the road, I could see a flock of cars travelling in our direction. All bunched at the minimum safe-braking distance as if they were lonely on their own. The cars coming the other way were much bigger now, so I expected Esteban to slow down, but he moved the Ferrari into the middle of the road.

'I love this bit,' he said.

I braced against the seat as we approached the cars, but they all braked, swerved and pulled off the road, like the parting of the waves. The Ferrari drove through the gap unhindered, the sound of the engine bouncing back at us off the cars as we flashed through.

'What happened?' I asked when we were past the cars and back on an empty road.

'They all have collision avoidance software. If you drive straight at them, they all chicken out and move over.'

'What about speed cameras?'

He winked at me. 'They don't work anymore.'

Same as the CCTV we needed, I thought.

'What about getting reported?'

'We don't have a signal.'

'But the people?'

'We're gone before they look up from their HUDs.'

As we approached a small village, Esteban braked, and the speed bled away from the car faster than I could imagine. We crawled through the village at 15mph, slower than a self-drive car would have gone.

'I thought you'd charge through here.'

'No, man. Out on that road, in this car, 120mph is safe. There's good grip and visibility. I know the roads.' He slowed some more to give a woman with a child and dog some extra room. The child beamed and pointed but his mum covered his ears to protect him from the noise. 'I know what all the press say, but speed on its own isn't dangerous. It was simpler for the politicians to drop the speed limit than get people to drive properly. Easier to get the car to drive slowly, even if they do have bugs.'

I was reflecting on his logic when he stopped and gave each of us a black hood. 'Put these on, the location of my home is private,' he said. I ignored a flash of unease and put the hood on. I was pushed hard into my seat again and enjoyed the thrill.

***

'Take the hoods off now,' Esteban said.

I blinked at the sudden daylight. We had stopped outside Esteban's home. A unique piece of architecture, all angles and splashes of colour mixed with glass. It was nothing like the boring uniformity of my flat. A long drive, set out like a French tree-lined boulevard, led away from the house.

'So, despite all the warnings from the government, you're both still alive,' Esteban said.

More alive than I've felt in a long time, I thought. Life outside the Model Citizen was intoxicating. It took me back.

Zoe still wore her smile – maybe she agreed with me for once, but her hand still tried to use her HUD. 'I can't get anything to work.'

Inside the house, Esteban removed his collar and rolled his neck.

'Beer?'

'I can't. I have an Excess Consumption Order.'

Esteban shook his head sadly. 'Fuck that shit,' he said. 'Your iMe won't work inside the house. It'll never know, and the alcohol will be out of your system by the time you're back on-grid.'

My HUD still had a blank screen with an *Unknown Error* message, but I wasn't sure.

'Don't do it, Boss. When I had no signal on a girl's trip to Spain, my iMe still logged everything and synced when we got back,' Zoe said.

'That's not the same. Abroad you're in roaming mode. You're out of range, but the system still works. Here, it's like your iMe is broken.' Esteban took our collars off, and I enjoyed the cool on my neck after the heat and weight.

He handed me a beer, and I took the frosted glass that must have been straight from the freezer. I twirled it, catching the sun in the golden liquid, savouring the moment. My first beer in two months was gloriously cold and refreshing. I took a second sip and wiped the froth from my mouth. *Sign me up for off-grid living.*

***

Esteban lived as a self-styled nemesis of the Model Citizen. His appliances were all older models, too old to be connected to iMe. Too old to tell tales on him. His technology was there to help him, not control him. An antique iPhone charged on the side table, with its cable disappearing from sight. His bar was stocked with different whiskies. He had leather chairs, red meat and cheese in a fridge with a handle, and red wine breathing in a decanter. Zoe looked appalled.

He lounged on a big corner sofa, legs up, both arms stretched along the back. Zoe and I took the armchairs facing him. He could look past us and through the huge windows to the uninterrupted view of trees and fields. 'So, just because I have no signal, you think I killed Karina,' he said.

'Well, you're the only person unaccounted for at the time.'

'I know that's not true.'

'What do you mean?'

'Ask Art,' he said. 'Anyway, I was at a quiet dinner with a few friends.'

'Give me some details and names so we can check,' I said.

He started, but Zoe wanted to make notes and looked lost without her iMe. Esteban gave her a pen and paper. She stared at them before opening the pad. She scratched awkward shapes, struggling with the unfamiliar action.

'Tell me about the neck collars we wore.'

'I designed the first Suppressor in the beginning. As a test case for the system.'

'What did it do?'

'You've seen already.'

'May I?' I gestured at his collar and picked it up when Esteban nodded his approval. It was lighter than the one I had worn, made of some composite material.

'I've made improvements over the years. The first one was a clunky old thing. Yours are the third generation.'

'So iMe knows you have them?' Zoe asked.

'Of course they know.' Esteban leaned forward, more animated. 'Every time I use it, alerts go off. Same as you – they know you're off-grid now.'

'But they said it's impossible,' she continued.

'They have to say that.'

'But they should've told us.' I felt aggrieved. They were obstructing the investigation.

'They can't. Their power is based on iMe's infallibility.'

'Are there other Suppressors?' *If there are, we've got a real problem.*

Esteban shrugged. 'I don't know… I made mine when I was at iMe, and it was extremely hard, even with inside knowledge of the technology.' He looked past us again at the view. 'I only have these few.'

Something in the way he said it made me doubt him. *If he can make these, he could make more.* 'You could be making them and selling them to whoever wants to hide.'

'I could…' He had a distant look in his eye. 'There would be plenty of buyers.'

22

DI Clive Lussac

As Esteban had promised, the alcohol had been out of my system before I was back on-grid, but I'd slept badly.

I acknowledged the insistent Buddy on my HUD who kept giving an exaggerated yawn and then pretending to fall asleep on his banner that said: *'You have had insufficient sleep for optimal health and performance'*.

'I'd sleep if I could,' I shouted, but the churning guilt over Karina and thoughts of living without being monitored the whole time consumed me.

It was good that the NHS was working well now. People were living longer. But were they living better? Was I? My marriage was over, I was living in a tiny flat on my own. I didn't want my life always to be in perfect focus. I wanted to forget how I had got myself into this mess. I needed a drink and comfort food when I got home.

I had tried a Purge club once, but what was the point in consuming, just to vomit it back up? I had to keep it down to get the alcohol charge in my bloodstream, the buzz from the caffeine and sugar. Purging didn't give you those – just a terrible after-taste and a sore throat.

It would be light outside now, so I told the house to go into heat recovery mode. The windows cleared the blackout image and let in the promise of a warm day. I shivered from the lack of sleep and enjoyed the windows magnifying the sun's weak, early morning heat as I stood in front of them.

My dismal flat was so small that it only took a few big paces to get around it. I could easily have kept the flat neat all the time, but I couldn't be bothered. Instead I binge cleaned: left the flat to get dirty over a few weeks, then I'd feel guilty and tidy up in one sustained blitz.

I looked at the message Sophia had sent last night for the 100th time: '*Don't worry. I thought you looked nice. x*'. I was sure I was reading way too much into the x at the end of the message, and I decided to sort the flat out. I shuffled around, picking up clothes and removing the shoe I used to trap the floor-cleaning robot in its charging dock. It emerged as tentative as a vampire stepping into the sunshine. It rotated left and right, scanning for obstacles and headed off to work. It always vacuumed and washed the kitchen first. I followed it.

'Two sausages, eggs, tomato and mushrooms, bread,' I said, then added 'cancel' before the fridge could respond. It was fun to order the breakfast I wanted, but I wasn't in the mood to hear the denial. My Excess Consumption Order ended at 6pm. One more crappy day, and I was planning a party for tonight. A solo, hedonistic party.

I tapped my jaw to make a call. 'Oscar, my friend. How are you?'

'Good, Clive. You want your stuff?'

'My Order is over today.'

'Sweet, come on up.'

***

I stood in the lift, with its walls of mirror and looked down. Denial was a wonderful thing, and mirrors never gave good news. With my usual hollow gesture, I touched the glass where it said fifth floor.

'Trips of two storeys or less are reserved for disabled users. Use the stairs and feel better,' the lift said.

'Can't make me.' I touched for the eighth floor, and when the lift arrived, I stepped out and then straight back in, making the lift think I was a new passenger and pressed for the fifth floor. My little trick only worked because ours was on an old software version. The new ones checked that the same person hadn't got back in.

Six doors along the corridor I stopped at Oscar's, and he opened up. He was sweating and smiling, in the glow of his mid-twenties and his perfect physical condition. His blue exercise gear clung to every muscle in his chest and arms. I avoided looking down. I'd made that mistake before and knew that his black leggings hid nothing either.

'Done 150km this morning,' he said, waving at his static exercise bike. He shot me an accusing look. 'Did you use the lift again?'

'I might have.'

'I keep telling you it's only two storeys. It would do you good.'

'You know me…'

'Yeah, too well, if the lift let you travel two storeys then you'd use the stairs instead.'

'Exactly… I shouldn't be forced to exercise.'

'Whatever.' He shook his head with a half-smile of exasperation. 'Your stuff's over here.'

Oscar went into the kitchen and lifted two bags. I heard an encouraging clink. Two months of Oscar's alcohol allowance in one bag, chocolate in the other. *I do love health freaks.* I approved a payment on my HUD and took the bags. *Party on.*

'What are you saving for now?' I asked.

'A new bike.'

'For an exercise park?'

'No, why risk falling off? Another internal one.'

'But I thought that one was new.'

He shrugged. 'Yeah, but there's a new model out, so…'

'And you pay for it by being a drug pusher to an old policeman. Very modern… See you soon.'

'You'll be sent to a Health Reorientation Camp if you carry on like this.'

He was right, but even so, I broke off a tiny piece of chocolate. I couldn't risk a big spike in my blood sugar, and I'd have to eat less today to stay inside the Excess Consumption Order, but I couldn't resist letting the chocolate melt slowly and deliciously over my tongue.

23

DI Clive Lussac

'So why didn't you tell us that Esteban had Suppressors when we were here before?' I asked, comfortable again in one of Art's office chairs.

Art said nothing, and the only noise was the cherubs spitting water into the fountain. 'It's protected by a non-disclosure agreement, but let's just say it was part of his settlement package.'

'Settlement for what? Leaving iMe?'

'I can't give you details.'

'I could get a subpoena and force you to tell us.'

'You can try, but everything related to iMe, including Esteban's behaviour, is protected by an absolute exception in the Official Secrets Act.'

We were pressed up against Art stonewalling to protect himself again.

'Could Esteban be making and selling Suppressors?'

'Maybe.' Art shrugged and spread his hands as if to say, *How should I know?*' He smiled.

I wanted to smack the smugness out of him, but I dug my nails into my palms to suppress the urge. 'I could arrest you for obstructing our case.' I said, settling for a verbal slap.

Art leant back in his chair and steepled his fingers. 'Don't challenge me, Inspector. It wouldn't be a fair fight.'

I let the silence drag, looking straight at him. 'Maybe, but I'm investigating a murder and a disappearance.' If I was going to get fired, I might as well go with a fight. 'Do you have a Suppressor as well?'

If I hoped that this would throw Art off-guard a little, then it failed. He stood and went to the door. 'I'm done,' he said, locking his gaze to mine.

He held his hand out to shake mine which surprised me, but, as I took his hand, it clamped hard, crushing my fingers. He was much stronger than I thought. Art moved his face close to mine, and I could see a small nerve jumping near his eye.

'Be *extremely* careful how you go, Inspector.'

***

After the meeting, Zoe and I both headed for the toilets. I left with a shudder – I couldn't get comfortable with the new vacuum tube urinals. Sure, the suction took all the liquid away with zero chance of embarrassing drops on your shoes or trousers, but it felt a bit perverted.

Zoe wasn't done so I loitered outside. That felt weird as well, so I paced away from the toilets and back again.

A call buzzed in my head and I checked the caller ID. 'Mary, it's a bad time–'

'The divorce demand is still in your checkout basket, Clive.' Her voice was a little shriller than normal. It always was when she was annoyed with me.

I didn't reply. Instead I watched Art coming along the corridor towards me, Manu Ameobi and Emma Bailey flanking him, half a pace behind.

'Sorry. Need to go…' I caught Mary saying 'get it done' but didn't focus on the rest of the verbal stream that came at me as I pressed my jaw to hang up.

'Trouble, Inspector?' Art asked. The warmth of his sincerity blew across me like a glacial wind.

'Just my soon to be ex-wife.'

'Messy divorce? Shame.' He walked off, tutting in mock sympathy, enjoying my discomfort.

Manu and Emma walked past, both looking a little embarrassed. I wasn't sure if they were sympathetic for my divorce or apologising for Art's manner.

After a couple of clicks and swipes, I found the divorce demand. My finger hovered over the words *'Click to Accept'* again. One little button to kill what had already died, but it still hurt when I pressed it. Two messages came in: one was the confirmation of the divorce, the second was a credit notice from the bank confirming the settlement.

'Fuck,' I muttered.

'What?' Zoe asked, coming up behind me.

I couldn't tell her that my divorce was now real after all that chat in the car. I never found that talking helped anyway. All that reliving the pain made it worse. It kept it raw and fresh. *If you pick at a scab, you make it bleed.* This was the same. I had a box for my emotions, and I visualised opening it and putting the divorce inside. However much I pushed down, the lid wouldn't shut. It snagged on my guilt over liking Sophia.

'The finality of my divorce just hit me.'

'I'm sorry, Boss.' Her arm moved like she was going to try and comfort me, but I turned to block her, and she withdrew her hand.

Mary ran in my mind: a sunset over the Dales, a fight on a beach. Thinking about it clogged my brain, and I needed to get back onto safer ground – think nice, logical thoughts. Think about the case.

There was something scratching at the back of my mind I couldn't quite reach. I shut my eyes and focused on the sensation of my breath going in and out of my nostrils, hoping it would give the idea the space to come to me.

'Right now, the only strong leads are the iMe people and Esteban, right?' I said.

'Yep. I talked to the dinner guests Esteban named, and they say he was there.'

'We can't use that to rule him out.'

As Zoe and I started walking towards the exit, she said, 'So what now?'

'We need to look for ex-iMe employees with a grudge.' A light seemed to go on inside me. 'We need to find anybody with a Suppressor.'

'How?'

'By looking for gaps. Esteban said that iMe Tech Support got an alert when our signal went, remember?'

'Yes, so they must have got alerts for others.'

'If there are more people with signal failures, then one of them could be our killer.'

24

Thief

I'd been away from the cage for a couple of hours, but could think of nothing else. My exercise session had gone in a flash – I had been on autopilot, going through the motions as I imagined the evening ahead. Savouring the details.

I dumped my gym bag by the chair and hopped in; letting its mechanical damping support my weight as I reclined. I flicked the light switch and looked at the monitors.

Alan's head snapped up with the sudden shocking glare. He snarled and spat. His stay with me had started all whimpering and subdued, but his truer, nasty side had surfaced. I hadn't expected it. I thought he would get weaker and easier to control the longer I owned him. Maybe this dual side of his nature was why he had done well in politics.

I pressed the intercom. 'How you doing, Number Two?'

I muted the sound when he started to shout. If he had been attached to a machine that bleeped out swearing, it would have fused from the overload.

He didn't have a shred of charm or humanity, so he was going to get the full effect. He would see it all live.

He was the star of the show.

***

As I opened the door to the cage, he charged at me, swearing and shouting. His chain stopped his run with a jerk as it snapped taut, like a rabid guard dog pulled up by its lead. He stood panting, a crazed stare from his bloodshot eyes. Now all the layers of pretence were stripped away, his feral core remained. He wasn't worthy of a human name – none of them were. He was my second possession. My Number Two.

The pistol I held had a gas canister on the front that looked a bit like a second barrel. I could see him considering it as I raised it and pointed it at him.

'You haven't got the bottle, you fucker.' He spat at me, the white globules scattering in the air and landing short of my feet. 'Shit scared to get too close.'

He was straining against the chain, trying to get to me, oblivious to the shackle gouging into his skin.

I raised my left hand and turned a dial on the side of the gun. A little red dot appeared on his chest.

'Turn around.'

'Can't do it to my face?' he shrieked, but I could see a little fear and uncertainty in amongst the bravado.

'Just turn around.' I moved the dot down to his crotch. 'I can shoot you there if you prefer, but it will really hurt. Your choice.'

He stood his ground for a few seconds longer, then reluctantly turned his body, keeping his eyes on me until the last possible moment. 'Fucking do it. Go on, do it!'

Adjusting the air pressure on the gun to allow for the distance and the thickness of his clothing, I moved the red dot onto his right buttock. I pulled the trigger and saw the red feather of the dart land exactly where the dot had been.

'Owww. What the *fuck*?' Two shouted. He reached around with his hand, flailing at the dart. Each lunge made the dart's head wobble and flop around. After a few failed attempts, he managed to grab the end and pull it out. Two stared at the dart, examining its needle and the red feather end. The clear middle syringe section, marked in millilitres, was empty now, with the plunger pressing up tight against the needle. I could see him work out what it meant.

'What was in that?' he asked.

'Best to sit down, Two. You're going to feel sleepy.'

***

Two's body was loose and floppy from the drugs, and it made lifting and moving him more like some strange, wrestling dance. By the time he was on his back on the bed, I was panting from the exertion. I took a minute to get my breath back and went to get the other things I would need: rope, containers, and my bleeding kit.

My four ropes were braided carbon fibre – light and strong, and their black satin sheen had a sinister glow. Each had an eye spliced in one end to create a loop. Grasping the first rope, I passed the eye under Two's leg and threaded the other end through the eye to create a snare around his ankle. The second rope trapped Two's other leg. Holding the free ends of the two ropes, I jumped up onto the bed. I wiggled the end of each rope through a separate pulley on the ceiling. They were small and a bit fiddly, but I knew that they were screwed into a solid structure hidden by the metal ceiling. Once the ropes were over the wheel of the pulleys, I went to the wall and threaded them into two ratchet hooks on the wall. Each time I pulled the rope through the ratchet, it gripped the rope and held it tight.

I repeated the whole process with the other two ropes, one around each of Two's wrists. By the end, his torso lay on the bed, with each hand and foot hovering slightly above it, held by the four ropes. He looked like a garden swing, with his body acting as the seat.

My bleeding kit waited on the table by the side of the bed: six central line catheters and a scalpel. I checked that the clamps on the catheters were all closed, and then taking each catheter in turn, found its place in Two's body. Each time, the skin dipped under the pressure of the catheter's needle, before the sharp point pierced it. His blood flowed and filled the catheter, the pressure building against the clamp, seeking release.

I hummed as I picked up the plastic tubing which always seemed to snag and knot however careful you were, but eventually I had a tube from each catheter, feeding into two empty black five-litre jerrycans.

I kept humming the same song as I waited for Two to regain consciousness. I remembered my father singing the old Stranglers' song while he made something, and I was his helper.

The words came to me with his smiling face: 'Death and night and blood.'

25

DC Zoe Jordan

Clive had chased and whinged, and Bhatt finally messaged us that she would send us extra help. My Sentiment did a little dance of celebration, and when Clive and I got back to the PCU, five new faces waited for us around the case wall. According to Bhatt's latest press MessageCast, these were, *'highly trained police officers added to the team'*, but blank expressions of the five trainees sitting at empty desks said otherwise.

I called them forward. 'I need you to find gaps in iMe signal data,' I said.

'But, like, basically, you always have a signal,' the one with the diamante earring said. He looked at the others. They nodded their agreement at such an unshakeable truth. Each face told me they thought I was mad.

I didn't need them to believe, just to work. Time for a bit of shock therapy. I threw the image of Karina's body onto the wall.

'Look at her. She didn't have a signal. Now she's dead.'

I waited, dragging the silence out, past awkward, well into weird and stressy. Until I could see that they got it.

I spent ten minutes or so showing them the step-by-step process I needed them to follow. They worked well, but after a couple of hours, they had to go home. New health and safety guidelines mandated that anyone under twenty-two couldn't work for more than five hours a day. Studies showed that being overworked generated long-term stress and mental health issues. They had arrived before Clive and I got back from iMe, so their time was up.

Good news: the crew had got through the last four years of gap data. Bad news: I had asked for all ten years.

'You're kidding me,' I said as Clive muttered some excuse and skived off. The rest was down to me. I needed to find the patterns and repeated names, but each search took an age.

Every five minutes, my Buddy rolled out her reminder: *Meet the girls*. I sighed and shot a wistful look at the door, but no way was I going to make it *and* get through the rest of the gaps data.

We were all members of an InnerCircle, a secure, opt-in TrueMe group where we could privately share chats, photos, and our location with each other all the time. The group was bouncing with excited *Nearly there*' and *There in five*' chats. In map mode, I could see their signals arriving at the bar where I should be.

'Going to have to bail on you guys. Stuck at work again. Sorry,' I said, and the words appeared in the group window next to my name.

The chat filled with *Miss you*' and hearts in reply.

I watched their signals sit around a table and checked out the photos of a group of men who approached. *See what you're missing*' was the caption. The sad face emoji tacked on the end didn't blunt the sting of the message.

Yep, my choice, but it was crystal clear what I was missing. Maybe it would be better not to be able to see what they were doing. Then, I could pretend they had bailed on a boring night and gone home early.

I'd been bitten by some insects when I was in the Great Park, and four angry bumps screamed for my attention. As I scratched at my elbow, I thought about Mum putting me in as the third wheel between her and

Clive. It really made my days more random when I was with him.

Sure, I wanted Mum to date, but no way was Clive right for her. He bounced between depressed, bored, interested, and back again. I never knew who would turn up, and now Mum wanted to talk about him at home as well. He was a mess – like a scruffy bear. And not in a good way.

I skimmed over Mum's messages about Clive and looked at the InnerCircle photos. Some of the girls were dancing and smiling. I wasn't going to have a fun night, but I was working on perhaps the most important case for years. Watching my friends at a bar wasn't helping Alan or getting me closer to finding Karina's killer.

I shut down the InnerCircle window. I could go out another night and celebrate solving the case.

I went back to my data to find a breakthrough.

I was going to be the difference.

26

DC Zoe Jordan

By 00:01, my Buddy was worried. Her eyebrows were pushed almost off the top of her head, and the edges of her downturned mouth were impossibly low. She climbed up on her *You have been at work too long. Your performance is suffering'* banner, fluffed a pillow and slept.

Sure, my eyes were gritty and a bit heavy, but I wasn't going to bail with only the first year of data left.

If someone had tried to develop a Suppressor in the beginning, there'd be signal gaps as they tested it.

My fingers drummed out a beat on the table through the mind-numbing minutes of my latest search. Buddy unfurled a *'Collating Results'* banner, not her usual *'No Results Found'*. I sat up and leant forward, even though it didn't make the image on my HUD screen any bigger.

Buddy threw the results at my HUD. There were lots of gaps in the first year and nearly all for a brief period of time. I drilled down on the first gap, hoping to see one person testing their Suppressor. I groaned as I saw loads of people centred around the location of a hole in signal coverage. The hole got fixed, and the gaps didn't reappear.

It was the same with the others.

Rocking back on my seat again, I pulled up my summary report from the crew's searches and mine. The only strong pattern with repeated data was Esteban. I looked down the long list of people, including us, whose signal stopped at the lay-by where Esteban picked us up. Must be Esteban's house guests wearing his Suppressors. They were all off-grid for a few hours and then came back on at the same lay-by.

I created a new heading, *'Guests'*, on the case wall, and stacked all the names under it. We had a lot more information but no new usable knowledge.

I moved six men who went to see Esteban a lot under a *'Friends'* subheading.

Except for the one name, I split the rest between *'Random',* like Clive and I, and *'Close Friends?'* for a lot of married women – some who were high profile.

The last name went to see Esteban a few times in the first couple of years. Clive would like the last name.

Art Walker.

***

The following morning, my InnerCircle showed me that I had missed out big style. The in-jokes that I didn't get were made worse by the *'You had to be there, babe'* messages. Work may have been pushing me to the edge of the group, but I'd let it.

After the gap data, I had worked a couple of hours more to follow another lead, and wow, could my Buddy nag. It was worth it. I had real news.

'Tell me what you found,' Clive said.

We were back in front of the display wall, bums on the corralled desks, looking at our case overview with Art and Esteban, and I talked Clive through the gaps.

I saved the best for last.

'Alice Bakaev and Tom Mitchell,' I said.

'Who?'

I threw two new pictures onto the wall, and Clive looked at them without any sign of recognition. I added an *'ex-iMe'* heading.

'OK, Zoe, enough with dragging it out, get to the point,' he said.

Alice's photo showed a woman in her thirties with pale skin and intense frown. Tom projected a laid-back smile, tanned face and a baseball cap perched backwards on a huge set of dreadlocks.

'Both of these two were programmers with iMe. Both know the system.'

'Where are they now?'

'Not where you would expect from the photos.' I had all my notes showing on my HUD. 'Alice dropped out. Apparently, she got upset about the civil rights issues with iMe. She couldn't live with what she saw as a violation of everyone's privacy and the control of her lifestyle.'

As I expected, Clive nodded his agreement with this point of view.

'So, she dropped out and joined the Druid commune in Glastonbury.'

'Jeez, that's an extreme choice,' Clive said. 'I get the off-grid lifestyle choice if you're Esteban. The cars, food and luxury would do it for me, but the Druids live under canvas and catch their own food – and they *still* have a signal.'

I didn't see either choice as attractive. Why bother when everything worked so well on-grid?

'Alice seems unlikely to be involved if she's with the Druids, but follow it up,' Clive said, and he moved her picture to the side next to Karina's boyfriend, Dave.

'Tom's much more interesting. Do you remember Doris Barclay?' I said.

'Of course I do. Old Ma Barclay, is she still going?' Clive seemed to shudder.

'Yep, I did a search and found some news articles about her crime family and you trying to make charges stick.'

'Yeah, a lot of witnesses disappeared or changed their minds.'

'What's she like?'

Clive half-smiled, I think he was enjoying reliving the past.

'Think of a stereotypical little old lady: small, big glasses, and grey hair.'

'Sounds like my old nan,' I said. I missed her now she was gone. I missed her no-nonsense view of the world.

'Now add big metal skull rings on all her fingers and the foulest mouth ever.'

'Not my nan anymore.'

'Add a love of hurting people, and years of practice doing it. This charming mixture is Mrs Doris Barclay.' Clive stopped reminiscing and focused on now. 'How is she involved in this?'

'Tom Mitchell works at a health club she owns.'

I threw pictures of Doris and Tom up onto the wall, dragged them together, and slid them to the *'Possible Suspects'* area.

Clive stopped his pacing and crashed down into a chair, staring at Doris and Tom. 'Shit, if she's involved, we've got trouble. What's the club?'

'The Health Bank,' I said.

'That's hers? It's expensive.' He paused to consider it. 'I guess the club's name is a play on her name. You know Barclays Bank.'

I was none the wiser. 'What?'

'You've never heard of Barclays Bank? What do they teach you these days?'

These days? Does he think I'm still at school? I shrugged.

He sighed in mock frustration and launched into lecture mode about the *'old days'*. 'Before iMe made all money electronic, we used to have banks. You would have an account and use it to pay bills. You could get cash out, coins and notes.'

'I remember getting some actual money from nan when I was little.' I smiled at the memory of her. She always slipped a folded note into my hand whenever I saw her. *Don't tell your dad,'* she would say, with a wink.

'Thanks for making me feel that old. Anyway, one of the old banks was called Barclays.' He stopped like he was waiting for applause.

I shrugged again. 'Anyway, Tom left iMe four years ago and went to work at the Health Bank.'

'What would a club want with an ex-iMe programmer?'

'Well, I don't think he will be doing their online presence or pushing custom-ads at people.'

Custom-ads were getting more intrusive recently. Of course, I had to buy things like deodorant, shampoo and tampons, but I didn't want every ad-screen I walked past to light up asking me if I'd run out of shampoo or reminding me to review my tampon purchase. The system shouldn't put my personal hygiene stuff on display for everyone to see.

'No, Old Ma Barclay would have had a serious profit squeeze on her illegal drugs and girls business when iMe came in,' Clive said.

This was all before my time. My history lessons had been filled with how the terror threat and mass migrations from Africa and the Middle East had swamped the country, forcing us to close our borders. Teachers droned on about how iMe had saved children from paedophiles, how the streets were safe again from muggings and violence, how tax avoidance led to centralised finance. They lectured us on why we should all aim to conform to the Model Citizen: the health benefits and the better, longer life. They hadn't spent any time on drugs and prostitutes – they were approved things you could spend your FUs on. They were *shopping*.

If Doris lost money, then it could be a motive. I let Clive continue.

'With iMe, we knew when people took drugs because the chemicals registered straight away. We could follow the user's signals back up the chain of meetings. It was like a spider's web. The user would touch the outside of the web, and each intermediary led us back to the spider at the centre. When we shut them all down, the government legalised the drugs to get the tax revenue and improve product quality.'

'What about the girls?' I asked.

'That was a little more difficult,' he said. 'We looked for patterns. We got iMe to write a search to look for buildings with one or more girls in. Anywhere that had a steady stream of men going for short visits, we'd turn up and arrest them. It got to a point where they didn't bother to set up a new brothel as they knew we would be straight round. Then the government legalised prostitution. Licensed sex parlours stopped the human trafficking and improved sexual health. And most importantly for the government, it generated more tax revenue and reduced policing costs.'

'Doris Barclay would have lost a lot of money every day?'

'Yes, she won't have taken it well – she's not a forgiving person.'

'Then she'd be motivated to get around iMe to replace the money flow, right?'

Clive nodded.

'But it's all legal, so why would people need to go to the Health Bank to get drugs and sex?'

Clive shook his head again with a dismissive flick, and I flushed with irritation. *He's so patronising.*

'Oh, Zoe, you're so naive. Just because it's legal doesn't mean you want every purchase on your permanent record and shared. I mean, if you fancy a...' He stopped. 'If you are a married man and fancy a... some...'

He's almost blushing, I thought.

'Some... horizontal *refreshment* with a lady who's not your wife. Then you wouldn't want it recorded, and you wouldn't want your wife to pay for a location check and find that you weren't in a meeting after all.'

I laughed. 'Horizontal refreshment? Do you mean a fuck?'

This time he did blush. His discomfort at discussing sex with me made me forgive his patronising tone a little.

The club was the breakthrough.

'We have a motive.'

27

DI Clive Lussac

As we waited for the car to arrive and take us to the Health Bank, the display wall showed Bhatt's latest brutal press conference. She was bombarded with endless streams of questions about the lack of progress. She was sure to pass her hurt on to us. Shit always flowed downhill.

I turned away from the wall. 'Tell me about Tom Mitchell,' I said.

'According to iMe's Human Assets department, he started soon after the prototypes were approved.'

'What did he do?'

'He was a programmer. Initially, he wrote the monitor software that we use to trace a signal. They said that he was bright and got more involved in the system.'

'Involved in the generation of the signal?'

'A bit.'

'Did he have access to enough of the technology to build a Suppressor?'

'Human Assets said not, but it sounded like a scripted answer.'

'So why did Tom leave iMe?'

'That he got a better offer from the Health Bank.' She stopped and looked towards the window. 'You hear that?'

'Yes.' I could hear shouts coming from outside.

Zoe threw a local map onto the display wall. The scale was large enough for us to see the surrounding area and a line of Uniforms keeping back a growing throng of people. They were mostly press, which wasn't going to improve Bhatt's mood.

***

As the police car drove up the ramp out of the PCU car park, we saw the press line shouting at us. Two Uniforms rolled on the floor, knocked flying by the people who burst through. Someone got in front of our car, and the pedestrian safety program stopped it with a jolt. We rocked back and forth in our seats as the people swarmed around the car. I could see a BBC News badge on one person's chest, pressed tight against my window. The car bucked and hopped from the people pushing and pulling at it.

So far, we'd managed to stay distant from the press storm flying around. Bhatt had taken all this heat, but now the storm had broken over us. The questions came from everywhere and swirled around in the car.

'Inspector, Inspector. Can you tell us where Alan Kane is?'

'Has iMe been hacked?'

'Who killed Karina Morgan?'

The press had linked Karina and Alan, and every question stung like we were surrounded by a cloud of angry hornets. I couldn't answer any of them.

I knew that images of Zoe and I would be on the news – the story edited to make us look scared and useless. They wouldn't have to try too hard, because we were useless. I wished I could get out and tell them we had solved the cases, that everything was OK and back to normal. I hated a lot of iMe, but now I was being forced to protect it, to repair the damage.

A uniformed sleeve pushed along the car window and in front of the BBC News badge. Another arm was squeezing along the other side. Little by little, the Uniforms got us some respite from the press. They made a blue ring around the car, and it stopped rocking. The car's panels popped as they flexed back into shape and I heard a gruff order shouted. The blue ring started shuffling away from our car. We had half a metre, then one. Daylight returned to us, and we had space to move.

Zoe found the right menu option to reset the car out of its crash mode before it started rolling. I mouthed my thanks to the Uniform sergeant as we made a left turn in the road. I was breathing hard, and Zoe looked shaken.

Six messages hit me all at once. They were all the same. 'We understand you have been involved in an accident that wasn't your fault. You are entitled to compensation for your injuries. No win, no fee.' The car's crash mode would have triggered alerts in the insurance companies and woken all the scumbag personal injury lawyers. I deleted them.

'Is it going to be like that every time we leave?' Zoe asked.

'I hope not, but probably,' I said. 'They'll have to put more Uniforms out to keep the press back.'

'That was scary.'

My heart rate was slowing. 'Yeah, it was.'

The case was up close and personal now, and Zoe and I would be under huge pressure from the press. And Bhatt.

28

Thief

Two groaned as he came around. 'What the fuck?'

'I'm glad you're awake. I want you to watch this.'

He started to scream more obscenities at me, like the animal he was, but then he noticed all the tubes coming out of him, then the ropes around his wrists and ankles. He choked on the words and his eyes jumped around the room, looking for some escape. 'What the fuck, you don't have to…' he stammered.

I pulled on the end of a rope, making the ratchet clack happily. With each pull, Two's leg rose, and I alternated between two of the ropes until both his legs swung about a metre off the bed. I went to the other end of the room and the two other ropes. More clacking and pulling resulted in Two's hands being raised half as high as his legs.

'Comfy?' I said.

'Please, you don't have to…'

'Life's not so great when you don't have control, is it?'

Releasing the locks on the bed's wheels with a toe, I pushed hard on the side of the bed to get it out from under Two's torso. His body dropped, the loops on the ends of the rope tightening. Expelled air grunted out of him as his weight was caught by the ropes. Now he really did look like a lopsided swing, swaying gently back and forward – his legs higher than his hands, and his head closest to the floor. Two lifted his head and tried to keep it up, but couldn't support the weight for long. It dropped backwards, exposing his throat, his eyes looking straight at the jerry cans I had positioned with precision.

I bent and held the catheter in Two's neck. His head was flushing red from all the blood rushing to it, so he tried to raise it again. I placed a hand on his hair to stop him and pushed his head down again.

'Just watch, Two.'

He whimpered with fear as I turned the clamp on the catheter. A ribbon of bright red appeared and snaked its way down the tube.

'No... please,' he said as he saw the blood in the tube reach the first of the cans and disappear inside.

'You shouldn't have corrupted everything at the beginning.'

I twisted the other clamps open. Each tube filled with blood. Two moaned.

'It will take a while and then be all over,' I said, in my best sincere doctor's voice – I even patted his hand reassuringly.

I needed a cup of tea – this was thirsty work.

Two sobbed and thrashed in desperation now, but each movement cut the ropes deeper into his wrists and ankles and made him swing more.

He stilled and watched his life drain away.

29

DI Clive Lussac

We were well into our journey, but I was still shaking from the press scrum at the PCU.

'There's something I need to tell you, Zoe,' I said. It wouldn't be fair to let her meet Doris Barclay unprepared.

'What's that, Boss?'

'Doris Barclay. She's going to be rude, vile, and offensive. She likes to find your weaknesses.'

'And…'

'And, try not to let her see that she's got to you. She feeds on conflict and aggression, but being nice winds her up… and…'

I hadn't forgotten how much Doris got to me in the old days. Unlike lots of people who'd met Doris, my scars were only caused by verbal wounds, but even so, they had never really healed. I didn't want them to open up again.

'Boss?'

The lips coming towards me, puckering in anticipation of a kiss. A thin red line, with deep wrinkles top and bottom like the legs of a wriggling centipede. The red lipstick feathering into the cracks. The lips opening, and the tongue escaping, darting from side to side…

'Boss?'

I shook myself free of the image, but I knew I would see it again soon. 'Er… my surname comes from a French town, it's near Bordeaux… Because of that, Doris calls me Frenchie… she pretends to give me a French kiss.'

'So?' Zoe looked at me, waiting for the punchline and not knowing I had given it.

'So…' *That tongue!* 'So, don't be surprised when she does.'

'Sure,' she said, as uninterested as if I had pointed out of the window of the car and said 'house'.

I would happily pick up spiders and let them explore my hand. Create a bowl with my fingers and let them tiptoe about. I didn't understand the fear people had of them, but I couldn't explain to Zoe that I was terrified of an old woman's tongue. Petrified it would force my lips apart and rummage around my mouth like a daring burglar. Scared I would taste her bile.

I stared out the window looking for something to distract me, but we were travelling through the urban sprawl of West London towards Chelsea. All the separate towns merged into one huge rat run. Bland buildings and garish shop signs.

'What do you make of Ameobi and Bailey?' I asked, dropping an old press photo of the 'team' from just after the launch of iMe onto the car's screen between us. Art, Esteban and Manu Ameobi smiled out in the centre, Tom Mitchell and Alice Bakaev on the left, Alan Kane and Emma Bailey on the right. She stood back a little from the group, like she had done in our meeting.

'Well, we always knew that Manu must have deep technical knowledge, but I didn't realise Emma used to be a programmer.'

'I guess she would know all the things that could go wrong and could test the code better.'

'She could still know the code well enough to get around it.'

'And Ameobi definitely does,' I said.

'So now we have more people of interest.'

To solve this, we were meant to narrow it down and eliminate people. Just be left with the killer. Instead, we were adding names to the list.

It felt like we were going backwards.

***

Lots of old banks had been converted into bars, restaurants and homes. The Health Bank still had its original stonework facade and leaded windows, which added prestige to the entrance to the club. Inside, the cashiers' booths and meeting area had been replaced by a small reception desk and a wall of metal bars. It gave the impression of something that might protect the entrance to a bank vault. Solid metal doors with large wheel handles and currency signs added to the illusion.

The other walls were white, broken with splashes of colour from stylised prints of old bank notes. I recognised the old fivers and tenners. They evoked fond memories. Behind the receptionist was an original Barclays Bank sign.

We approached the desk and threw our IDs at the receptionist. 'We need to see Tom Mitchell,' I said.

The receptionist's eye shadowed as his HUD displayed our IDs, and it looked like he picked them up and passed them on to someone else. He paused and said, 'Please wait here.'

Behind us, a thin, elegant woman in an expensive looking silver tracksuit approached one of the metal doors and touched the centre of the wheel. It opened with an electronic click as the lock released.

Time to bend the rules. 'Come on, Zoe,' I said.

'We don't have a search warrant.'

'It's not a search, we're just punters taking a little look at the facilities,' I said. Over my shoulder, I called to the receptionist, 'We're going to do a tour.'

I could hear his protests behind us as I put my left hand on the metal door the woman had used. Instead of opening, I heard a harsh little buzz of denial. It must be programmed for members only, I thought, so with my left hand still touching the door, I used my right hand to select the *'Menu'* in the top left of my HUD. I then selected *'PCU'*, then *'Overrides'* and then *'Locks'*. After a second, I was rewarded by the electronic click of the door opening, and we stepped through.

***

The short corridor went straight and then made a sharp right. Through the glass wall to our left we could see into the gym area. All sorts of bikes and equipment that I didn't recognise were in use by the beautiful members. They would be following an exercise schedule from their training Buddy. The staff members looked bored with nothing to do unless someone messaged them that they needed more water. The gym was huge but split by short partition walls to provide a more private and intimate experience. We could hear controlled breathing and the clack of weights being dropped. This was all way beyond my 'do as little as possible' approach to exercise.

We passed a couple of doors marked *'Private'* and reached the end of the corridor. On our left were the changing rooms, and on our right, a single door with the badge *'Resistance Training'*.

I pushed the door to the changing room and Zoe and I went in. Obviously, the changing rooms were multi-gender. A simple male/female classification of an old-style gym wouldn't have been appropriate in our multi-gender society, and the changing rooms were made up of lots of private single person and family booths. This wasn't the 'all change and shower together' forced naturism of my school changing room. Touching a door with a green vacant sign, I went inside a booth. 'Oh, they have Halo showers,' I said.

'I love those,' Zoe said, and popped her head in to look as well.

The shower was a tall glass tube, with a door to get in and out. I had seen videos of them working: the chrome disc at the top could be locked in place to provide a basic, top-down shower, or it could traverse up and down to create an all-torso shower. The more expensive showers had more than one water halo to create a total immersion experience a bit like a vertical bath, but with a fraction of the water usage. The showers here had six halos, and would each cost more than half of my salary.

Back in the corridor, we stopped at the resistance training door. I pushed it, but it was locked by an old key-code lock with a handle and buttons labelled 0 to 9. Years back we had been trained in picking locks, but only on locks with keys, and the override option on my HUD wasn't going to work on something so old and mechanical. Without the code, we weren't getting in.

I heard a door open behind us and turned to see three walls of muscle coming towards us. Each had a shiny shaved head and wore a tight blue vest and trousers in the same colour as the Barclays badge. The vests were probably 5XL, but they were still stretched tight across every bulge and bump. The first one got to us and the other two stopped right behind him. They filled the corridor. *They must spend all their FUs on protein*, I thought. Almost in perfect sync, all three crossed their arms over their huge chests and stuck their hands under their biceps to emphasise the muscle mass. I thought it looked choreographed and almost laughed. Luckily, I stopped myself. *Fuck, their arms are bigger than my legs.*

'You shouldn't be here,' the front one said. His two friends scowled and nodded in unison.

'We were just looking…' I said.

'Come with us,' he said.

We had the muscle in front of us and the locked door behind us. Nowhere to go.

'How?' I asked.

The question seemed to confuse him for a second, but then he got it and started to turn. All his muscled bulk didn't make for agility, and he turned slowly. His two friends turned as well, getting themselves into a temporary beefcake gridlock. It was like watching three big lorries trying to reverse and manoeuvre in a tight space. All that was missing was the warning beeps when they went into reverse.

They sorted themselves out and led us to one of the private doors we had passed. First Muscle opened and went through the door. The other two stood across the corridor like a roadblock forcing us onto a diversion. We followed the first guy. We had no choice, and the other two closed up behind us, trapping us between them.

After some twists and turns in the corridors, First Muscle stopped outside an open door and waved us inside.

I heard the words I had been dreading: 'Give us a kiss, Frenchie.'

***

Doris' voice was deep and gravelly from a lifetime of cigarettes. I looked at the desk to avoid seeing the tongue that would be waving in the air. A snake's tongue tasting the air for the scent of its prey.

A big hand pushed me down into a seat and Zoe appeared in a chair next to me.

The hand forced my head up. I looked at Doris, relieved that the tongue was away. She still looked like a sweet little old lady, except for the rings: skulls of all designs, skulls in flying helmets, or sombreros, some with crossed-bones. Most were metal, but it looked like some white ones could have been carved from bone.

'Who's your pretty little friend, Frenchie?' Doris said.

'I'm DC Jordan,' Zoe said, a challenge in her tone as she held Doris' gaze.

'Got some spirit this one, eh?' She leered at Zoe.

'Are you slipping her one, Frenchie? If you're not, I bet you're gagging for it…'

'No, I'm—'

Doris steam-rolled on. 'You gagging to grind away on top of her? Tasty bit of skirt like that.' She turned back to me. 'Bet you want her to replace Mary now you're divorced.'

I wasn't surprised she knew about my divorce. She had always been well-informed.

Doris looked back at Zoe and winked. 'Does he put the privacy glass on in the car and interfere with you, Zoe? Good thing about driver-less cars, eh, plenty of time for a fumble with *Uncle* Frenchie.' She leered some more. 'Is he making you earn a promotion on your back?'

I looked at Zoe, trying to give her some support. 'We have a professional relationship, Doris,' I said.

'Doris?' she spat. 'Doris? You always were *filth*. Always taking a fucking liberty. All my days, I've always come down hard on disrespect. It's Mrs Barclay to you, scum.'

'I'm sorry, Mrs Barclay, please forgive my rudeness,' I said, seeing my politeness causing anger to flare in her eyes.

'Professional? You?'

'Mrs Barclay, as DI Lussac said, our relationship is strictly professional,' Zoe said with a sweet smile.

I was proud of her, standing up to Doris' foul mouth in the perfect way, and I took advantage as Doris paused for breath.

'You must be Tom Mitchell.' I said to the man sitting next to Doris. Even in a smart blue suit with a white shirt, hair neatly clipped and gelled, he was still recognisable from the photo of the man with the hat and dreadlocks.

'Yes,' he said.

I said, 'We need to ask you some questions.'

'You've got a fucking liberty, Frenchie. You come in here without so much as a please and nose around.' She slid a wrinkled hand on top of Tom's and patted it. 'Tom's a good boy, and he's done nothing wrong, so you can both fuck off and don't come back.'

Two hands slid under my armpits, and I was yanked airborne and towards the door. The muscle carried me with my feet skimming the floor. I could hear Zoe protesting behind me.

'Fucking liberty,' Doris said, as we were hurled into the corridor and marched out.

30

Thief

I put a funnel into the neck of one of the jerrycans, picked up the razor-sharp scalpel and sliced a smile into Two's throat. I wanted as much blood out as I could get. His heart had stopped a while ago, so I left gravity to finish the job.

I put a thick plastic sheet on the bed and slid it back under his shoulders. After spinning the back of the bed under his bum, I released the ratchet on the first rope. To avoid a nasty burn, I made sure that I wasn't holding the rope as it ran through the ratchet. Two's left leg thumped down onto the bed. I visited each ratchet, and when all his limbs were down, I pulled the ropes back through their eyes and spent some time cleaning and drying the ropes as best I could. I left them in neat coils in their cupboard.

Now I needed to tidy Two away.

I pushed his bed out of the cage, along the passage and into the garage. I had put lots more plastic sheeting on the floor under the saw. It was old, but new to me, and gleamed in the middle of the room. I had picked it up at a bargain price a few years before from a butcher who was forced out of business by the red meat restrictions. It looked a little like a scorpion: four bent legs supported a flat, metal body, and a large metal 'tail' curved up and over the metal bed. The 'sting' was the bandsaw's blade.

The green button made the bandsaw whirl into life. The long, narrow, rotating blade sang in anticipation. I pushed Two's wrist towards the blade and paused. *Better make sure my fingers are out of the way.* The butcher had promised that the blades were specially designed to slice through meat and bone with no clogging – just a nice clean cut. I pushed again, the blade sliced through the wrist as promised. Two's hand plopped to one side.

My plan was to do all the cutting in one go, but I couldn't resist trying my other new toy. With a hiss, the lid lifted and slid back. *So cool.* Two's hand slipped into the bag, which I placed onto the machine's bed, making sure the open end was straight and flat on the rails. I reread the instructions to make sure I was doing it right. The lid hissed down, the compressor hummed for a few seconds and then the light turned green. I opened the lid again and examined Two's vacuum-packed hand. Airtight – no mess and no smell. *Perfect.*

It took me longer than I expected to do everything, but by one in the morning I had a nice neat pile of Two bags stacked into a large trunk. The blood had gone down the drain, followed by ten minutes with the jet wash and lots of drain cleaner. Two's clothes and the sheeting I put into the incinerator and I spent another hour cleaning and storing the saw.

I needed some sleep.

I needed to decide who deserved me next.

31

DI Clive Lussac

'That went well,' I said, landing on the pavement outside the Health Bank.

Zoe turned and looked at me, eyebrows raised in two little arches. 'Really?'

'Doris is hiding something.' I rubbed my armpits and biceps to ease the pain from the 'help' the muscle had given me out of the building. 'She wouldn't have been so nice otherwise.'

'Really? She was being nice?'

'Well, it's all relative.' I gave her an apologetic half-smile, half-shrug gesture. 'But for Doris, yeah. She must have liked you.'

Zoe shook her head.

I called the car, and as we waited for it to come to pick us up, I felt the glare from one of the muscles who still stood in the doorway.

I could see Zoe was reliving the shock to the system that Doris gave you. 'You did well. That was the right way to handle her,' I told her.

'Thanks.'

'Let's go,' I said, watching our car's silent approach. It stopped and opened its doors. It was weird, but I felt better since the meeting and getting thrown out. I didn't know if it was the adrenaline, but I felt more alive than I had in a long time. I was starting to feel like I had a purpose again. Maybe it was the confrontation with an old adversary. Maybe it was the message I had just received from Sophia: *When are you going to take me out for dinner?*

***

On our crime wall at PCU, Zoe pinched the photos of Doris and Tom Mitchell and dragged them up to the top of the *Possible Suspects'* list, settling them next to Art and Esteban. She moved Ameobi and Bailey to form our second row. It didn't feel like much progress.

I was staring at the screen, stuck in a thought process, trying to pick the killer. My eyes flicked between Doris, Esteban and Art. *Ip dip sky blue, who's it–*

I dragged my focus back into the room. Zoe waited, bored with my silence. She slid onto the corner of her usual desk and waited.

'We should look at *why*, not how,' I said. 'Why Karina was killed or why Alan Kane is missing.'

'I've been thinking about that.' Zoe took a big breath in to prepare herself, and then started. 'Art has the position and the knowledge, but already has power and money.'

'There's never too much power. He's hiding something, I can feel it.' I tapped the table for emphasis.

'But why would he kill Karina or take Alan?'

'You saw Karina, she was beautiful, and we know Art has a roaming eye.'

She looked thoughtful and said, 'And Alan? That won't be sexual for Art.'

'No, but Alan was involved with iMe from the beginning. Art could be out for revenge for something Alan did.'

'So could Esteban.'

'Maybe. Can you check into Alan's time with iMe? Also, check if Art or Esteban came into contact with Karina.'

Zoe's fingers danced in the air as she made notes. 'Yep.'

My eyes went back to Doris on the display wall. 'Doris' background says she has the will and the money to build a Suppressor. She also has Tom Mitchell.'

'So, what are they doing?'

'I don't know,' I admitted, 'but...'

Zoe shifted, uncomfortable on the desk, and looked at me again. 'But what?'

I held my hand up to stop her. 'That door with the old lock seemed out of place. Everything else was new and controllable.'

'You want to check it?' she said.

I nodded, and I watched as she turned on her HUD and started to move things around. The crime wall cleared, and a map of the Health Bank appeared. Zoe scrolled and zoomed so that we could see a section of the corridor where the resistance training door was. We couldn't see CCTV-style images, just a line drawing of the floor plan that was compulsory for every building to provide. White lines on a black background straight from the architect's plans.

'This is live,' she said.

The corridor was empty, and Zoe zoomed out a bit so that we could see part of the layout of the gym. The area had about ten green dots in it, each where a person was presumably on some piece of exercise equipment or mat.

'Can you rewind the history to find someone going through the door?' I said. 'I'd like to follow them through and see if it tells us anything.'

The time display on the screen counted backwards in jerky twenty-second intervals. Dots came and went along the corridor, others moved between exercise stations in the gym, then after about fifteen minutes of time had rewound, two dots went through the resistance training door.

'OK, now let's go forward and follow them,' I said. I felt that we were onto something, and the anticipation fizzed in me.

The two dots on the screen stopped in front of the door.

Zoe moved the cursor over the dot on the right who would be operating the key-code. 'That's Zac Prentice,' Zoe said as his picture and personal details came up. 'He's one of the bouncers we met yesterday.'

'Yes, the one who lifted you out of your chair. Who's the other one?'

'It must be a member – she's a city lawyer.'

'She's being escorted. That's weird, all the members we saw moved around without needing escorts.'

The two dots moved again, passing through the door and Zoe scrolled the display to keep them in the centre of the screen. They went along a short corridor and down a spiral staircase. At the bottom, both dots were stationary for about thirty seconds, and then Zac Prentice went back up the stairs, leaving the lawyer to carry on.

'What did they do at the bottom of the stairs?' I asked.

Zoe stared at the screen, not wanting to miss anything. 'Don't know, there's no additional detail,' she mumbled.

The lawyer went past two empty rooms, then past another with people in. The two dots in the room were almost on top of each other.

'Hold it there,' I said, pointing at the dots in the room. 'Who're they?'

Zoe paused the screen and checked the details of each of the dots. 'Lucia Rossi is one of them. She's twenty-four and works at the Health Bank as a personal trainer. The other is Toby Robertson, he's sixty-two and works for a civil rights charity.'

'That's a very small room to exercise in.'

'And the main gym had a lot of mats for stretching, I doubt they need more.'

This was significant, I thought. If it were legitimate, then the room would be in the main member's area. A locked door and an escorted member meant some form of two-tier membership, and the second tier had to be getting better benefits than the ordinary members. Toby looked like he was benefiting from Lucia's intimate attention.

'Follow the lawyer again,' I said.

The lawyer's signal continued past more small side rooms, which were either empty or with two dots showing in them. The last room was a little larger, with three dots in it, so close together that the dots merged into a large ellipse. Zoe brought up the details: A member with a personal trainer on each side. I raised my eyebrows. It was easy to imagine what was going on in there.

The lawyer got to the end of the corridor where it opened out into a large area with at least fifty people in.

'That looks like a casino,' I said, getting up to cross to the screen. 'Look here.' I pointed at a line of dots with two dots opposite them. 'That's a bar. See the line of people waiting, and the two dots must be the bar staff.'

Zoe nodded, seeing the meaning of the dots on a black background.

She pointed at the rough circles of dots. 'Then these people are gambling.' Some circles had four dots, others more.

'Yes, they're card tables, and this long table could be roulette.'

***

Nisha Bhatt rocked back in her chair and pondered her screen. Zoe had run her through what we had found, and now we waited for her verdict.

'OK, I'll buy it,' she said. 'And Alan Kane is a member?'

'Yes,' I said.

'What about Karina?'

'Well.' I scratched my neck. 'We're not sure how she fits but there has to be a link. We need to find it.'

Bhatt shook her head. 'So, now what?'

'We have to get in to see what's happening for ourselves. All the members in the resistance training room are wealthy. They'll go silent and get their lawyers if we don't surprise them and catch them red-handed.'

'So how do you want to do it?' Bhatt asked, sitting forward.

I spent the next few minutes going over the plan Zoe and I had come up with.

'Do it,' Bhatt ordered.

32

DI Clive Lussac

An old bank would have been secure, but the Health Bank was a gym and run by all sorts of health and safety directives. That meant multiple escape routes for the occupants and back doors. Zoe found the details of all the door locks from the building's plans before we left, and she had already pre-programmed them to open for us.

We waited, leaning against the brick wall at the back of the Health Bank. We were about halfway down a narrow alley that ran behind the parade of shops. Opposite us, the other wall was a designated street art site. The psychedelic patterns intermingled with faces and animals. I loved the vibrancy of the colours and the sheer scale of the artists' imagination.

While we waited, a man with greasy hair and a huge beard walked down the alley with a group of tourists.

'What does it all mean?' one of the tourists asked, pointing at the wall.

The man's beard and moustache parted like a sudden opening in the bushes of a garden maze. 'This piece expresses the isolation of the individual trapped in their hostile environment.'

'The art's good but the explanation's bollocks,' I muttered to Zoe.

'I've done one of those tours,' she said. 'You'd learn something if you tried.'

I spent a minute trying to think of a quick comeback, but I had nothing. I'd come up with something brilliant when it was much too late.

'The crew are outside,' Zoe said. 'Bhatt has just approved the search warrant.'

'OK, send them in. We'll go when they're causing the maximum noise.' My pulse rate reading on my HUD started to climb. 'Get them to confirm when.'

Zoe relayed the message to her crew, and then we waited. We were both breathing hard despite not moving. I zoned out the alley and the lecturer droning on. All I could see was the door.

'OK, the three bouncers are coming into the reception area. The crew are flash messaging their IDs to everyone in the vicinity.'

I put my hand on the door and it clicked open. I stepped into the darkness of the entrance.

***

We jogged down the corridor. I was worried that the crew wouldn't detain the bouncers long, so we needed to hurry.

My heart was banging away, but I could barely hear Zoe breathing behind me. 'Left here should bring us to the back of the changing rooms,' she said.

I stopped and glanced around the corner and saw the door. Zoe almost barged into me. 'Come on, Boss.'

Here goes, I thought, while opening the door to the changing room. A couple of people looked our way as we entered, but we didn't face any bouncers or nasty surprises. We skipped through the changing room, and I peered out into the corridor with the locked door. A small white trainer and pink leggings appeared around the corner, followed by a woman dressed for the gym. Not staff, just a member.

I stepped out into the corridor and Zoe held the door open to let the woman go into the changing room, then followed me out.

I put down the small box I was carrying, fished around in my pocket and found a red tube covered with 'Highly Corrosive' warnings and the name 'Arbor-ate'. The tech guy from the terrorist section said it was some sort of genetically engineered organism that ate wood, and promised it would get through the locked door quickly and silently. The tube ended with a short nozzle and a twist cap. I snapped off the cap and placed the nozzle on the door where the lock was attached. Squeezing the tube, I saw a white paste emerge from the end. It looked like toothpaste with metal flecks in it. As soon as it touched the wood the paste started to fizz and hiss. Small white bubbles seethed around the lock and started to turn brown as the paste ate into the wood. I traced the outline of the lock with the nozzle, trying to make sure that I got a good fat bead of the paste everywhere. The whole area around the lock was bubbling brown now. Wood splinters danced and writhed in the darkening foam and the lock moved a few millimetres, slumping towards the corridor.

I grabbed the handle, then pulled and wriggled it around in a circular motion, trying to wrench it clear. Each rotation freed the lock a little more, and I could hear the wood tearing over the fizz of the Arbor-ate. With a sudden release, the lock came away and the door sagged open. I could see the other side through the foamy hole in the door.

'Let's find out what's going on,' I said.

***

At the bottom of the spiral staircase we stopped in a short corridor, trying to find why the bouncer and lawyer had spent time there. In the glow of an automatic light, I looked around the simple space. Other than some pictures of historic sporting events, the only thing on the walls was a large metal cabinet with another mechanical lock.

We hadn't been sure if the door with the key-code lock had a metal core underneath the wood, so the tech guy had given us a second tube just in case. This one was blue with all the same corrosive warnings on it, and its green paste ate through the thin metal door in a couple of seconds.

'Suppressors?' Zoe said.

'Let's find out,' I said, and opened the door.

The cabinet didn't hold Suppressors. Inside were rows of shelves, each one had a line of velvet covered stands and looked like something in a jewellery shop display. A lot of the stands were empty, but the rest held small, shiny bracelet-like objects with straps and leads. Every lead was connected to the power, and each bracelet's LED light stared back at us like a set of little green eyes.

I picked one up and passed it to Zoe. As I did, the lead over-extended and popped out of the bracelet. The LED changed from green to blue.

'They must be on charge,' Zoe said as I pulled down another bracelet and removed the lead. I turned the bracelet over in my hand. It was wider than my wrist and seemed to be made of some synthetic woven composite. The straps on the outside looked like they were designed to adjust the size. Like the Suppressors Esteban had, the bracelet was getting warm.

'What do you think, Zoe?'

'It's kind of like a Suppressor but much smaller than Esteban's ones.'

'That's what I was thinking. Let's carry on.'

We walked on, then stopped outside the door where we had seen the signals from Lucia Rossi and the charity worker. I pushed the door open and we looked in. The room was empty except for a bed and a chair. The subdued light, the purple wall coverings and matching fabrics made everything seem soft and sensual, like an intimate boudoir.

I looked at Zoe and she nodded, seeming to share the same conclusion: Lucia was providing *personal* training.

We stopped outside the next door and we could hear voices.

'Do you want more?' a male voice asked.

'Oh, please, please,' replied a woman's voice, husky with desire.

I opened the door and stopped, trying to make sense of what I was seeing. The room was decorated in the same seductive style as the first room. A woman lay on the bed, her hair fanned out on the pillow that supported her head. She wore a fluffy Health Bank robe with the Barclays Bank logo over her left breast. A man knelt on the bed, close to the woman's head. He was toned and had one of the club's fitness instructor uniforms on. She was looking up at him, full of expectation. She didn't even notice us, but the man glared at us and jerked his head behind him, like he was indicating the room we had just come from. 'Room one is free,' he said.

The woman's left hand clutched the sheets and I could see one of the bracelets strapped tight to her wrist. The man dropped his hand down into the bowl by his side. He brought out a golden-brown chip, heat steaming from it, and dipped it in a sauce. He rested it on the woman's lips.

Zoe and I stepped backwards out of the room and looked at each other.

'He was feeding her chips and mayonnaise, right?' Zoe said.

'It looked like it,' I said.

We went along the corridor and ignored two empty rooms. The final room held a couple with another fitness instructor. The couple both wore robes and bracelets, and each grasped a small fork. The instructor held a tray with fruit and marshmallows on it. The man speared an item on the tray, held it under the dark, running chocolate fountain and placed it in his partner's mouth.

I felt more like a voyeur watching their indulgence than if they were in bed together. Something weird was going on here.

***

The main room wasn't what we expected either. The tables weren't for cards or gambling but for eating and drinking. We were in a restaurant. We could see steaks and pizza, wine and beer. The sight and sounds of happy, carefree people enjoying themselves made me nostalgic. It was like a scene from before iMe. Quite a few people looked like they were well over their FU alcohol allowance.

'Bring his signal up,' I said, and pointed at a man in his forties in an expensive grey suit. He had taken his tie off and stuffed it in the breast pocket of his jacket. He sagged in the upholstered chair and his head rolled as if it wasn't firmly attached. From the sheen of sweat on his brow and flushed cheeks, I was sure he was drunk.

'OK, got it,' she said.

'What are his readings?'

'Normal.'

'Normal? He's pissed.'

'His signal says there's zero alcohol in his blood.'

The man grabbed the last piece of pizza from his plate and stuffed it in his mouth. He chewed, savouring the flavours, and drew his left hand up to flick his hair back from his eye. As he did, the cuff of his suit rose and I could see he also wore a bracelet.

'Calorie intake?'

'Low, Boss. Like he's not eaten for a few hours.'

I looked around the room. Everyone was wearing a bracelet. The only thing we had guessed correctly was the bar.

I was about to go and talk to the man when I heard a familiar voice.

'Frenchie...'

***

You're the person who has committed a crime, Inspector,' Alfie said. 'Criminal damage to the door and cabinet at the very least.'

Alfie stood on Doris' left. To her right was Tom Mitchell, as smart and silent as before. The three bouncers made up the group. Alfie's bald head shone like the bouncers'. He hadn't changed much in the years since I last met him. His seventy-year-old body was still big and the lack of fat said he looked after himself. He could have been a prediction of what the bouncers would look like in fifty years. Not surprising as he had started in the same way – bouncing at one of Doris' clubs. Recognising that he had the brains as well as the physique, Doris had sent him to university, and he had been her lawyer for years.

'But all these people are eating and drinking,' I said.

'We all have to eat, Inspector. That's not a crime.'

I looked at Zoe for help and she gave a tiny nod. The shadowing in her eye showed that her HUD was active.

'That man was eating and drinking, but he shows no alcohol in his system,' she said, indicating the drunk.

'What's your point?'

'Those bracelets must be interfering with the iMe monitoring,' I said.

Tom Mitchell squirmed at the mention of the bracelets and looked down at the floor.

'People are consuming taxable food and drink, using their FU allowances and your bracelets are stopping it being reported. If nothing else it's tax evasion and fraud, *Doris*.' I enjoyed saying the name. Like Al Capone, Doris had got away with so many crimes and killings and maybe it would be a tax charge that took her down. I smiled at the thought.

I knelt down and released the top of the box I had been carrying since the alley. An immediate angry buzz started, and six micro-drones came up and out of the box, hovered and then scattered. The diners looked up at the noise as drones buzzed around them. They started to panic. People jumped up, looking for an escape, upending tables, smashing glasses and spilling chairs as they tried to get away. The pissed guy waved a lazy arm to swat at a drone like it was all a drunken hallucination.

Doris screamed, 'Frenchie, you'll fucking pay for this! I'll rip you and your little girlfriend apart.' She motioned to the bouncers to grab me, but they stopped when they heard people arriving behind them.

The crew piled into the room, clearly having a wild time, and took in the scene: the drones, the diners, the mess. Their huge smiles disappeared when two bouncers stepped towards them.

Doris chuckled. 'That's your backup? Five little kids. Don't make me fucking laugh.'

Then she heard the heavy boots on the stairs and the first of twenty black helmeted counter-terrorism cops stormed into the room, almost running the crew over. 'No, Doris. *That's* our backup,' I said.

I had a huge, stupid grin on my face. Finally, after all those ancient defeats, I had got her. Finally, I had beaten her.

I didn't see Alfie's fist until it smashed into my right eye and sent me flying.

33

DC Zoe Jordan

Clive and I waited in the sad space called Interview Room One. We only had one interview room, so I didn't understand why someone had bothered to number it. When it was last decorated, beige paint must have been cheap as it covered everything. The walls and table showed chips and knocks from the years since the paint had been slapped around and the original battleship grey was visible underneath. It gave the room a camouflage feel.

I looked at Clive. His right eye was a small bloodshot slit surrounded by a sea of yellows, blues and purples. It could have been the inspiration for some of the street art outside the Health Bank. Worst of all was the massive egg swelling on his cheek.

'That looks nice, Frenchie,' Doris said, laughing. 'I hope it's hurting.' She tapped the backs of her rings on the table to create her own metallic applause. The liver spots dotted her hand like the chips in the table's paint.

'Yeah, it is,' Clive said. He reached up and his gentle fingertips explored the egg. 'I've never been able to see my cheek before.'

Alfie kissed the big ring on his right hand. The gold band held some sort of gold coin that doubled as a decorative knuckleduster. He stared at Clive.

Doris patted Alfie's arm as if to congratulate him. 'Embarrassing, Frenchie. Little peck from an old man and you go flying. I did laugh. You landed like the useless sack of shit you are.'

Clive shrugged. 'That little *peck* resulted in Alfie being charged with assaulting a police officer.' Clive stared back at him. They were locked into some bullshit macho stubbornness competition. *Why do they think it matters who blinks first?*

Clive should be the boss, but I was the one trying to keep the interview running in a professional manner.

'You claim to never have heard of Karina Morgan?' I said.

'That not what I said, dearie.' Doris could do a convincing little old lady act when she thought it might help her. 'I said that I saw her in the news but that's all.'

'And Alan Kane?'

'As I said, he's a member of the club. I've met him a couple of times.'

'Well, you'll go down for fraud, *Doris*.' Clive couldn't resist jumping in again. Even then, he still stared at Alfie.

He was taking us off topic, and after all the grief he gave me for doing it once with Art, here he was doing it again and again. One rule for him and another for me.

Alfie dropped his stare, and Clive wiggled in his chair, a jubilant smirk on his face. *Jesus, he thinks he's won something.*

Clive was still staring as Alfie reached for his case. With a clack, he released the catches and put his hand inside. 'I've sent you this electronically, but I thought paper would make the point clearer.'

He slid a few sheets of paper across the table to us. Alfie was as old-school as Clive.

I glanced at the front cover:

The Health Bank
Wilde Membership
Terms and Conditions

'What's this?' I asked.

'Every one of our members in that room joined our Wilde Membership,' Alfie said.

'Clever name,' I said, enjoying the nice play on words.

Doris grinned her appreciation of my understanding. 'Thanks, dearie.'

Clive was trying not to look lost.

'Explain it to him, dearie. He always was as thick as shit.'

'Wilde as in Oscar Wilde,' I said to Clive, but he looked blank. 'All those people are giving in to temptation. They're indulging themselves.'

'And?'

I had to spoon-feed him. 'Oscar Wilde is quoted as saying that he could resist everything except temptation. Like the members. It's why the room is called Resistance Training – it's a double meaning with the resistance training in a gym and Wilde's lack of resistance.'

Doris nodded along with my explanation, but Clive said, 'So?'

I gave up trying.

Alfie turned the pages over to get our attention. He pointed at the highlighted clauses. 'You will clearly see that my client has no fraud case to answer. Any FU reporting issues are the responsibility of the member.'

I pulled the paper close to read the smaller print.

7.3 The Member is liable and responsible for their Freedom Unit allowance, reporting consumption to the Ministry of Well-being and Health and any tax liability arising from their use of the Membership.

7.4 The Member fully indemnifies the Club and its Employees for all and any claims brought against the Club and its Employees in relation to the Member's use of the said Membership.

'I've also sent you the audited accounts and tax returns of the Health Bank. They show that the fees paid by the members have been properly declared and taxes paid.'

'But your bracelets suppress the signal – that's a criminal offence,' Clive shouted, and banged the table so hard the sheets of paper bounced.

'Again, I thought paper would be easier,' Alfie said, delving into his case again. 'It's an extract from the Sovereignty Protection Act.'

A single sheet of paper came across the desk, covered in text but with only one highlighted sentence.

'It is a criminal offence to block, suppress or hide the iMe signal.'

'There you go. You've proved my point,' Clive said, a smile of triumph playing on his face.

'No, Inspector. The signal was not blocked, suppressed or hidden. At no time did the members' signals get lost. Your records will show that.'

'But you changed the content of the signal.'

'My client cannot possibly know the intent of the lawmakers, and there is no mention of the content of the signal in the act. She can only go by the letter of the law, which she has not broken.'

Now it was Doris' turn to look *very* pleased with herself.

***

Clive was sulking in the corner of the PCU by our crime wall. He kept touching his eye and looking down at the floor. I'd give him a minute more and then we need to get on with it. We still had Alan to find and Karina's killer to catch. Moping around in the office wasn't going to do either.

Fuck waiting, we needed to get on with it now. 'Boss, we have work to do.'

He looked up and slumped his dispirited shoulders. 'I can't believe she's going to get away with it.'

'As Bhatt said, the case has been passed to Fraud. It's up to them now.'

'Yeah, but did you see the Wilde membership list she forced Alfie to give her. It's all celebs and lawyers. It's going to get hushed up.'

'Maybe.' I was sure that the fraud guys would fight hard to make a case.

'They can't prosecute. It's an all-inclusive membership. They can eat or drink anything and there are no records of who had what.'

He made a good point. Without records of consumption, the fraud guys couldn't prove how much each member owed in undeclared FU tax. 'I'm sure the CPS will find something in the Sovereignty Protection Act that makes the bracelets illegal.'

'I hope so. I finally thought I'd got Doris.'

I picked up Doris' and Tom's photos on the screen and slid them away from Art under the 'Possible Suspects' list. I didn't want to move them out completely yet. 'They could still be involved. Alan Kane is a member.'

'Not a Wilde member,' he moaned, and stared at his hands. Finally, he said, 'Let's start again. Can you check the signals of all the suspects and track Art again?'

I didn't get Clive's certainty about Art. *Sure, Art's a bit pervy, but there's nothing linking him to anything.*

I clicked into a stored search and threw the summary screen for last week up onto the crime wall.

'Knew it,' said Clive.

In bright, full colour I could see nice solid signal lines for Doris, Ameobi and Bailey, even one for Esteban.

Art's signal was encrypted over the weekend.

***

Clive was being unbearably smug, but I couldn't argue with the data. Art's signal had been encrypted over the weekend, and now he was in Parliament. We would have to see him after he left, so I went to see how the crew were doing.

They had formed a tight little clump in the office. Connected enough to sit close to each other, even though they never talked amongst themselves. They messaged each other instead, using their HUDs, hands waving in the air: poking, swiping and pinching the items on their screens. Just the hand-dance that you saw everywhere. It was what I did with my friends.

'Anyone got anything?' I asked.

'Nothing new on Ameobi,' Ezra answered, his diamante earring sparkling.

Ava, the brightest crew member, was bouncing in her chair. If she was still at school, she would have had her hand up in the air and be shouting, 'Miss, miss' waiting to be asked.

'Ava?' I said.

'Well, basically, it's Emma Bailey.'

Her blond hair was held in two ponytails, which flicked and jumped in time with her excitement. I was tired and drained and felt a flash of irritation at her energy. I stopped myself saying anything in case I sounded as old as Clive. After a breath, I asked, 'What have you found, Ava?'

'Well, it's her TrueMe account. She's posted some photos of food and recipes. They're from her house.'

'Show me.' Ava threw her display at my HUD, and I flicked through them. 'But these were posted last week.'

'Yes, but look at the meta-data embedded in the photos.' She pushed into one of the photos. 'See, the location shows her home address which is where her signal says she was, but look at the time stamp. The photos were taken on the evening Karina went missing.'

This confirmed that Emma Bailey was at home on that evening. She was so quiet and timid that she didn't really fit the profile of Karina's killer anyway.

Ezra interrupted my thoughts.

'There's a new message on Alan Kane's TrueMe account.'

'What does it say?'

'I'm home.'

34

DI Clive Lussac

Alan's TrueMe account and his *'I'm home'* message made us think he was OK, but he still didn't have a signal. I booked a car to get us to his home to see what was going on, but it was mid-morning and the streets were choked with cars. To save time, I sent a forensics drone ahead of us.

When people used petrol cars to get about it ruined the air quality, but rush hour would come and go. People commuted, parked and then roads became quieter. Now people got their self-drive cars to drop them off at work and told them to circulate. The cars drove themselves around and around the roads close to their owner in case they were needed at short notice. The cars found a recharging point when they were low, but otherwise they were on the roads. Rush hour lasted all day now.

We had become commuters of habit: I travelled backwards, Zoe faced forward, the screen between us. Zoe connected our car's screen to the drone's image feed. It hadn't arrived at Alan's yet, and we stared at the blank screen as the car crawled along, our frustration growing with each slow mile. Finally, the screen flickered into life and we could see the road Alan lived on. The drone approached Alan's house, its image focused on the wide-open front door.

'He must be there,' I said. 'We definitely shut the door after our search.'

Zoe said, 'The drone's too big to get through the front door.'

'OK, tell it to park and deploy the micro-drones.'

We watched as the drone got closer and closer to the ground. As it settled on the tiny patch of land in front of Alan's house, the screen changed to a useless view of the dense weeds that were higher than the drone.

The car's screen blanked and divided into six separate sections. One by one, they filled with a view of Alan's open front door as each micro-drone got airborne and came online.

We followed the screen, our eyes scanning the different images as the micro-drones scoured the house. Except for a couple of closed internal doors that the drones couldn't get through, it was a bare shell. Alan's house, but not his home.

Except it wasn't exactly the same. 'Expand number four,' I said.

Zoe touched the segment of the screen showing the image of the lounge and it redrew to take up the whole screen. We had a much better view now. The armchair had been pushed back against the wall, and a big silver trunk occupied the middle of the floor with its lid shut. Marks led to it across the carpet from the doorway. They were solid unbroken lines. Not like drag marks, but more like a trolley had been used to wheel the trunk in.

'There's a label on the lid,' Zoe said, nudging the controls to move the micro-drone closer to the box until the lid filled the image. She frowned when she saw what it said. 'What does that mean?'

Stencilled on the lid were the words *'Home sweet home'*.

***

After the scan, we shut the drones down and when we arrived at Alan's the main one was in sleep mode, with the micro-drones stowed away and the lid shut. We wouldn't have seen it resting in all the weeds and grass if we hadn't known it was there.

Zoe went into the house first and paused. I took a pace past her and then another towards the trunk.

After a third step, I reached out and opened the lid of the trunk. I peeked in.

I swayed, and my mouth filled with saliva as I fought to control my body.

'What is it, Boss?'

'Don't.' I tried to grab Zoe's arm to stop her looking, but I was too late.

She stood transfixed by my side staring into the trunk.

On the top lay Alan's severed head. The mottled, bluish grey of his skin was made shiny by the plastic covering that pressed tightly against each crease and fold. His eyes were open, staring at us, and his tongue was sticking out.

'His tongue's been pinned in place,' I said, shuddering. Three round metal pin heads held Alan's tongue tight against his bottom lip and chin: one in the tip and one on each side.

The head was exactly in the centre of the bag and parallel to the edges. Someone had taken time and care with the vacuum packing to get the positioning so accurate. It reminded me of the care that had been taken over Karina's body.

On either side of the head, two smaller bags were taped to the head's bag. Each contained one of Alan's hands and were positioned so that the fingers were splayed out and Alan's thumbs were touching his temples.

Whoever had killed Alan had made him look like a kid in a playground – tongue out and hands rotating at his temples, rudely gesturing to his friends and singing, 'Ner, ner, de, ner, ner.'

***

The micro-drones hadn't found any fingerprints but to be safe Zoe passed me some new gloves which I snapped onto my shaking hands. I separated the bags and turned Alan's head over. The metallic ends of the severed probes glinted in amongst his flesh. His iMe had been cut out and explained the lack of a red signal from him.

'There's someone else in the house,' Zoe said.

'Who? Where?' If it wasn't Alan, then was it Alan's killer?

'I've just scanned the building. There's a man in the kitchen.'

We both looked at the closed kitchen door. We had no weapons, no way of protecting ourselves, and someone sick enough to kill Alan and bag him up was behind the door.

But I could shield Zoe. 'Stay close,' I told her.

Zoe moved behind me, and we tiptoed towards the kitchen door. *Jesus, I'm scared.* What would I even do against an armed killer?

We completed our slow motion, two-person conga across the room and I reached out to the door handle. I could hear movement inside – it was coming straight towards us.

My hand was millimetres from the handle when it jerked down and the door opened. A scream made Zoe and I jump. I brought my left arm up to parry any attack and pulled my right arm back, ready to throw a punch. 'Police! Police!' I shouted, hoping the noise would buy me a second or two.

But I wasn't attacked.

'Thank fuck,' the man said. 'You scared the shit out of me.'

I wasn't going to take any chances, so I jumped forward, grabbing the man's wrist, yanking and twisting it behind him and up into an arm lock. I frog marched him across the kitchen and slammed him into the wall.

He was in his early thirties, a little shorter than me with a wiry build. I held his wrist in my right hand and my left arm pushed his back and neck into the wall. The left side of his face was tight against the wall and I glimpsed something wet on his lip, nose and down his cheek. *What's that smell?*

The sweet, putrid aroma of fresh vomit bit into my nostrils and triggered my gag reflex. I looked around the room to find the source of the smell. The sink held a puddle of brownish liquid and lumps that I didn't want to identify.

'Gross,' Zoe said as she caught the smell and saw the sink. 'He's a journalist, and he's already posted photos of the trunk.'

I pressed him harder into the wall. 'Shit. Do you know what you've done? This will go viral and everyone will question their safety.'

He smirked as he said, 'Yeah, but the people have the right to know what Alan's TrueMe message really meant. They deserve to know iMe isn't foolproof.'

'You bastard,' I said. 'You only care about the money.'

'No, it's about the truth.'

I pushed the guy harder into the wall, wanting to hurt him, then snapped my head around at the loud buzzing sound in the lounge. I let him go, then sprinted to the noise.

'Shit, shit.' I pulled my jacket off. 'Zoe, shut the front door.'

A TV news camera drone hovered over the trunk, streaming the image of Alan to a shock hungry world. My jacket hung like a matador's cape as I approached it from behind, not wanting to be seen on a screen.

I got closer and threw my jacket over the drone, wrestling it down using the sleeves of my only jacket, smelling the burning as the drone's hot motors attacked the lining. Now I really would have to get a new suit.

The drone kicked and bucked but stopped buzzing. As I lay panting on the floor next to it, I answered the call ringing in my head.

'Clive, what the fuck's going on?' Bhatt bellowed at me. 'The images are everywhere. The PM's screaming for an answer. Get to my office *now*.'

***

My thoughts swirled and crashed around in my head. Each dark one attacked me.

I had the sunshine and safety above me and I knew I should climb back up, but I had earned my monuments to failure. Black, twisting grotesque shapes sculpted by my pain and despair. I laboured hard over many, many hours to make them strong. I couldn't leave them because I couldn't forget. Now, I had new shrines to failure to build.

Karina, she's dead because I didn't find her.

It came at me like a broiling noxious cloud. I shut my eyes to it, but it snaked up and around me. Writhing along me, then down my leg. My failure weighed heavier than any ball and chain, and it dragged me further down.

Another thought came to encircle me. *So is Alan – I'm useless.*

The cloud grasped my other leg, adding to the pull. I was falling. The others joined in – all my old shames and mistakes. They all had their claim, and I let them take me. How could I fight the truth?

'Clive!'

I lifted my head from my hands to look at Bhatt.

She stood above me. I could feel her frustration pushing down on me. She was going to attach more blame and doubt.

I looked at her and waited. I felt like the real me was a small black silhouette stored inside my body. My true face, hopeless and despondent, was hidden by the bigger mask that the world saw.

A tender, gentle hand touched my face. Something in her eyes made me see the pain she carried as well. How can we all be so carelessly blind to the despair of the people we see every day? We had our own burdens to carry. Maybe we would break if we added their load to our own.

'Clive,' Bhatt said again.

'Am I fired?' I said.

'No.' Her laugh was the last thing I expected. 'No, but nearly. I've spent some shitty hours with the PM, the home secretary and the chief constable.'

'Sorry.' I let my head drop and roll.

'I had to sit and take a bollocking. Lots of threats: none of them subtle. But I eventually managed to calm them down.'

'So, what's happening?'

'I finally convinced them that they needed traditional policing methods to solve this case. I said that technology wasn't going to help – in fact, the technology is the problem.'

I tried to make myself think a positive thought. 'Ain't no school like the old-school,' I sang, flat and off-key, the words to a half-remembered song.

Bhatt winced. 'Don't sing, Clive. It's not helping, and you haven't exactly got anywhere with the case.'

'No. Sorry.'

Even the tiny criticism of my terrible singing added to the downward suck of my failures.

'It was a battle,' Bhatt said, and then threw me an unexpected lifeline. 'I told them that I trusted you. I told them that you were the only person who could solve this.' Her words came down to me, fastened under my arms and started to draw me up.

'I will,' I choked.

35

DI Clive Lussac

The indoor roof garden of iMe's office in Richmond displayed West London's greenery at its best on this bright afternoon: uninterrupted views of Richmond Park, round to Kew Gardens, and even a glimpse of Hampton Court. We'd been told that all the meeting rooms were booked but that everyone used this less formal space. Manu and Emma sat opposite Zoe and me. We each had a colourful balance-ball to perch on. I couldn't keep the stupid thing still while I puzzled over the drinks menu. Eighteen different types of still water. How could they be different? I clicked a random selection.

'Excellent choice,' Manu said. 'It's my favourite.'

The chilled vibe of the iMe offices felt like nothing was wrong. Manu and Emma looked too relaxed.

'I've got two dead bodies, your current boss with an encrypted signal and your old boss running around with a Suppressor,' I said, irked and venting. 'What's going on?'

Manu looked shocked. 'We're all working flat-out to resolve the situation.'

Gentle laughter drifted over from a group nearby. 'Sounds like it,' Zoe said, looking past Manu at the group.

'Why doesn't it work then?' I stared at Emma, trying to get her to contribute something, anything.

Eventually, through a tight mouth, she said, 'It does.'

'Then show me who my killer is.'

Manu and Emma exchanged a glance, and Manu spread his hands. 'We're all trying.'

Emma just stared.

'Try *harder*,' I shouted, and lost my balance. I caught myself and stood but my foot hit my balance-ball and sent it bouncing across the floor. All the heads spun towards the noise.

'Let's go, Zoe.' I raised my voice so that whole roof garden could hear. 'No one here seems to give a shit.'

***

'I don't understand the problem, ma'am,' I said. 'Before Alan's body showed up, our next step was to talk to Art about his encrypted signal.'

I was pushing for a full, public confrontation to rattle Art as much as possible and pile the pressure on him. Either as Art left Parliament or in his office, but Bhatt smiled as she vetoed the idea. 'I'm brave, but not stupid. You've no evidence against him,' she said. 'I'll get him to come here for an interview. Tread carefully until we have something concrete.'

'But—' I protested.

She held her finger up. 'But we have to live with him if we can't prove anything.'

I had a feeling about Art being more involved than he was saying, but what if I was wrong? He would make a powerful enemy.

'And what about Esteban?' Zoe asked.

True, there were Esteban's Suppressors to think about.

All the years of not having to think made me indecisive. Every cop was warned about paralysis by analysis, but I was more a case of paralysis by indecisiveness. But what was that phrase Esteban had used? 'Fuck that shit.' I liked it; it was like reliving a favourite flavour. I let it play around in my head.

'Boss?'

'FTS.' Time for action. 'We'll interview Art first and then Esteban.'

***

Now Art stretched out in his chair in Interview Room One, relaxed and confident despite the contrast of the small room to his own luxurious office. Bhatt and the chief constable were both watching the interview through the one-way mirror. I couldn't afford to screw this up – my leg jiggled up and down under the table.

'Mr Walker, I'll ask you again. Where were you when your signal was encrypted?'

The side of Art's mouth rose a little, letting his contempt show through. 'I don't have to tell you that.'

'We are investigating two murders, and you're refusing to help us. Why would you do that if you have nothing to hide?'

'It's not relevant to this case and you know iMe encryption is covered by the Official Secrets Act.'

We had anticipated this response and the CPS was looking for a legal route to force disclosure. It was time to switch to Alan.

'Tell me about Alan Kane.'

'What about him?'

I couldn't decide if Art was being unhelpful out of spite or whether he was buying time to compose an answer. 'Did you like him?'

Art's relaxed demeanour seemed to get pushed out by an inner tension. He didn't stiffen so much as solidify. 'The man was a fool. Always self-destructing over some woman or other.' Art flashed a brief smile.

I wondered if he had enjoyed Alan's fall from grace. 'What was he like to work with?'

Art dismissed Alan with a flippant hand wave, like he was flicking at a fly. 'Average.'

'Did he share your vision for iMe?' I put my hand down to stop my leg jiggling and waited for Art to reply.

Art blinked several times. Maybe this was getting stressful for him.

'No. iMe was intended to be all about convenience. It was meant to take your smart phone and give you the HUD to replace it. You'd always be connected and no more passwords or identity theft.' He took a sip of his water.

'We've got all that.'

'We were younger and naive then. We sold our vision of convenience and didn't think through the consequences.'

Like me, I thought, *when I brought iMe into policing.* 'So how was Alan's vision different?'

Art had a wistful look on his face as he thought back, then it hardened, and he snapped, 'You're old enough to remember the years of terrorist attacks. The Islamic fundamentalist violence and the Christian fundamentalist retaliation. The violence trying to split the UK into separate countries.'

'I am,' I said. Watching the news had been misery – all violence and senseless killing. Kids killed on buses by one group and then different kids killed in the name of justice and revenge. The calls for London to be a walled city again.

'All the technology back then, like the pay-as-you-go phones and encrypted messaging made catching terrorists difficult,' Art said, outrage crackling in his voice. 'We wanted the location services to be for finding your friends, shops and restaurants. To enrich your experience of wherever you were.' He paused again. 'Survivor Mia changed all that.'

'I remember her,' Zoe said. 'We held a vigil for the kids at our school.'

I remembered her as well, the shock wave it sent through the country and the pressure it put on the police. She was the only surviving kid from a school minibus taken by a paedophile ring. No one had tried to help the children or stop the abduction. Some were scared, their fear driven by all the *'Don't be a Hero'* posters. Others were too busy filming the children being taken and boosting their social media profiles by posting their videos.

The bus had been found easily as it had a GPS tracker in it. Mia only survived because the abduction was on her birthday and she was given a brand-new phone that morning. She handed her old phone to the paedophiles and kept the new one hidden. When she finally had a chance to turn it on, we had tracked her signal.

I said, 'And Alan used that?'

'Yes, he sold the idea to the government. Safety always trumps privacy.'

He was right; the government had leveraged the suffering of the parents. Why would you object to the police knowing where you are if you have nothing to hide? Why would you vote against stopping little kids being rescued from paedophiles? Are you that selfish that a little loss of personal freedom would mean that we can't catch terrorists? The rhetoric had gone on and on.

'That was Alan's idea?'

'Yes. The government took the momentum from all the attacks and Mia and built it up and up until people were demanding location tracking of everyone.'

And so, the government watched everyone. Every second of every day, but not like in a sci-fi film. No sinister master criminal, no alien invasion, no rebellion of machines or a catastrophic weather event. The people hadn't rebelled against it, instead most had voted for it in the referendum. Many had queued overnight to ensure that they were amongst the first to get iMe.

For me though, it was like all the free people rushing to climb aboard a cruise ship knowing it was run by His Majesty's Prison Service.

Art is being too nice, too helpful, I thought. *It's not normal.*

'And you were upset about it?'

'Well, yes. We all were. The government had promised not to use the technology for tracking and what's the first thing they do? Track people.'

'So, Alan betrayed you.' I pulled myself up in my chair, trying to make myself bigger and more intimidating.

'He betrayed the technology. He took what we made and twisted it, corrupted it.'

'And that made you angry?'

'Of course, the lying shit tricked us.' Art ran his hand over his hair.

'Then, in an act of revenge, you took him and killed him?'

'Hah. You're an idiot, Inspector.' Art slumped back into his chair, and I could see the tension in him evaporate.

'Answer the question, Mr Walker. Did you kill Alan Kane?'

Art went very still again. With a dead-eyed stare said, 'No, I did not kill Alan Kane.'

'You didn't cut him up and put him in the trunk?'

I pushed some photos of Alan in the trunk at the display wall.

Art flicked through the photos. I would have expected some revulsion or shock, but he took his time examining each one.

'I did not put Kane in that trunk,' he said, and glowered back at us, but he couldn't stop himself glancing at the photos every few seconds.

'Is that why you arranged Alan like that? Are you taunting us, saying we can't solve this?'

'It looks like an accurate message, Inspector.'

***

'He's lying, and we've let him go,' I said back in Bhatt's office. She was at the hand-wash station again.

'His body language was weird,' Bhatt agreed. 'There's something there.'

'He was enjoying looking at those photos of Alan Kane,' Zoe said. 'He kept staring at them like he was savouring the experience.'

Was she finally beginning to see it?

'He looked like he overcompensated with the direct eye contact. It seemed like he was trying not to look like he was lying,' Bhatt said.

Yes. Yes. I was going to get him, and I knew how.

36

DC Zoe Jordan

Our office was besieged with press camera drones. They were like rabid bluebottles, swarming and tapping the glass, trying to get in. If we didn't solve this, who would get sacrificed? Bhatt? Clive? No, I was at the bottom.

Art had said he didn't know Karina and we hadn't found any links between them so, unless she was a victim chosen at random, Art had no obvious motive. We only knew one person who had a Suppressor, and that was Esteban. He had witnesses saying that he was at a dinner, but he could have taken Karina and then gone to eat.

Doris and Tom were Fraud's problem now. They had the staff to put the case together and deal with all the legal arguments there would be between the Ministry of Well-being and Health and the members.

We finished taping covers over the windows to stop the drones seeing in and now couldn't see the bright and sunny day outside. The investigation seemed in the dark as well.

Clive was pacing and muttering in front of our crime wall as he rehearsed the next interview with Esteban. When I got the message that Esteban was here, I grabbed Clive's arm to stop him.

***

'What was your relationship with Alan Kane like?' Clive asked.

The more time I spent in Interview Room One, the more depressing it was. I pushed my fingernail under the edge of a chip in the paint. A leaf of beige popped up, revealing more grey.

'It was OK in the beginning, but it collapsed into arguments,' Esteban said.

Clive leaned forward in his chair. 'Heated arguments? Were you angry?'

'Yes. He betrayed all the promises that were made before we started.'

I uncrossed my arms. 'Angry enough to kill him?'

'Of course not,' Esteban said with a small laugh. 'Why would I? I have too much to lose.'

'Why should that put you above suspicion?'

Esteban said nothing, so I threw the photos up on the wall again. They were the same ones of Alan in the trunk we had shown Art.

Esteban glanced at them.

'Did you arrange him like this to show us how clever you are?' I leant forward across the table so I could invade his space as much as possible.

'No. But...' Esteban swept his hand up to wipe his forehead. It was the first time he hadn't looked in complete control.

'But?'

'Alan could be incredibly childish,' Esteban said. His hands came to his temples and he stuck out his tongue. He rotated his hands a couple of times. Each one going in the opposite direction, like kids do. Like I had. 'Alan did that at the end of the meeting where we were forced to agree to the tracking. It was his victory gesture.'

'That must have wound you up,' I said. I could feel Clive's leg bouncing up and down again under the table.

'We were all upset and angry, and it really rubbed salt into our wounds.'

'And you decided to kill him then?'

The sweat was back on his forehead. 'No, I didn't decide to kill him.' Esteban was staring at me now. A silent challenge.

I stared back. 'OK, we'll come back to that later.' I paused, allowing the pressure and threat of the question to hang in the air.

Thankfully, Clive's leg stopped bouncing as he shifted his weight in the chair. 'Was that when you left iMe?' he asked.

'No. I was angry and I felt betrayed, but tracking made sense because of people like Mia. The government couldn't be selective on the cases, so it got applied to everyone.'

Clive scraped his chair back from the table. 'What made you finally leave?' he asked. I could hear him rubbing his leg with his shoe.

'I drew the line at the Model Citizen. Being tracked all the time was one thing, but controlling everything you ate and drank… Taxing your enjoyment was too much.'

Clive nodded. 'Was that Alan's idea as well?'

'Not directly, but you remember the financial pressure on the NHS. It drove the Prevention is Better than Cure campaign. Model Citizen only works if everyone has iMe.'

'So, you left?' Clive rolled up the sleeves of his shirt. The warm weather had given him the excuse not to buy a new suit despite the burns.

'Yes, around the same time as Alice Bakaev.'

'And took your Suppressors and got immunity from prosecution for being off-grid.'

He shrugged. 'I've told you before. I signed the Official Secrets Act.'

'That's convenient. It lets you do what you like.'

'Yes, it does.' He smiled.

I wasn't going to let him off that easily. 'And you decided to kill Alan Kane because you thought you could get away with it?'

That wiped the smile away.

'No,' Esteban said.

'What about Karina Morgan? Did you know her?'

Esteban paused a long time. 'I did not know that woman.'

The pause and his formal speech raised a flag in my mind. 'Really? Because it sounds like you did.'

Esteban paused again, apparently going through some internal dialogue. 'OK, OK. It will come out anyway,' he sighed. 'I didn't really know her, but I did meet her at a party.'

37

DI Clive Lussac

We had Art back in the interview room, but I decided to let him stew a while. I had turned the thermostat up, hoping that the stuffy room, uncomfortable chair and the heat would help piss him off enough to make him angry and careless.

I looked at Zoe. Rightly, she seemed pleased with herself. She'd got Esteban to admit to having met Karina at a party, and we had a link.

'How are we going to solve this?' she asked.

'The truth?' I said. 'If it stays like this then we won't solve it. Not without proof. We need luck or a mistake.'

'A mistake as in someone else getting killed and the killer leaving evidence?'

It was the grim reality. 'Yes, like the old days, unless we get a confession, we're going to have to wait.'

Zoe shivered. 'Waiting means going through that press scrum every day. My mum's got TV drones all around the house.'

'I know. She said.' I knew Zoe didn't like me talking to Sophia, but it wasn't really her call.

Zoe crossed her arms and frowned. If I had kids it would have been my job to object to their choice in partners, now I was the one being judged unworthy.

Sophia and I were going on our first date tomorrow, and we hadn't told Zoe yet. I bottled it. I'd tell her later.

***

I smiled at Art, hoping to goad him. Trying to get under his skin.

He wasn't as relaxed as before – he dabbed at his forehead with a monogrammed handkerchief.

'Let me tell you what I think,' I said. 'You have a Suppressor and you used it to kidnap and kill Karina Morgan and Alan Kane.'

Art banged his fist down on the table, leaving a small dent in the flimsy top. 'I did *not...*' He seemed on the verge of saying something else, but he stiffened and stared at us.

I looked at Zoe and nodded. She threw a document onto the room's display wall.

Art turned, and as he read it, the colour drained from his face. He dropped his head into his hands.

Now I had him. I let the silence stretch out. I wanted him to think through the consequences.

After a long pause, I said, 'Mr Walker, you're normally the only person who can authorise the release of encrypted iMe data. Is that correct?'

'Yes,' he said through his hands.

'But in special circumstances the prime minister can also authorise it.' I was enjoying myself. I pointed at the display wall. 'I arranged for the chief constable to write that letter. Explaining how you are the prime suspect in a double murder and are refusing to cooperate with the police. Asking for the prime minister's approval for the data to be released.'

I looked across at Art, who still had his head in his hands.

'We'll leave you to think about whether you'd like me to send that letter.'

We left the room, and I clanged the door shut.

'You still think he's innocent, Zoe?' I asked.

'He's certainly hiding something,' she said.

***

As we walked back into the interview room, Art looked up at us. I had dragged Bhatt and the chief constable in to watch the confession I hoped to get. I could feel their gaze again.

Shuffling my chair around in a noisy little dance to get comfortable, I brushed a flake of loose paint off the table and looked at Art. He seemed diminished, like his suit was now too big for him.

Here goes.

'Mr Walker, where were you and why was your signal encrypted when Alan Kane went missing?' I asked, and waited, praying it wasn't going to be another stonewall response and that I had dragged the chief constable in for nothing.

Art hesitated and then straightened the lapels of his suit and cleared his throat. Even then, it took another visible effort of will to get him started.

'Um, I want your assurance that this won't go any further,' he said.

I looked at him, trying to blank out my reaction, not wanting my excitement to show. 'I can't possibly promise that. This is a murder investigation.'

He nodded, seeing the obvious dilemma. The arrogant, self-important front had gone. His insecure core continued. 'I... I was in London with friends.'

I shook my head. I needed more than this pathetic reason. 'Why would you need to encrypt your signal just to see friends?'

He was obviously still holding back, so I pointed at the letter that was still on the display wall. I entered the prime minister's ID in the *'Send To'* section at the top and hovered over the *'Send'* button.

'Wait… Wait,' Art said.

'We need the truth. All of it, not some useless half story about friends.'

'OK. OK.'

I glanced at Zoe, seeing in her eyes the same excitement I felt. We were so close to the truth, we needed him to start, and then it would all spill out.

'Please, Mr Walker. Take your time and explain it to us,' she said.

Art straightened in his chair. 'You understand that I'm an important man…'

I had to bite my tongue. *Arrogant shit.*

'And as such, people come to me asking for favours,' he continued.

'OK,' I said, trying to nudge him on.

'Some of these favours I feel I can accommodate… for people who need some anonymity.'

Just confess, I wanted to scream at him, but I couldn't risk it.

'And you accommodated a favour at the weekend?' Zoe said.

Art looked down again. 'Yes. For some friends.'

'Who?'

Art mentioned some old actors and musicians and lots of names that I didn't recognise.

Zoe nodded, she seemed to know them. She was busy with her fingers on her HUD.

The display wall cleared the letter to the prime minister and redrew with the signals of Art and the names he mentioned.

'This is the trace for the weekend,' she said. 'All of these people's signals are encrypted.'

'I thought the encryption was only for the police and state secrets, not a bunch of celebs,' I said.

'We need to see the data,' Zoe's voice was firm and commanding. It seemed to shock Art.

'OK,' he said, and typed out a message on his HUD. 'Wait a minute.'

We endured an awkward silence, like an unplanned interlude in a show, waiting for the truth.

'OK, refresh your query,' Art said.

Zoe refreshed the display, and the signals now showed normal. She changed the screen to a map. All the signals were in London. When she zoomed right in, the signal dots stayed clustered in the same place. Art and the celebs were in a nine-bedroom mansion in Princess Gate, opposite Hyde Park. It was nowhere near the location where Esteban said he met Karina.

This wasn't what I expected. 'What's going on?'

'My friends wanted some privacy for a party, and I was able to oblige.'

'You were hiding the signals of celebs just so they could have a party?' We'd been here before. 'You denied that.'

'Well, it wasn't really relevant,' Art said. His ego seemed to be re-inflating now his actions were out in the open.

'How often do you do this?' Zoe asked.

'Maybe once a month.'

'So, you're selling celebs a way to hide their parties?' I demanded.

'They need respite from the paparazzi, and I don't sell anything. Check my accounts. My only income is my salary.'

'Oh, we will,' I said. The little bastard was playing with us.

'What do you get out of it,' Zoe asked.

'I'm invited to the party,' Art said with a satisfied smile.

'They're not your friends. They're using you to hide from the press.'

Art looked straight back at me. 'Oh, I'm not naive, Inspector. But I'm the one in the position of power. I can turn their signals back on at any time. They know that.'

He beamed at me with the self-satisfied recollection of nights partying with celebs while I was probably alone in my lonely flat feeling hungry.

I had to grip the table to stop myself hitting him in the face.

***

I looked out of the window in Bhatt's office. She had reflective privacy glass that let the light in but kept the press drones out. Her office was much higher in the block than PCU, and usually, you could see a long way. Today, all I could see was cloud and a curtain of heavy rain coming towards us.

'But Art's confession to the parties could simply be a way of deflecting the suspicion of the murders,' I said. I could hear the whine in my voice, and I didn't like it.

Bhatt shook her head. 'You've no evidence. We have to let him go.'

I slumped back into my usual chair in Bhatt's office. It had all gone wrong. When we got close to Doris the case started disappearing: now it was the same with Art.

I couldn't bear to think of him smiling in the rain or in a car going back to his office.

I said what was going around and around in my head.

'The killer's still out there. They'll kill again.'

38

Thief

I was drawn to the emptiness of the cell. It needed filling, and the worm in my head kept wiggling and calling to me: *another, another.*

I was outside and walking. The heavy rain passed and the air smelt damp but clean. The swamped drains left puddles everywhere. I swore as I put my foot in one, trying to avoid a bloody HUD Zombie who wasn't looking where they were going.

I stepped to the side of the pavement to try and shake the water out of my shoe, and watched a car splash through a puddle and drench a woman who was walking and talking to her HUD.

The police were a problem. They hadn't got any proof yet, but they wouldn't stay useless forever. At some point they would try and search my home. They might find the hidden entrance to the cell. I had cleaned and bleached it lots of times, but I could still be undone by a stray hair or a print that showed Karina or Two had been there.

I needed a way to deflect the police. There must be something that I could do to mislead them. Maybe I could manufacture some evidence and leave it somewhere to get the police to look elsewhere.

I stopped with my shoe halfway back to my foot and let a big smile spread over my face. I could steal Zoe or Lussac.

The woman with the wet leg glared at me and shouted, 'What you looking at? Think it's funny? You can fuck off.'

As she stormed away, I shifted my weight and felt the squelch of water in my sock. I started walking and thinking again.

***

Back home, I slumped into my control chair and rocked backwards. The lights were off and I was bathed in the gentle green glow of the monitors. I flicked through the individual views from each of the infrared night vision cameras. They all showed the same empty cell.

My need was an itch I couldn't reach. Zoe could be fantastic to own. I would savour her, but she might be a repeat of Karina.

Lussac had pissed me off.

39

DI Clive Lussac

I had a strange feeling that I was being watched and, for the twentieth time, I checked the local iMe signals for someone who might be following me. I couldn't see anyone interesting, but it didn't stop the hairs on the back of my neck standing up.

The tranquillity of my apartment block foyer soothed some of my apprehension, but I couldn't shake a nagging ache of foreboding. I pushed the button for the lift. Three storeys up, so no need for the double journey messing around I used to get to Oscar's flat. As I waited for the lift, I scanned the area, grateful when a gentle *bing* announced its arrival.

'Hello, Clive,' the lift said as I got in, 'are you going home?'

'Yes,' I replied, and the indicator for the third floor started glowing.

Shit, I thought, *the lift software has been upgraded.* Now I'd have to use the stairs to see Oscar.

***

I closed the door to my flat. I was safe in here, but even so, I felt the need for a soothing drink. As I went into the kitchen to find one of Oscar's bottles, a message on my HUD stopped me in my tracks.

'Sender: Alfie.'

Doris' lawyer.

'Subject: Thinking of You.'

What the hell does that mean?

I opened the message and saw a press release from the Ministry of Well-being and Health. It described the period of consultation for the use of helmets by pedestrians. People busy using their HUDs were walking into things, while others had slipped or tripped. The published studies were crammed with statistics on accidents and images of people who had suffered severe brain damage from a relatively minor impact to the head.

I had seen the press release before and it wasn't relevant to me or the Health Bank. I wondered why Alfie had sent this message, and then the tag at the bottom of the message crashed into me: *'It appears that a little tap on the head can be dangerous. Be careful out there.'*

On its own, it seemed innocent enough. Alfie would laugh off any suggestion that he was threatening me. I reached for a bottle, splashed two week's FU allowance into a glass and took a big gulp. I savoured the burn as the liquid traced its way down my throat, but it didn't stop my hand shaking as I put the glass down on the worktop. My Buddy ran out, waving his finger at me in rebuke, and unfurled another banner: *'Freedom Unit violation reported to the Ministry of Well-being and Health.'*

Doris knew I would understand the real meaning. In the old days when she wanted someone killed, she pulled Alfie aside to say, 'They've gone too far, Alfie. Get someone to give them a little tap.'

***

Zoe had tracked down one of the celebrities who was at Art's party. Some pretty boy from a funk-rap boy band I'd never heard of. The band were the latest winners of a TV talent show that churned out the next superstar every six months, and who would be gone before the October chill stripped the trees bare of their autumnal reds and golds.

Zane E was staying in the majestic luxury of Cliveden. The historic hotel seemed a strange choice of location for a brash rap star, but it was a good excuse for an afternoon drive through the countryside to the Buckinghamshire town of Taplow.

As the car crunched up the long drive, I felt as green as the manicured lawns. I was nursing one hell of a hangover, and my head banged so hard that it was difficult to think straight. I wasn't doing a good job of being a decent boss, let alone a suitable date for Zoe's mum. I had booked a restaurant for tonight and Sophia had messaged me to say that Zoe knew about our date and wasn't happy. She had given me the silent disapproval treatment on the whole journey and now, full of virtue and offensive good health, she looked down at me with obvious distaste from her moral high ground.

The noise in my head got louder, and I had to shut my eyes to suppress the vomit rising in my throat. It took me several seconds to realise that the additional ringing was actually a call.

I tapped my jaw and winced at the volume of the voice in my head.

'Clive, Clive, is that you, man?' Oscar shouted.

Bright white flashed before my eyes. I needed to lie down in the dark room. 'What's up, Oscar?'

'Jesus, man, I got an assessment from the Ministry of Well-being and Health.'

'So?' We all got them this time of year as part of the taxation regime.

'So? *So?*' he screamed. 'They've got a new cross-referencing process. They've checked my alcohol purchases over the last six months and compared it to my alcohol intake. They say there's a discrepancy that they want to talk to me about.'

'They've asked for a meeting?' That wasn't a good sign.

'No. They've demanded a full audit.'

'Oh shit,' I blurted. A full FU audit was brutal, and the Ministry used the most humourless staff they could find.

'Exactly, shit,' Oscar agreed. 'I'm going to have to tell them the truth, Clive. I mean, there are the payments as well.'

He was right. He couldn't deflect an FU audit, and my payments to him would be unexplainable any other way.

'OK, Oscar. Just do what you have to – I'll deal with it when it comes back to me.'

I was screwed. This close after my Excess Consumption Order, I would be looking at a three-month stay in a Health Reorientation Camp run by the Ministry. I wasn't sure I would survive.

***

As we walked into the calm oasis of Cliveden's great hall, my head eased, and I felt a bit better. It was the sort of place I would like to become used to.

I smoothed the jacket of my new suit, hoping that I looked like I belonged. I'd heard that people with money dressed down as shabby chic, but all I saw were beautifully dressed people, their modern style contrasting perfectly with the large fireplace, suits of armour and tapestries on the walls. I was the only shabby thing in the room.

A receptionist came over – it was obvious that her tailored uniform must have cost three times as much as my new suit. 'May I help you?' she said to Zoe after dismissing me with her eyes.

'We're here to meet with Zane E,' Zoe said.

'He's expecting you and asked if you would join him in the library. I'll take you through.'

We followed her, and Zoe muttered, 'You're a disgrace. You're hungover and you stink of alcohol.'

I had no defence, so I followed Zoe like a naughty little boy following their angry mother.

***

Zane E was dressed in a sharp, elegant bluey-silver suit with black shoes that outshone the silverware on the table. It showed how out of touch I was. I was expecting a baseball cap on backwards and big jewellery. He was at home here, and his good looks and sense of style were really intimidating. I dropped down into a chair and hid my scuffed shoes under the table.

He looked around the room. Even here people were staring, red dots blinking in their eyes to show they were filming Zane. The images would be flashing around the world, joining all the other people commenting on someone else's life rather than living their own.

'The library has been reserved,' the receptionist said, and shooed the people out.

Zoe started with a gentle lead-in. She was clearly a fan. Some questions about the band and his background. I nudged her leg to get her to bring the questions to the real subject.

She shifted in her chair as she adjusted from fan to police officer.

'Do you know Art Walker?' she said.

'I don't know the guy, but I met him once at some nice pad near Hyde Park,' he smiled at the memory. 'Great party.'

'Did Art Walker invite you?'

'No, my agent did. He's in with Art.'

Zoe threw a photo of Karina at Zane. 'Have you seen her before?'

Now Zane lit up. 'Sure, Karina. She's fantastic fun. Gorgeous and smart. We chatted together a few times.'

Zoe looked at me to make sure I wasn't asleep, but I was concentrating hard.

'What happens at the parties?' I asked.

Zane looked a little shy. 'I was brought up by my aunt, and she always said that a gentleman should be discreet.' A hint of moisture touched his eyes. 'She's gone now, but I try to make her proud every day.'

Maybe his aunt's influence was why he seemed so well adjusted and modest, despite all his sudden fame.

'I can see that,' I said, softening my tone.

Zoe asked, 'Was Karina at a lot of parties?'

'I've only been to three, but she was there every time. She said she had been to a few, but it sounded like a lot,' Zane said.

'How often are they?'

'Every month, my agent said.'

We had already checked – the iMe technical briefings were held at most once a quarter. These parties could be the networking events that Karina told Dave she went to. The monthly frequency seemed to line up.

We'd found a link between Art and Karina.

Zoe was thinking the same thing because she asked, 'What was Art Walker like at these parties?'

'Not cool. He acted like he was the big man. Full of himself at organising the parties and the privacy.'

'What else?'

'Lots of staff and people who weren't celebs, like Karina, weren't happy. Art pushed them around, you know, controlling them, telling them what to do all the time.'

Zoe threw another photo at Zane, and I knew who it was. 'Did you ever see him?'

'Yeah, Esteban. I met him at a party. He was cool.'

'Anything else you remember?' I asked, noting Zoe's pointed glance at me.

Zane looked a little upset now. 'Some of the women made a real effort to avoid Art. They said he had *interviewed* them before letting them come.'

***

As the car made its way back from Cliveden, I sent a report to Bhatt telling her we needed to talk to Art and Esteban again. We would need to talk to Dave as well and perhaps shatter his illusions of Karina. Or maybe he had found out, and we should move him to the top of the suspects list.

I let my mind drift ahead to my date with Sophia tonight. My first date in years and I was both nervous and excited. Zoe was back giving me the silent treatment, so I imagined the perfect evening instead of talking.

The *bing* of another message from Alfie broke my daydream. An old iMe press release about the benefits of always knowing where people are. The meaning was clear: they were tracking me. The message ended with the sinister words *'Tap! Tap!'*

The car pulled into the secure basement of my block. I had told Zoe that I wanted to avoid any waiting press drones, but I didn't want to risk bumping into one of Alfie's men outside on the pavement. I got out and stood in the empty concrete loading area as the car pulled away to take Zoe home. The harsh light cast dark shadows into the corners of the bays. I began to think that this wasn't such a good idea. The lights were controlled by movement sensors and the ones around me started to shut off, deepening the darkness and my unease.

I knew that I needed to move to keep the lights on, but I froze when I thought I heard a footstep from near the door. My pulse coursed through my head and I panted as if I was running on my treadmill. *There can't be someone there, can there? The light would have come on.*

I stood straining to hear movement. The last light timed out and pitched the whole area into darkness. All I could hear was my own breathing. I was going to have to do something. I couldn't stay here.

I took a tentative step toward the door, and the lights overhead came on and dazzled me. It made the area near the door seem even darker. I shuffled forwards, peering into the black, wishing to get close enough for the light by the door to come on, but knowing that would be the moment anyone waiting would rush me and give me a tap.

I felt so exposed moving towards the darkness while being floodlit. I inched and inched, my whole body tense, and my left hand held up as a defensive shield.

The light snapped on. I flinched and jumped to my right. I hoped that any blow would most likely come from a right-handed attacker and this would move me away from their hand and the weapon it contained. I guessed that if they had a gun, I would be dead already.

I looked around, but I was alone. I felt like a complete idiot, smiled and breathed out. I had been so scared that I hadn't even scanned the area for iMe signals. I checked now and confirmed that no one was there, but I didn't trust the system anymore.

I walked the remaining paces to the door, still feeling that there was some sort of threat. I put my hand on the door and it clicked unlocked. As I pushed the door open, a hand shot out and grabbed my wrist, pulling me through the door and up against the wall. I hadn't even seen the person, but I could feel their weight against me and their breath on my neck.

'Inspector Lussac, I've been following your signal. This is a strange way in, are you trying to avoid someone?' the man said.

'Who are you?'

He said nothing, but I felt the pressure ease from my back and his hand locked on my wrist pulled me around to face him.

He looked about forty, his hair was shaved into short stubble, and his eyes glared a cold menace. His signal wasn't showing, and his suit bulged with muscle. If he wanted to smash my face in, I'd have no hope.

'Did Doris send you?' I said.

'Who's Doris?' the man answered and pushed his ID into my HUD.

'Special Investigator Winter, Freedom Unit Enforcement, Ministry of Well-being and Health.'

I sighed with relief that I wasn't going to get a tap from Doris, but then I realised that I was in just as much trouble.

'You need to come to our offices tomorrow at 9am. I've been chatting with Oscar. He has all sorts of stories about you.'

With that, he released my wrist and patted my cheek. 'Don't be late,' he said, and stepped through the door into the loading area.

I slumped back against the wall and tried to control my breathing. I needed to get to the safety of my flat and to calm down before my date with Sophia.

If I'd known what a bad idea that was, I would have run after Winter and begged him to take me there and then.

40

Thief

I was going to attack tonight, but still needed to complete my preparations. The clock in my HUD showed just before five in the afternoon. I had enough time if I didn't make any mistakes. I walked up to the gleaming metal worktop in the garage and traced shapes over the surface, my fingertips touching with gossamer lightness, caressing it.

I slid my hand down to a drawer, pulled out a rubber anti-static mat and laid it out on the worktop. Kneeling, I opened my sports bag and carefully extracted the large carbon fibre box. The lid unclipped with two solid clacks and I looked inside.

My greatest achievement. Much, much harder than a Suppressor. Years and years of my own sweat to finally work out how to get it to work.

It was much bulkier, but as I didn't have to wear it, the size didn't matter. I stroked its outer cover with deep pride, picked it up as if I was handing a sacred relic and put it on the mat.

I hinged up the top of its shell and looked at the array of circuits and electronics inside, replaying the hundreds of hours spent making it but, in its current state, it was useless. The security encryption for iMe was beyond military grade and impossible to generate a signal without DNA. I allowed myself a smile. After one of our meetings, I had collected the used drinking glasses. They had been waiting in case I needed them.

Earlier in the afternoon, with diligent and patient work, I had extracted his DNA from the nucleus of the skin cells left behind on the glass. The next step was to map his DNA into the key that iMe needed to recognise the signal as him. Lastly, I transferred it onto a tiny ID wafer.

The wafer nestled in a small padded carrier about the size of my thumb and I eased back the carrier's shiny lid. With a low purr, the carrier mechanism opened, and the ID wafer came up and out. The bronze coloured translucent film glimmered under the bright garage lights.

I didn't have time to repeat the whole process, so with great care I used my tweezers to lift and transfer the wafer from the carrier into the receiving slot in the shell. When I was sure it was in place, I pressed the small button on the side and listened to another purr as the shell closed over the ID wafer and lowered the wafer into the body of the electronics.

I pushed a second button and a small fan started inside the shell. The display changed to say *'Initialising'*. After a couple of seconds, the display changed to *'Test Mode'*. I waited. Test mode wouldn't get as far as generating a signal, but if I had done the DNA extraction wrong, then nothing would work and my night would be ruined.

The display changed again as it went through the test sequence. *'Connecting… Connected… Login… ID Lookup… ID Test… Complete.'*

The display cleared. I held my breath for the moment of truth. I smiled as it redrew and blinked. *'ID Mimic: Lussac, Clive. Verified.'*

***

The two Suppressors I needed were already waiting on the table in their protective carrying cases, fully charged and ready to go. Lussac was the right target. It was two-for-one: he'd pay for challenging me and, as a bonus, I'd derail the investigation.

There were a few holes in my plan, but I couldn't control everything. Anyway, Zoe was too young to know how to think for herself. All her generation knew was iMe. She'd never work it out.

I turned my display wall on, selected a movie-streaming channel and selected two films I had seen before. My Mimic, home alone, would transmit my alibi that was unchallengeable now that iMe was so ingrained in the legal process.

His Mimic would cause havoc.

***

My Suppressor let me ghost through all the tracked masses and, at 6pm, I approached the entrance of Lussac's apartment block. This was my moment of greatest exposure as I had to use the Mimic's signal to open the front door.

Shit. Two press drones in standby mode crouched by the door. They might catch Lussac's signal and start to power-up – all lights, propellers and cameras. I hustled over to the drones and spent a few vulnerable seconds removing their power supplies.

I hit the *'Pulse Mode'* switch and the Mimic powered up, logged in and generated Lussac's signal for a fraction of a second before shutting down. The signal was on long enough for the door to recognise Lussac's signal and open. Of course, he would have two signals during the pulse from the Mimic, but I knew that this would be treated as a glitch and Tech Support wouldn't see a flag to investigate it.

I stepped through the door, pleased that no one had seen me and that the drones were disabled.

The lift call button did nothing. It must need a signal to work but I wanted as few pulses as possible, so I used the stairs to climb to Lussac's apartment. Outside, I flicked the *'Pulse Mode'* switch again and was rewarded by a soft click.

I stepped into his home.

***

Lussac's flat was small and messy. There wasn't anywhere near the front door to hide, so I threaded my way along the hallway trying to avoid the discarded clothes. I couldn't see a suitable hiding space in the open plan lounge or kitchen area.

I paused at the bedroom door to check where Lussac was. My HUD drew a location map and showed him stationary in the loading area under the building. I didn't have much time.

I scanned the bedroom. There only seemed to be two choices: bathroom or wardrobe. The bathroom door was open wide, and I could see the shower and toilet. If I hid in there, I would have to close the door and he might remember leaving it open. He lived alone and maybe he never closed it. I decided that I couldn't risk the bathroom. That left the wardrobe.

I jogged over to it, slid open the left-hand door and looked with dismay at the shelves covered in jumbled clothes. A couple were folded, but the attempt at organisation had stalled early and a tangle of shirts and jumpers were dumped on top. Socks and T-shirts peeked out of the drawers and stopped them closing fully. I closed the door, making sure it was in the same position it had been, and slid open the right-hand door.

The area was a hanging section and the rail was all but empty. It left plenty of space for me and my bag. I pushed aside the two hangers: one had a clean and ironed shirt, the other a crumbled suit jacket. I stepped into the wardrobe and slid the door shut behind me.

My side of the wardrobe was dark, but I could see a thin section of bedroom wall through the other door. I would be able to see Lussac come into the bedroom without having to rely on my HUD. I settled in to wait, relaxing my muscles but staying alert. I would need to explode into action when he arrived. I delved into my pocket for the syringe and wiggled the cap off.

The wardrobe smelt musty, but I caught the undertone of a burnt smell as well. I took a quick look around to find the source and saw that the back of the jacket was burnt through. Why had he kept it? I waited, trying to ignore the smell.

I rechecked my HUD and saw that Lussac was in the lift.

I flexed my shoulders in anticipation.

41

DI Clive Lussac

My heart was still thumping around in my chest as I waited for the lift.

'Shit. That's all I need.'

I was beginning to buckle under the weight of it all: two murders, no arrest, pressure from Bhatt, threats from Doris and now FU Enforcement.

Calm down, I told myself. *Get a grip.*

'It will be alright,' I said, but I had no idea how.

I looked at the counter for the lift. It was on the 35th floor. I watched the slow countdown as the lift descended and tried to slow my breathing to keep time with it. *Thirty-One*. Breathe in. *Thirty*. Breathe out. It helped, and by the time the lift arrived, I was feeling calmer.

I greeted the lift's 'hello, Clive' like an old friend and settled into the short trip back up to my floor.

***

I stepped inside my flat and shut the door, collapsing back against it in relief. My wrist ached from where Winter had grabbed me. Rubbing it to try and ease the soreness made it worst.

'Fucking FU police,' I muttered.

I looked into the flat. Messy, but at least I was safe. I could block my problems out. Like a child, I closed my eyes as I rested my head on the door. If I couldn't see the world, then I could pretend that it couldn't see me.

I enjoyed some moments of tranquillity, allowing all the bad things to drift out of my mind and be replaced with my date with Sophia. I could picture her eyes smiling at me and her beautiful face framed by her lustrous hair.

What she saw in me I had no idea, and I wasn't going to risk it by asking her.

I spent a few minutes dreaming of how the evening might go and how perfect it would be.

I was interrupted by a message from the car I had booked saying that it was five minutes away.

'Shit, look at the time,' I said. I didn't want to screw this up by being late. Sophia was out of my league, and she might not give me a second chance. I could relax in the car.

No time for a shower, but I had time to wash quickly, clean my teeth, and get changed. At least I ironed my only nice shirt last night.

Fuck the world. I was going to have a great time tonight. The rest could wait.

I splashed around in the bathroom and glanced at the result in the mirror. I managed to convince myself that I looked pretty good and wetted down a stray piece of hair. It needed three more attacks with the water before it stayed in place.

Perfect... well, maybe not perfect but as good as it was going to get.

No solitary dinner for one for me tonight. I would sit at the table with Sophia and watch for the envious looks thrown in my direction. It would make a nice change from the pitying looks I usually got.

All I needed now was my shirt, and I could head out of the door for the best night I had enjoyed in a long time.

42

Thief

I heard the front door open and Lussac slamming it shut and collapsing against it. I caught a muttered, 'Fucking FU police' and then silence.

What's he doing?

I listened to him come down the hall and into the bedroom.

Lussac rushed across the bedroom – I could hear taps running and water being splashed around in the bathroom. I tensed as he flashed across the section of wall I could see and came towards the wardrobe.

The door started to slide open and I raised the syringe. His hand and bare forearm pushed through the gap and waved around, searching for a hanger.

As his hand found the shirt, I pushed the syringe into the exposed wrist and pressed hard.

***

I could hear him blundering around as his heart pumped my special drug cocktail around his body. I had maybe overdone the strength of the drugs a little, but I wanted to be sure of a quick takedown.

The sounds of movement in the bedroom stopped and I heard the whooshing noise of a compressing mattress mixed with the exhalation of breath as his body lost the fight with gravity. I stepped out of the wardrobe.

Lussac was on his back with his arms splayed out like he was on a crucifix. His bum was only half on the bed, and his legs bent in an untidy mess under him. His body seemed to match how he kept the place.

I lifted my bag, careful not to bang the contents against anything, and put it on the bed next to Lussac's head.

The bag unzipped with a nice clicking sound and I picked out the Suppressor from on top of the Mimic. Both were off and were cold, inert mixtures of carbon, silicon and copper. My power came when they were on.

The travel bag gaped as I opened it and lifted the Suppressor out. I unclipped it to make a neck sized opening, used my left hand to lift Lussac's head and manoeuvred it with my right. After a bit of jiggling, I had one end of the Suppressor under Lussac's neck and I eased his head back onto the bed. I closed the ends together and adjusted the tension in it to give secure contact with his skin.

Next, I lifted out the Mimic and placed it on the bed next to Lussac's neck, I pressed and held the power button and waited for it to initialise. The display blinked *Ready*. I clicked a switch down to start the connection to the iMe network. I had a finger of my left hand over the power button of the Suppressor and stared at the Mimic's display. It stepped from *'Connecting'* to *'Login'* to *'Connected'*.

As soon as *'Connected'* came up, I flicked the switch on the Suppressor. There would be another fraction of a second of a duplicate signal I hadn't been able to engineer out, but I was sure that it would get ignored. A duplicate was better than a momentary period of *'No Signal'* which would hit the alert screens at iMe.

Either the tension or the weight of my Suppressor was stiffening my neck up. I rolled my head around to try and release it.

From here, the evening was going to one of two ways: Plan A or Plan B. I unclipped two small latches on the

Mimic and pulled the flap down. It revealed a small keyboard with little black keys and back-lit blue letters.

I typed out a message, made a small change, and then was happy.

'Mary, I know I have been a bastard recently, and it's too late for us, but I want to say sorry. I want to do it face-to-face so you can see that I'm genuine this time. Can I come over now?'

I pressed send and waited. The answer would tell me if I was going with plan A or B.

Please let it be A. Lussac in my cage would be fun, but he wasn't really part of the cause. Plan A would be sweet payback and generate the most disruption and doubt in the police.

The Mimic beeped, and the reply showed on the display.

'Clive, I want to believe you this time, I really do. Come over. I've programmed your signal for the front door and lift.'

Yes! Plan A.

***

I took the stairs again as they were empty and headed outside. The waiting car recognised Lussac's signal from the Mimic nestled in my bag and opened its door. I reprogrammed the destination from a little Italian restaurant to Mary's home.

Had Lussac planned a hot date? It would explain him washing and the ironed shirt. That added an unexpected edge to the evening.

I fantasised about what was to come.

43

DC Zoe Jordan

I filled up when I saw Mum dressed up for the date. She looked so beautiful. I dabbed at the corner of my eyes.

The simple black dress showed her figure off, and the silver necklace emphasised her neck and drew your eyes down.

'You're a bit showy, aren't you?' I said with concern, looking at the amount of cleavage the dress presented.

Her eyes glittered, and she fluttered her eyelashes in mock innocence. 'I want to look my best.'

The scene in the hall was the perfect replay of my first teenage dates. Mum full of pride, but also worrying that I had too much flesh on display. Me full of excitement and defiance, saying that I wanted to look my best before storming out. Her concerned, 'Be careful' while waving me off.

'Oh, Mum,' I said, hugging her. 'You wait all these years to date again, and then you choose Clive when you could have anyone.' Why couldn't she see it?

She shrugged. 'I like him.'

'But he's a scruffy mess. He always tries to cheat on his FUs and he's on his third Excess Consumption Order.'

She shrugged again.

'You're wasted on him. You can do so much better.'

Her car arrived and she opened the door and stepped out towards it.

'Don't be late… and be careful,' I called.

As the car departed, I shook my head. When had I become my mum's mum?

***

I couldn't settle. I wasn't sure if it was because of Mum or because of the case. I refused to admit to Clive that I enjoyed his old-school policing, but it was more interesting than relying on iMe, and it felt good that I was making a difference to the investigation.

I spent some time attaching notes on possible interview approaches to Art's and Esteban's files. They would be replicated onto our crime wall at the PCU office and I could talk them through with Clive in the morning. I hoped that it would be after some insincere comments about how sorry I was that the date had gone wrong, and that Mum didn't want to see him again. It had been years since Dad left, and I wanted her to be happy. Just with someone else.

Mum pinged me a message and my Buddy dragged it onto my HUD: *'I'm here, but he's not.'*

I felt for her, sitting at the restaurant, waiting on her own, but I was pleased that Clive was messing the date up before it started.

'Don't worry. He'll be there,' I messaged back, hoping that he wouldn't.

I went back to my notes and only three minutes later I got another message.

'He's still not here.'

He was only a few minutes late, but that was Mum. One minute late was still late.

'I'm sure he'll be there soon,' I replied.

Clive had been looking forward to the date, so I expected him to be there early, ready and waiting but he had told me about the messages from Alfie and what a tap really meant. I was beginning to worry.

Five minutes later, I could feel Mum's anger. *'He's really late. It's pissing me off.'*

I didn't have a chance to reply before the next message arrived.

'Can you find out where he is for me?'

I wasn't meant to do searches for personal reasons, but I guessed I could use Alfie's threats as an excuse. I moved my notes aside on my HUD, brought up the search screen and put Clive in. I waited, and the screen redrew with a map.

I spoke out my message and the HUD converted it to text. *'Don't worry. He's in a car about five minutes from you.'* Then, as an afterthought to soften it, I added *'He probably stopped to get you some flowers.'*

44

Thief

Mary's home was broadly in the same direction as the restaurant. He must have been going on a date, I concluded. He was probably taking his date to the same restaurant he and Mary always went to. I bet he'd even asked for their usual table.

I brought up the map on the car's screen and touched the displayed route. With my finger, I pressed *Previous Destinations'*, selected the restaurant and then chose *'Go via'*.

The map drew a new route past the restaurant and then on to Mary's. The arrival time had gone back ten minutes, but it was worth the delay if Lussac's date paid for a signal trace on him. She would see him come towards her, pause briefly and then sail straight on by. It would be like he had stopped, considered the date and then rejected her in favour of his ex-wife.

I enjoyed the rest of the journey with a big smile on my face.

***

The outside door of the block of flats opened as promised and the lift greeted me with a happy, 'Hello, Clive. I'll take you to Mary's floor'. When the doors opened, I slipped my mask on and strode along the corridor.

'Hi, Clive,' Mary called.

She must have been waiting for him by the door – that blew my plan of sneaking up on her out of the water before it had started. I rolled my shoulders in preparation.

The door clicked open as Mary pulled it towards her. I shoved against it and heard her surprise and confusion as she was sent backwards off balance.

I stepped past the door, pushing it shut behind me, and stood in front of Mary, my bag in my hand.

'Who the fuck are you? Where's Clive?' she screamed. 'Get *out*.'

I put the bag on the floor as she charged at me and tried to push me out.

We grappled – a sprawl of arms until I got a good grip. I shoved her back to give me the space I needed, and I punched her hard in the face, hearing the crunch of her nose breaking and seeing blood appear on her top lip. Mary was stronger than I thought – she was still standing – until I landed another two blows.

***

Mary sprawled face up on the entrance hall floor, groaning. She was semi-conscious, and I couldn't risk her using voice control on her HUD. I tore off a strip from a roll of silver tape, reinforced with fibres, and pressed it over Mary's mouth and around her cheeks to her jawline on both sides. Next, I rolled her over onto her front and pulled one arm behind her back. The other was stuck under her torso, so I had to wrestle it out before it could join its twin. I put one of her hands on top of the other and taped her wrists together. Now she couldn't use her HUD keyboard either.

'Shame,' I said to her back. 'I was going to frame Lussac for assault.'

I whirled three or four loops of tape around her ankles and pressed it tight. Seeing her bound like that tugged at a memory of an image I had seen.

'But you know I'm not him.' I removed my redundant mask.

Now she had to die slowly enough that I had time to get back to Lussac's house and remove his Suppressor before Mary's signal went red. Otherwise, I would be risking the forensic drones and the police getting to Lussac's before me. Walking into a room full of police surrounding a drugged detective inspector would be a certain way to get arrested.

An interesting challenge. I needed to be creative with what I could find in the flat.

***

Lussac's flat was a mess, but Mary's was tidy. While he lived in a sterile box with no pictures or any attempt at homeliness, Mary had made a real effort at personalising her space. One of her video walls showed a loop of her favourite pictures. Different places around the world: Paris, Rome, New York, with smiling groups of friends, their tanned faces mouthing a silent cheese for the camera. I watched for a few minutes until it started to repeat. Not one photo of her ex-husband.

I rummaged around in the kitchen and found various chemicals, but none would do. Strong bleach would have worked for a slow and painful death – but that had been banned years ago. In a high cupboard in the utility area, I pushed aside some spare cleaning products and found a toolbox.

I lifted it down. It was big, but from its weight I didn't expect to find much in there. I popped the catches and took a look inside. The top layer held a small hammer and a set of screwdrivers in clip holders. Underneath were two plastic boxes; each with ten compartments that held different sized screws and nails. It all looked unused, and I guessed she must have got the toolbox when she moved in, along with the selection of 'just in case' tools and fixings, but never needed them.

I heard some grunting and sounds of a body struggling from near the door.

Mary was still on her front but flopping about like a seal trying to get across a beach. Her bound struggling crystallised the memory: a celeb who'd died when an auto-erotic asphyxiation experiment went wrong. His partner had fled, leaving him bound at the wrists and elbows, hanging in a hotel room.

I rolled Mary over and was rewarded with a series of grunts that I assumed was a stream of abuse. Her eyes bore into me. Pure anger and hatred. If she got free, I would have a real problem.

I banged her head on the floor to still her, then reached under her armpits and dragged her to the bedroom, dumping her on the bed. I fetched the toolbox and stood looking down at her.

'Let's get started,' I said, while placing my bag with the Mimic in it next to her on the bed.

Mary's eyes still poured out anger, but as she looked around the room for an escape, I could see the beginning of real fear as well.

I watched it intensify as I got onto the bed beside her.

45

DC Zoe Jordan

Mum hadn't sent a message for the five minutes she allowed for Clive's car to come. Now I was getting an update almost every minute and had stopped reading them. It wasn't that I didn't feel for her, but there was nothing I could do about it. I needed to focus on Art and Esteban.

Art had said that he went to the parties, but Zane made it sound like he was the organiser. More than that, he was the provider of pretty young things of all genders to the celebs. I shuddered at the idea of the casting couch and Art murmuring 'of course you can meet the celebs, but there's something I want you to do for me...'

I thought about the way he had looked at me and felt grossed out. Was he planning to invite me?

Even if we hadn't found any iMe signals of the two of them close together, it meant that Art must have known Karina. Definitely at the parties. Art didn't attend the actual iMe technical sessions even though they were held in the iMe offices, but maybe that was where she first caught his eye. She was certainly pretty enough.

I opened my notes and typed out *'Art: Suppressor on Karina and encrypted signal to "cast" her?'* just under *'Dave: revenge?'* and *'Esteban: Parties?'*

***

Another message from Mum buzzed in my ear. *'Clive's still not here.'* I couldn't ignore her any longer.

She had ordered a glass of wine when she arrived, but said she was drinking water now. I could picture her, beautiful and stylish at the lonely table, an empty chair opposite her. I pressed my jaw to call him, but he didn't answer. *Where is he?* Was he feeling guilty at standing Mum up and too cowardly to talk to me, or had Doris got to him?

I touched my jaw again, this time to call Mum. She answered on the first ring, and I could hear the resentment in her voice.

'Where is he?' she whispered.

I expect she felt exposed being at the table alone and didn't want to make it worse by letting everyone hear.

'I don't know, Mum. He was nearly there. I tried calling, but he didn't answer.'

'Why didn't the car arrive?' she asked. 'Is there a work emergency?'

'No.' How could he leave her there? 'Come home. You're too good for him.'

All I got back was silence.

I sighed. 'Wait a sec.' I'd have to risk another trace to give Mum the full story, so I started the trace when Clive left his home.

'He was on the way to you...' I paused as I watched a fast-forward of the journey.' He got to the restaurant and stopped...'

'But he didn't come in,' Mum said.

'No, he just waited there for a few seconds and drove off.'

'Why? Where to?'

'Wait, I'll check.' I fast-forwarded again. Clive's signal trace stopped outside an apartment block. 'He went to a flat. Not his.'

I followed Clive into the block and to a front door. Someone was in the flat and I checked who it was. I gasped.

'What?' Mum said. 'Where is he?'

'He went to his ex-wife's apartment.'

'Why would he?'

'I don't know, Mum.' I followed the trace on and saw where they were. 'Mum—' I couldn't say it. The words caught in my throat.

'Tell me,' she said.

'I can't.'

'Zoe, tell me.' She used her strict parent voice.

'They're in the bedroom.' My voice cracked and faltered. 'They... they're on top of each other.'

I heard a small 'no' and the call dropped.

46

Thief

Mary thrashed around on the bed like a landed fish, desperate to escape.

She was wearing a short satin skirt and I was treated to a flash of her white knickers as it rode up her legs. She was pretty and full of spirit. Her make-up subtly enhanced her eyes and lips. Her formal shirt was sexy in a slightly severe way and the effect with the short skirt and her brown legs was spectacular. She must have wanted to put a full on, *see what you can no longer have* show for Lussac. He was a fool, but she had probably been too much for him to handle.

I tried to flip her onto her front, but she pushed back against me. I bent in close to her ear. 'You can fight me, or I can pluck an eye out. Choose.'

She screwed her eyes shut, and her body went limp. I rolled her over and taped her elbows together to mirror the images of the celeb I had seen. I couldn't complete the image with the things I had, but her wardrobe should have what I needed.

A couple of her handbags looked promising, with nice heavy chain loops to go over a shoulder. They were long enough but made of a shiny plastic substitute so wouldn't be strong enough.

I rummaged around and selected an old dusty leather belt from the back of the wardrobe. It had a strong buckle and the leather would take her weight. Perfect.

I put the Mimic on Mary's back for a few seconds. I was thinking about how Lussac's tracks would look when replayed by the police: he gets there, is taunted by her and punches her in the face. Then he takes her to the bedroom tapes her up and climbs on top.

Then he gets all kinky.

***

I moved the toolbox over to the en-suite bathroom door, took out the hammer and the box of nails and headed back to the bed. I rolled Mary onto her back and pushed the end of the belt through the buckle to form a noose and looped it over her head. With the buckle positioned neatly on her windpipe, I pulled the belt tight. She whimpered. I pushed her legs over the side of the bed and pulled her up into a sitting position. I slipped the handles of my bag onto my arm and pulled on the belt. She resisted, trying to pull away but stood up as the buckle bit deeper. She hopped after me, like a reluctant dog on a lead. Pull, resist, hop. Repeat. Each time I moved, my bag banged against my leg. The signal would look like Lussac had done it.

The bathroom door opened inward and I pushed it through 90 degrees until the handle on the inside of the door touched the wall. I turned Mary, so her back was flat against the open door, and flipped the spare end of the belt over the top of the door where it dangled in the handle-sized void between the door and the wall. I fished two nails out of my pocket and held them close to Mary's eye. 'Stay still.' She stared at the points and nodded.

I moved the nails and pressed them into the leather of the belt. They wobbled but held, so I picked up the hammer and invaded Mary's personal space. She cringed away from me.

Holding the belt flat against the door, I tapped the nails with the hammer, pushing them through the leather, but not into the wood. Now I could hold the hammer in one hand and the belt in the other. Grasping the belt, I pulled it up, tightening it around Mary's neck. She started to go red in the face. Her body was rigid with fear and, as she snapped her head back to me, she was pleading with her eyes.

'Up,' I said, and pulled up on the belt some more. Mary's heels lifted off the floor as she came up onto her tiptoes.

'More.' I pulled the belt so that only her toes were taking her weight. Mary's breathing was ragged with panic, but she didn't dare move in case the belt tightened even more. I held the belt in place with one hand and tapped a nail with the hammer. I was gentle with the first couple of strikes until the nail went into the wood of the door. I checked Mary – she was still up on her toes, so I drove the nail fully home, making it nice and tight in the solid wood of the door.

I banged four more nails into the leather to secure the belt to the front of the door above Mary's head. She seemed to be saying please repeatedly, but I couldn't tell through the tape. Her eyes were begging me.

I ignored her and stood back to check my work. I was happy – well, almost. *Lussac would be a bit pervier,* I thought. I grabbed Mary's shirt and ripped it apart. Buttons flew, and the shirt gaped to show her white bra and tanned, flat stomach. My final flourish was to pull her knickers down and leave them around her taped ankles.

'Your calves will burn up, and your toes will ache,' I said. 'But you should be able to manage at least fifteen minutes on your toes.'

I checked around the room and remembered what I had forgotten.

I took a tissue from Mary's bedside and rubbed it against her nose, making sure it caught at the blood drying there before putting it into my pocket.

I had the time I needed. Mary wouldn't last forever on tiptoes, but she would fight to live. It would look like Lussac was a vindictive, sadist killer who had left her to die.

'Actually, you might last more than fifteen minutes,' I said. 'Given what you have at stake.'

***

The car was waiting where I told it to, and I made it back to Lussac's flat in eleven minutes. I was really tempted to see if Mary's signal was still green, but I couldn't risk the police finding that a search had been run.

Lussac was still in drug-induced oblivion when I got back into his bedroom. I put the Mimic back on his bed next to the Suppressor, timing the switches on both so that the Suppressor turned off just before the Mimic. Lussac's true signal was back on the grid, so I removed the Suppressor from his neck.

I had one last job. I went to the bathroom and held the tissue with Mary's blood on it under the tap. The water ran through the thin paper, and I caught some of the blood-tinged water in my palm. I mimed careless hand washing over the sink, making sure that a couple of drops of the pale pink water splashed against the wall.

A little bit of forensic proof to supplement the signal evidence. I was pleased with the touch. I stuffed the tissue in my pocket so that I didn't leave any of my DNA behind.

***

I stood outside in the darkness of some trees and waited. It would all depend on Mary. When her signal went red, the police would go to her flat. They couldn't possibly treat it as a suicide, so they would run a trace and then come here.

I waited eight more minutes. Twenty-seven minutes since I had left Mary. She had been a real fighter.

I walked away from Lussac's road when I heard the sirens.

47

DC Zoe Jordan

Mum tottered up the drive. I wasn't sure if it was because she was upset or because she was walking in high-heels on gravel.

'Oh, Zoe,' she cried, opening her arms. I pulled her in and hugged her. I know I wanted Clive to screw the date up, but not like this.

'I'm sorry.' How could he leave her at the restaurant and go straight to his ex-wife's bed?

I couldn't say anything that would help, so I made the same small soothing sounds that Mum had used when my now ex-boyfriend kept going back to his ex.

An urgent message came up on my HUD. I kept a half cuddle going while I tapped the air to open the message.

Unexpected RED Signal alert. Deceased: Mary Lussac.

Oh, shit. I jumped out of the cuddle as I saw the name. There can't be many people called Mary Lussac.

Mum looked at me, startled by the sudden movement and the change in my attitude. 'What is it, Zoe?'

'I…'

Mum looked scared. 'Is it Clive?'

My head buzzed with a call. It was Chief Superintendent Bhatt. I could guess why she was calling me.

'Jordan,' she barked.' You've seen the message about Clive's ex-wife?'

'Yes, ma'am.'

'Get there now. Uniform are there, but I need to hear the details from you.'

She clicked off before I could say anything. What the hell was happening?

I ran a search on Clive again and followed his movements. I felt relieved. He was at home. Although he was the last person to see Mary alive, he had left more than twenty minutes before she died. Did she kill herself after he left?

***

Mary lived quite close to us, so it was a short hop to her place, but I fretted all the way in the car.

A big, gruff Uniform stood in the doorway of Mary's flat. He glared at me until I threw my ID at him and his face softened.

'Take it easy, luv,' he said. 'Trust me, I've seen a few and this is a rough one.'

I should have been pissed off at him calling me luv, but his tone was caring not mocking. He seemed genuine, so I let it slide. I could hear the forensic drones in a room ahead on the left, and I followed their noise to where I assumed the body was. At the doorway, I peered into the room.

Jesus. I dropped my hands onto my knees and gulped air to stop myself throwing up. Mary wasn't chopped up like Alan Kane, but somehow, he had seemed less real cut into pieces. Mary was whole and hanging. A leather belt cut across her neck and her head hung at an unnatural angle. Her painted toes brushed the floor.

I shut my eyes, but I could still see her purple bloated face. I shook my head to try and clear the image, but I couldn't. Mary still floated in front of me.

The forensic sweep was in full flow, so I had to stay in the hall and wait as the drones buzzed around, landed on things, swabbed them and photographed the whole room.

'The forensic checks and data gathering are complete,' said the forensic controller finally. 'It's all yours.'

I forced myself upright and leant against the door frame as the drones left the room a few inches above my head.

I could see Mary's taped ankles and wrists.

You have to go in there.

It took all my strength to push my foot over the threshold and into the room.

Mary's blood was smeared around her nose, which was bent at an unnatural angle. Tape covered the lower part of her face. I couldn't look into her glassy eyes. The rest of her face was a dark, red mess.

I stepped through the bathroom doorway and cringed as I accidentally bumped the door, which caused Mary to bang against it. The belt holding her up had nails driven through it and into the door to take her weight.

This obviously wasn't suicide or even an accident. This was a cold-blooded and callous murder, and Clive had been the last person to see her.

He couldn't explain it as a crime of passion. He would have used a knife or heavy object. Something that came to hand. This was cruel and deliberate. The open shirt and knickers done for humiliation. I felt I didn't know Clive at all. How could he be capable of this?

I shuffled backwards to avoid confronting the thought that flashed through my mind: *Better Mary than Mum.*

***

I called Bhatt and she answered immediately. 'Well?'

'You've seen the drone images, ma'am?'

'Yes. Is it as bad as it looks?'

'Worse, ma'am.' I was struggling to keep my voice even.

'Take your time, Zoe,' Bhatt said in a kinder voice than I thought possible.

'She has a broken nose and has been hanged. She's all taped up. There's no way she could have done it herself.' I sobbed.

224

Bhatt waited in silence, giving me a chance to recover.

'It looks like she was left on her tiptoes with the belt tight around her neck. She only died when her strength failed. She must have been terrified and in agony. The bastard left her to die.'

'Who was there?' Bhatt asked, but I knew that she knew the answer.

'Only Mary. The signal trace shows that Clive left before she died. He must have strung her up and then left her.' *How could he?*

I cried then, sobbing and gasping, the tears rolling down my cheeks as I imagined Mary's last minutes. The pain and desperation. The final inevitable panic. Her white knickers caught on the tape by her ankles could almost be a flag of surrender.

Again, the guilty thought: *Mum's OK, but it could have been her.*

I sniffed, rubbed at my wet cheeks and tried to stand up.

'Zoe, are you OK?' Bhatt was still connected and must have heard all my weakness. Shit. This wasn't the way to impress her.

'I'm OK, ma'am,' I said, but I knew that I wasn't.

'The evidence says that Clive strung her up and left her to die,' Bhatt said.

'Yes.' It seemed completely out of character, but the iMe signal didn't lie – not in Clive's case. There's no way he could get around the technology. He didn't have a Suppressor and certainly couldn't make one.

'I can't believe this,' Bhatt said. 'I was a guest at their wedding. Mary was lovely.'

Bhatt's tone hardened. 'Get over to Clive's. I'll meet you there. I'll send Uniforms and full forensics. We're going to put him away for a long time for this.'

48

DI Clive Lussac

Colours wheeled and morphed into crazy shapes that turned in on themselves, twisting and writhing like a pit of multicoloured snakes. One minute I was being carried on a cloud, the next I was walking through a field of corn, hand in hand with Sophia, with the sun warming my neck.

I watched a dark spot in the distance getting closer and turning into a black cloud. All my secret fears were in the cloud. The cloud buzzed with terrifying intensity as it chased me. The cloud turned into black flies as big as my hands, swarming around me. I turned to run but I was stuck to the ground. The corn was twisted around my legs and held me tight.

I glanced at Sophia. She was backing away from me. I reached and called for her. She mouthed my name, but I heard Bhatt's voice. Sophia's face morphed and whirled into Bhatt's. The flies pressed down on me.

***

I woke with a start and tried to open my eyes. I could feel something heavy on my chest.

My eyes seemed to be stuck together. I panicked, rubbing my hands against them to free them.

It didn't work. I needed to use my fingers to push my eyelids open but, when I looked around, I thought I was still in the dream. Bhatt stood over me, and a big black fly tramped around on my chest.

I shut my eyes and reopened them, but the scene remained the same.

I was in my flat and Bhatt was at the end of my bed. She looked at me with such disgust that it confused me.

Zoe stood next to her, but it wasn't the normal, happy Zoe. This was some angry, shaking, furious version of her, and what scared me was that the violence was directed straight at me.

'What're you doing here?' I croaked. My throat was dry and hoarse.

'Be quiet, Inspector,' Bhatt said. 'We're not finished.'

Inspector? She never called me that.

The fly on my chest moved again, and my brain finally rationalised it for what it was. A forensic drone. It shuffled over to my wrist and extended a long, clear probe. The probe touched my wrist, with the end sitting on a vein. With a flash of silver, a needle shot down the tube and I felt a prick of pain as it went through my skin. The tube filled red as the drone took a sample of my blood.

A buzzing to my left dragged my eyes from the drone. A second drone was in the bathroom, hovering over the sink with its blue scanning laser tracking over the handles and walls. It crabbed to the right, approaching the wall slightly above the taps on one side of the sink. The laser snapped off, and the drone extended a DNA probe and touched the wall with it. It stayed like that for a few seconds and then retracted the probe and sped into the bedroom to hover by the door. The one on my chest joined it, waited for four others, and then they flew out of the room in formation.

I looked at Zoe. Hoping for some flash of understanding, but she glared at me.

What have I done?

I could see the glow of Zoe's HUD change as she read something. She shook her head and spat the word, *'Bastard.'*

Bhatt looked at her and Zoe said, 'The DNA from his sink is a match to Mary's blood.'

What were they talking about? Why would Mary's blood be in my sink?

I couldn't make sense of Bhatt's words: 'Clive Lussac, I am arresting you for the murder of Mary Lussac...'

***

They had left me in Interview Room One for the last hour.

I couldn't have killed Mary. Even after the divorce and everything else, I still cared about her.

I tried to use my HUD, but it was disabled. Everything I tried resulted in my little red Buddy shaking his head and waving a finger at me. The banner he rolled out flashed *'Access Denied'*.

I'd done it enough times to people and watched their reaction. The young ones took it the worst. They had never really been without the constantly connected world in their head. They looked more scared of being offline than charged with whatever crime they had committed.

I had to sit there and wait.

***

After what seemed like a lifetime, the door opened.

Zoe came in, her suppressed anger visible in her clenched fists. She was followed by DS Martin Adams and the duty solicitor dressed in a shiny suit. Martin and I had worked together over the years – Bhatt must have forced him to help – bad back or not. He wore a sheepish *I don't really want to be here* grin as he hobbled to the desk with one hand pressed at the small of his back to ease the pain.

Chairs scraped back on the floor as Zoe and Martin planted themselves opposite me – a wave of suppressed hostility in the simple actions. The solicitor sat next to me. Zoe leant forward, elbows on the table, glaring. Martin fidgeted in his chair, unable to get comfortable. He went through the procedural preliminaries, and then Zoe said, 'Why did you *murder* Mary?'

I didn't say anything. I heard the words, but my brain couldn't process an answer. My blank eyes looked back at them.

'Are you refusing to answer?' Zoe said.

There had been such emphasis on the word murder. She made it sound like a terrible, cold-blooded death.

'It wasn't me. Whatever happened, I wasn't there.' I regretted saying it as soon as the words were out.

Martin laughed, and Zoe rolled her eyes in disbelief.

'Clive, come on,' he said. 'You of all people couldn't have said that, could you?'

How many people had I laughed at over the years for saying exactly that? It was a stupid defence with iMe knowing where everyone was, but what else could I say?

'Look, I remember getting home and starting to get ready to go out last night, then I remember waking up with drones and police in my bedroom.' As a defence, I knew how pathetic it was. 'I can't recall anything in between.'

'Really?' Zoe said. 'Really? *That's* your story?'

She blanked the wall in the room and threw up the floor plan of my empty flat.

'This is just before you got home yesterday evening. After I dropped you off,' Zoe said. 'You say you can't remember but we can show you exactly what happened.'

She said, 'Play, fifteen,' and the time stamp in the corner of the wall started counting forward in fifteen second intervals.

A signal dot appeared at my door.

'Pause,' Zoe said.

She touched a spot in front of her face: the signal dot on the wall pulsed once and an ID window popped up with my details.

'Do you agree that is your signal, Clive?' Martin said.

What else could I say but, 'Yes?'

I watched the display wall and my signal moving on it in brain-numbed shock as Zoe talked me through my arrival, washing, getting clothes from the wardrobe, sitting on the bed a while, and then leaving.

Her face glowed red with anger as she talked me through the car stopping outside the restaurant.

I couldn't believe that I was late for my date with Sophia and then driven off. That date was going to be special.

Zoe stopped the signal with me outside an apartment block. 'Do you recognise this address?'

My mouth went dry. Oh shit, no. It couldn't be.

'I didn't... I wasn't...' I tried, but it would be the same lame denials. 'It's Mary's building.'

No. No. No, repeated in my head as I watched on.

'This is where you punched Mary,' Zoe said. 'There is blood splatter on the floor. Then you went to find her tools and came back and dragged her to the bedroom. Then... then...'

Zoe stopped and gulped and couldn't go on. She shook her head and concentrated on her breathing.

Martin touched Zoe on the back to comfort her. 'Do you want a break?' he said.

She shook her head and Martin picked up the story. 'You got into bed together.'

Mary would never have done that, I thought. *Once, but not now. There's no way she did that voluntarily.*

It wasn't going to help me if I vocalised my thoughts, so I said nothing.

Next, my signal and Mary's went to the bathroom door. Her signal stayed in the bedroom and I stood close in front of Mary.

'What did you do there?' Martin asked.

I shook my head and shrugged. I only had a gaping black hole in my memory.

I looked down at the table, not sure where else to look. Definitely not at Zoe. I couldn't take the disgust in her eyes.

The colour of the reflection in the tabletop changed, and it made me look up at the display wall. I stared at the image of Mary, hanging and broken. Her eyes, the eyes I had gazed lovingly into for so many years, bulged. All the life in them gone.

I heaved and threw out a violent and noisy jet of vomit, which pooled an acid yellow on the concrete floor. The stench of it filled the room.

I hadn't done that. I couldn't do that. Not to Mary. Could I? Had I blacked it out? Was I *that* sick?

'Recognise your work?' Martin said, his hand over his nose to block the smell out. 'Some pervy experiment?'

'No. No,' I said with the taste of vomit in my mouth.

'Could Mary have done that to herself?'

'No.'

'Who else is there? Who is the only person who could have done it to her?'

'Don't answer that,' the solicitor said, but I had to face it: the data allowed only one answer.

'Me.'

49

DI Clive Lussac

I was doomed.

They dumped me back in my cell and left me to stew. Left me to come to terms with my inevitable guilt. But I couldn't have left Mary there, fighting the cramp and pain in her calves and toes, the muscles eventually failing and her body weight tightening the belt that last, terrible bit.

I knew I didn't do it, but the evidence was all there: the signal trace and a speck of Mary's blood on my wall from when I had washed her off my hands. What other conclusion could a jury make?

I sobbed and sobbed. Part grief for Mary, part fear for what would happen next.

I needed to work it all out. I thought of Suppressors and encrypted signals. I thought about Mary, replaying the good times and glossing over the bad. Were my instincts about Art right? How did Esteban fit in? How did Mary's murder link to Karina and Alan? I bounced the formless thoughts around. Grasped at stupid ideas, then crushed them. I was helpless in here.

I spent all the desperate, dark hours of the night trying to work how to prove it wasn't me.

***

After the lunch they gave me congealed next to my untouched breakfast, I made a lot of noise, screaming and shouting until they agreed. Now I was back in Interview Room One. The vomit was gone, but it had etched a light grey stain into the floor. The smell was worse now: a heady mixture of vomit and disinfectant that stung my eyes.

Zoe and Martin were in their seats. Their noses crinkled against the smell as they tried not to think about the content of the airborne particles hitting their sinuses. I knew Bhatt would be behind the wall watching everything.

Last night should have been a pleasurable first date with Sophia. It was meant to lead to a second date, not to me in prison for the violent murder of my ex-wife. It would be a brutal way to spend the rest of my days.

I had one chance before they processed me and I disappeared into prison for the rest of my life.

'Well. What did you want to say?' Zoe said, with no diminishing of her hostility.

I took a breath. They might laugh at my brilliant idea. Martin would be too cynical but maybe I could convince Zoe. I needed her to save me.

I had rehearsed what I wanted to say, but the pressure of my one chance chased the words from my mind.

My mute mouth gaped half-open. They must have seen me as a gormless fool.

They shook their heads and started to rise.

'Wait,' I said. 'Please.'

They resettled, and I found my missing words.

'Please, Zoe, Martin,' I said, and glanced at the wall. 'Chief Superintendent, please take a minute and look at me. You all know me. You know I couldn't do this.'

They stared back at me. This wasn't working.

'OK, OK… Forget that.'

Here goes nothing.

'Just do your job properly. *Look* and *think* and do some real police work instead of believing iMe.'

They bristled at the insult but didn't start to get up.

'I didn't do it, so there are two things you need to do.'

I paused for effect.

'Number one,' I said. 'I must have been drugged. Your drone took a blood sample. Get it analysed for any drugs that would knock me out.'

Now the key point. The one I couldn't believe I hadn't thought of before. Finally, in the bleakness of the cell with tears on my face and dried vomit on my shoe, my old detective's brain had started working again.

It was the answer to everything. It explained Karina and Alan and Mary.

'Number two,' I said.

50

DC Zoe Jordan

'Number two,' Clive said. 'What's the opposite of a Suppressor?'

He wore a pained expression, like he was willing us to know what he meant and not understanding why we weren't in perfect sync with him.

I didn't get it, and it must have been obvious on my face. Martin said nothing.

'OK, look at it this way.' His tone reminded me of my algebra teacher explaining simultaneous equations for the tenth time. 'Remember when we used a Suppressor and went off-grid. No one knew where we were.'

'Yes, of course I remember,' I said.

'All of our suspects had signals when Karina and Alan went missing and again when their bodies were found, didn't they?'

'Not Esteban,' I said.

'OK, not Esteban.' He seemed exasperated at the interruption. 'But all the others. Yes?'

I said 'yes' to let him finish his argument. I would pick it apart at the end.

'And the killer had to wear a Suppressor to abduct Karina and dump her body. Otherwise, we'd know he was there, yes?'

Martin and I nodded our agreement.

'So how can he be wearing a Suppressor and still have a signal?'

'You can't,' Martin said. 'You just said the Suppressor blocks the signal.'

'Come on. *Think*.' Clive's frustration was clear. He stared at me, willing me to understand what he was talking about.

There was a far-fetched explanation. 'Perhaps, if you could somehow have a copy of your signal somewhere else,' I said.

'*Exactly*, Zoe.' Clive beamed at me like I was now his star pupil. 'Let's say you have something that can mimic your signal. You could leave it at home, go and kidnap Karina, and iMe would give you a guaranteed alibi.'

I squirmed in my seat. It didn't feel right to be praised by Clive anymore. Not after Mary.

Suppressors should have been science fiction, but they existed. I had seen them. Now he wanted me to believe in a device that could somehow duplicate a signal?

'Yeah, but that would mean you've done the impossible and broken the iMe encryption algorithm,' I said.

'You don't need to break the algorithm if you work at iMe and have access to the system,' Clive said.

***

I stood in Bhatt's office.

'Do you believe him?' she asked, still using her gentle voice with me.

Clive had moaned about his ex-wife, but I hadn't really sensed the hate necessary to inflict this sort of suffering. I wondered if he had hidden it, the years of suppressing his feelings, and the pressure building and building until he finally popped. Don't men block out their feelings? I lived with mine every moment.

'I don't know,' I said, emphasising my doubt with a shrug. I couldn't wipe away my faith in iMe so easily. 'It's plausible I guess, but the simpler answer is that he did it and now he's trying to get away with it.'

Bhatt steepled her hands as she turned it all over in her head. She seemed to decide.

'I've known Clive a long time, so look into it. We can give him that.'

***

Back at my desk at PCU, it seemed strange to have Clive's empty chair opposite me. The crew couldn't take it in, and any discussion on the subject stilled when they saw the photos from Mary's bedroom. A few of them rubbed their necks in subconscious empathy.

Martin lay on the floor. The prolonged hours spent in a crappy chair during the interviews had done his back again, and he was trying to ease the pressure before an emergency appointment with his specialist.

It was down to me to check Clive's theory, but I wasn't sure if I wanted to try too hard. I couldn't live with getting Clive off if he had done it. I would have to sit and talk to him every day. Every smile would feel like he was gloating. Worse, if he patched it up with Mum.

If they went out, I would be frantic the whole time worrying that Mum would be next.

51

DC Zoe Jordan

I tried to suspend my natural scepticism, keep an open mind and think it through, but all this talk of Suppressors and mimicking signals made my head spin. Until last week, iMe always worked. Now Karina and Alan were dead, and if I shut my eyes I could still see Mary in her last seconds as her twitching muscles screamed *enough*.

I needed a break so headed to the vending machine. As I approached, its synthesised human voice said, 'How can I serve you, Zoe?'

I scanned the array of food and drinks, not sure what to have.

'Your iMe reports: you are inside all of your Freedom Unit allowances. You may choose anything.'

My eyes settled on a Mars bar, but the FU tax was too big, so I said, 'Give me the low-calorie nutrition bar, please.'

'Certainly.' The machine whirred, arms moved, and a flap opened. My nutrition bar appeared, and I took it. 'A pleasure to serve you, Zoe.'

I chewed on the bar as I headed back to the office thinking about Clive. His defence was that someone was able to generate his signal. They had drugged him, left him in his bedroom while they went off and killed Mary as an elaborate frame.

We were also meant to believe that because Clive had a dream where his neck was warm, the killer had put a Suppressor on him. The small bruise on Clive's wrist where he said the drugs went in could have been anything. OK, there was a puncture mark you could see in an extreme close-up of the forensic photos, but he could have done it while killing Mary.

I replayed Clive's signal from last night. A smooth track to Mary's flat and back again, with no gaps and nothing out of the ordinary.

I checked the others, all at home watching different films. Esteban and Dave chose generic pulp, but why did Manu watch the fourth re-imagining of *Blade Runner* when the original was way better? I couldn't forgive Emma for *Legally Blonde 8* and *9*, and as for Art watching the new version of *1984*, what was that – guilt, irony or research?

Even if I didn't believe Clive's words, his vomiting at Mary's photos was real.

I thought about it for a long time: Was Clive a killer? Should I even try and save him?

***

It wasn't about feelings or belief, I decided. It was about the truth and being the best cop I could be. I would find all the facts and then decide. So, I started with the blood test.

The forensic drone took the blood as a 'tick the box' procedural thing. We didn't usually need it as we knew the amount of alcohol, tobacco, cannabis, cocaine and all the other legal drugs from the iMe readings. Tax rules meant that they were all measured accurately and stored.

I composed a full toxicology request on Clive's blood, sent it off and made a call.

'Hi, Bella,' I said.

'Zoe, how's tricks,' she said, knowing it was me from the caller ID.

'Favour to ask.' We had met on the ten-week intern programme run by the Justice and Rehabilitation Service and become good friends. She had chosen forensics when I chose the police.

'Go for it,' she said. 'You want to hassle some guy with a drone?'

'Nooo.'

We both laughed at the memory of the prank when we used a drone to buzz all the sleeping beds in the men's dorm at the training centre. How did men make such a mess and not care?

'Look, I've just sent a blood tox request. It's urgent. Can you push it through?'

'OK, give me a couple of hours. Still on for Friday?'

A night out with the girls was what I needed. I'd missed so many recently.

I crossed my fingers. 'Obviously.'

***

Next was Clive's duplicate signal story. When we had first met, he had gone on and on about old-school policing. He had said 'think like the criminal'. *What would I need if I was the killer?*

I would need Clive's DNA to generate his signal. Clive had drinks at Esteban's home, Art's office, and in the other meetings. Dave had made us tea.

OK, assuming I knew how to get the DNA off a cup or glass, then I could get Clive's DNA. But then I would need something that took the DNA and generated a valid iMe signal.

How would you do that? Who would be able to do it?

An iMe employee made the most sense, but that just took me back full circle to the suspect list. I made some notes on the wall and pushed a little yellow flag next to the notes as a reminder to come back to it.

Next, the killer would need to get through both the outside door of Clive's block and the door into his apartment. Clive's signal, real or fake, would open the doors.

I searched through the menus on my HUD. Under 'Locks' I could see how to give myself access to unlock a lock and disable a lock, but no way of seeing if a door had been opened.

I called Tech Support.

'Hi, Zoe. It's Rob. What's up today?'

I had called him so many times during the investigation that he was treating me like part of the team.

'I need the detailed history of a lock opening and closing,' I said.

'Sure, I'd need the address and when. All that data gets stored for the manufacturers in case there's a claim.'

I told him Clive's address and asked for all of yesterday's data from Clive's apartment door.

'It's not like I don't have anything else to do.' I caught the impatience in his voice.

'Please, Rob.'

'That's the guy who killed his wife, right. He's a sick bastard.'

'Looks that way,' I said. 'But I need the data to make sure.'

'OK, no probs. I'll message you the results.'

***

By the time the report arrived, the day had darkened to dusk and the PCU office was empty. I shivered. It felt creepy to be in there on my own.

I created a new file on the crime wall and threw the report onto it. It was easier to see on the big screen.

The report was simple, with one row for every time the door opened and only two columns: Time and User. The nine rows displayed in chronological order.

Time	User
08:27	
18:52	Clive
19:17	Clive
19:25	
21:07	Clive
21:15	
21:25	PCU Override
21:33	PCU Override
22:02	

The time of the first row had to be Clive leaving in the morning at 08:27. I frowned at the empty 'User' column. The last row also had no user data but the time of 22:02 matched when Bhatt and I left with Clive in handcuffs. The two rows showing the user data as 'PCU Override' matched the times of the forensic team's arrival to scan Clive's flat and then when Bhatt and I had arrived. The meaning of these rows seemed obvious and didn't help me with Clive's guilt or innocence.

If I discounted these rows and had five remaining data rows: three rows showed Clive as the user, two had no user data.

I touched my jaw to make another call.

'Zoe,' Rob said. 'That's quick even for you. Just a sec.' I heard clicks then huffing. 'OK, what?'

'What does it mean when there's no data in the user column?' I asked.

'Because the doors are never locked from the inside, there's no user data going out. It's a fire safety thing, so people can always get out. The last thing you need in a fire is a lock with a technical fault trapping everyone inside.'

'So, you get user data when it unlocks going in but no user data going out?'

'Exactly.'

I said, 'Thanks.' Rob repeated his usual 'no probs' as I hung up.

I checked the report again. Five rows.

Five made no sense. Two rows had User data as Clive. That meant Clive went into his flat at 18:52 and twenty-five minutes later he went in again, without having first gone back out of the door. That wasn't possible unless he'd jumped out of the window, and his flat was too high for the safety rules to allow it.

I scanned the rows again, struggling to see a pattern. I shook my head and added my thoughts to the display wall to help to get the whole thing straight.

Time	What Does It Mean?
08:27	Clive going to office in the morning
18:52	Clive coming home from work?
19:17	Clive going in again. How can he go in twice?
19:25	Clive going to restaurant then Mary
21:07	Clive coming home
21:15	Clive going out, but he was still there when we got there
21:25	Forensic team going in
21:33	DCS Bhatt and me going in
22:02	All leaving with Clive in handcuffs

I looked again at the first time Clive went in and furrowed my brows. 18:52. I double-checked my signal trace from yesterday evening. Clive and I were still in the car together at 18:52. We didn't arrive until just after 19:00.

'Zoe,' Rob said again, more than a little exasperation in his voice at my next call.

'Can you look at the report you sent me,' I said.

'You owe me, Zoe. Wait a sec…' I heard sighing and clicking as Rob searched for the report. 'OK, got it.'

'Look at the second and third rows. They don't make sense.'

'Clive went in,' Rob said as he read the lines. 'And then – weird. Then he went in again.'

'Exactly. I knew I didn't misunderstand.'

'No.'

I hung up and went back to the problem of making a second signal for Clive, a duplicate signal. *Mimic… duplicate… copy… signal… shit.* I slapped my palm against my forehead in frustration, then settled myself, trying to think clearly.

As I scanned the empty office, bathed in the glow of the display wall, I caught myself muttering. 'Mimic. Same as copy, simulate, duplicate. How can you duplicate a signal?'

'Was that the answer?' I said, testing the idea with the dusty desks. I said it again, louder and clearer. 'How can you duplicate a signal?'

It wasn't a new thought, but somehow saying it out loud made me hear a second meaning. When I said it next, I changed the emphasis and it all fell into place. 'If I *duplicated* Clive's signal, then I might get a *duplicate* signal as well. One real signal and a fake one from the duplicate.'

I called Rob again. The excitement surged in me, then got swamped with doubt. *You can't have duplicates. iMe works.*

'Zoe, I do have other stuff to do, you know.' Rob sounded even more pissed off than before.

'Yes, sorry, but I need to test an idea. You told me at the beginning that gaps in signals automatically generate an alert, right?'

'Yes. And?'

'You didn't get an alert from Clive last night?'

'No.'

'Do you ever get duplicate signals?'

'Sometimes an echo from a building in the right weather conditions can show up as a duplicate.'

My excitement fought back against my doubt. 'Do they generate an alert?'

'No. We only care that you have a signal.'

'Please tell me that you keep the duplicates?' I held my breath. I couldn't prove anything without the data.

'Zoe, you should know by now that we keep *everything*.'

'Can you send me a report for Clive showing if he had any duplicates yesterday?'

'Sure, but the search isn't optimised to find duplicates. It will take a while.'

I hung up again, churning possibilities. If Clive's story had any truth, then there would be duplicate data for him.

The process of working this out was exhilarating. Clive was always saying it and, reluctantly, I realised that he was right.

***

My fingers tapped an impatient beat on the desk as I waited for the report.

Finally, my HUD binged, and I threw the report up on the wall and opened it. Clive's signal was duplicated four times.

The time of the first two duplicate signals were when he was still in the car with me. These could be when the killer got into his building and then his apartment.

Then Clive got home, and the next duplicate was seven minutes later. Again, it matched the timings of his story of being drugged, his real signal being hidden by a Suppressor signal and his fake signal being generated. Then Clive's signal left, travelled to Mary's and back and re-entered the apartment.

The final duplicate was just before the last time the door opened from the inside. It could match Mary's killer turning the fake signal and the Suppressor off before leaving.

I crossed things out, moved things around and scribbled on the wall until I had the duplicate data mixed in with the door data. I stood back to look at the sequence and reran it in my head.

Time	What Does It Mean?
08:27	Clive going to office in the morning
18:46	**Duplicate** - Is the Killer mimicking Clive's signal to get in the building door?
18:48	**Duplicate** - Is the Killer mimicking Clive's signal to get in the apartment door?
18:52	Clive was in the car. Is this the Killer?
19:17	Is this Clive really getting home?
19:24	**Duplicate** - Is the Killer putting Suppressor on Clive and turning a duplicate on?
19:25	Clive or Killer going to restaurant then Mary
21:07	Clive or Killer coming home
21:13	**Duplicate** - Taking Suppressor off Clive and turning a duplicate off?
21:15	Clive was still there when we got there. Is this the Killer leaving??

Time	What Does It Mean?
21:25	Forensic team going in
21:33	DCS Bhatt and me going in
22:02	All leaving with Clive in handcuffs

The data said that maybe Clive was telling the truth. Yet everything inside me was still screaming that I should believe iMe. *The obvious answer is that Clive is lying, and the signal is right.* All this could just be data errors.

But I had worn a Suppressor. It had shut my signal and HUD down.

There weren't meant to be errors.

52

Thief

Lying back in my chair, I was comfortable, re-watching Karina and Two in a highlights movie. I could lose myself in them again and again.

I had downloaded the images from my old digital camera onto my similar vintage laptop. Connections to the outside world would risk exposing the content. I definitely wasn't going to use the camera on my HUD.

Even in the old days, I had never put data into the Cloud. Why would I be that stupid? The marketing, I had to admit was brilliant. People imagined a soft and fluffy place that their files lived, floating above them safe from hackers and misuse, not an industrial data centre. Sure, your files were safe if the hard disk in your computer failed, but they were scanned by Microsoft, Apple, Google and all the others and turned into data. If the hosting company could sell the information, why not the employee they treated like shit? Organised crime infiltrated the data centres and went digging for the gold: the files with your bank details, your passwords, your credit cards.

DataGate had been the tsunami wave of ransom demands emailed to the unsuspecting world. How much was that naked photo of your partner taken on holiday worth? Less than the ones of someone who isn't your partner? Less than the video? What price for that letter from your doctor, the tax office or social services? The governments had taken over the data centres and put them behind military firewalls. Of course, they still scanned the data. For terrorist or criminal activity. To audit your tax return. For the greater good.

Everything on the HUD was held by iMe. Nice and safe from loss but scanned and searched and sold.

***

When the *Best of Karina* movie was over, the only light came from the pale glow of my laptop's screensaver.

My eyes were shut, and I was imagining Mary. I wish I could have stayed and watched her eyes: the hope, the panic, the pleading, the pain.

Karina had gone so peacefully that it was almost poetic. The flow of her blood in the tubes and the gentle sagging of her body as her heart stopped.

With Two, I had set up a camera to focus close in on his face. I watched the hope drain from his eyes when he saw his blood in the tubes, replaced by fear and anger. He was primal as he thrashed against his chains. I told him that he was making his heart beat faster and the blood would be gone quicker, but he didn't listen.

The real drama was at the end. He stilled and panted. I hadn't gazed into someone's eyes before and really understood them. Two was so expressive. He had resigned for a few seconds before his brain's survival instinct kicked in again. A flash of hope. No, determination. More struggling, but fainter this time. The chains rattled and stilled, and his eyes dimmed and faded.

I watched Two's last moments again and again, finally acknowledging a part of me that had lurked in the shadows for so long. I wished I had the footage of Mary's eyes.

I hungered to watch it live, and I knew what I wanted to do with my third guest. My number three.

***

The trees of the street rustled in a gust of wind and disturbed the calm of the evening. As I approached Number Three's house, I scanned for other signals. Three was alone in the kitchen.

A big dog barked in the distance, but it wasn't close enough to worry about. Three's only neighbours were distant and out. I knocked and waited. Three came to the door all in a fluster and saw me.

'Oh, hi. Wasn't expecting you,' Three said. 'Come in, come in. My sauce will burn if it's left.'

The burning sauce explained Three's preoccupation and why my Suppressor and bag had gone unnoticed. Careless? Yes, but my familiar face was trusted. I stepped across the threshold and clicked the door shut behind me.

In the kitchen, Three was stirring a creamy sauce. Vigorous, constant movements accompanied by mutterings about it splitting and burning. 'Won't be long. Just need to catch this. Don't want to have to start again.'

I put my bag down on the floor and picked a large, heavy metal frying pan from a rack on the wall. I held the strong silicon coated handle, made for grip and burn prevention, and I tested the balance of it in my hand.

I stepped closer to Three, who was still preoccupied with the sauce. I thought if I set myself sideways it would give room for my swing and allow more of my body weight to come through with the pan. I could use my back and legs and twist into the blow. I drew the pan back.

'Never mind the sauce, Three,' I said.

'What are you talking about? Three what?'

'You.'

Three's head turned to question me, but I timed it to perfection. My arm flew, driven by my shoulders and the extra power as I pivoted my hips. It was like a perfect horizontal golfer's swing. The flat of the bottom of the pan connected with Three's turning cheek. The long sonorous bong from the pan sang with the purity of the blow and echoed around the room. The crunch and crack of Three's cheekbone collapsing didn't have the same musical quality.

***

I felt happy now that the cage held my new possession. Number Three didn't look so amused and was giving me the silent resentful treatment. Or maybe it was the smashed cheekbone and wild bruising on Three's face which must hurt like hell, so I slipped a needle into Three's vein and pushed in something to take the edge off.

'Is that better, Three?'

'Why are you calling me that?' Three asked, through the broken lips and all the swelling.

'Karina was first, then Two, who you called Alan. You're my third guest. My number three.'

Three saw the sequence and knew what I was capable of.

'Do you prefer Number Three, or just Three?' I asked. 'Number Three sounds a bit too formal.'

I was using both but couldn't decide which I preferred.

As I got no reply, I made the decision myself.

'Number Three for introductions and when we have company. Three when it's only the two of us, and we're cosy together.'

***

I was finding Three's silent malevolent stare enjoyable, so I decided to work in the cage. I wanted Three to try and guess what was coming.

I was sketching designs. The belt mechanism I had used for Mary was fine in as far as it went. In fact, I was pleased with my ingenuity and creativity on the spur of the moment. A smile played across my face as I wondered whether Lussac appreciated it as much.

But for the games I was planning, something so coarse and rigid wasn't acceptable. Different competitors would be different heights. I would need something reusable and adjustable so that I could get the extension of the toes just right.

Trying to ensure adjustability was giving me problems. I had sketches of sliding mechanisms and simpler designs with slots in the metal that I could move and tighten in place, but none of them worked. All the designs needed too many hands to get tight and accurate. With annoyance, I screwed them all up and threw them across the cage.

'It's more difficult than I thought, Three,' I said.

Three spat at me. The spittle had a pink tinge to it as it sailed high, arching and falling well short of me.

'That's not a nice.'

'Fuck off.'

I stood and strode over to Three, my clenched fist millimetres away from the smashed cheek. 'What have I told you?'

Three cringed away, not wanting any more pain. 'Sorry.'

***

My design, in the end, was simple, if disappointingly basic. A hook on the cage wall and, above it, a hook on the ceiling. In between the hooks, I ran a ratchet luggage strap I had found in the garage. One end I could loop around Three's neck, over the hook on the ceiling and down, through the ratchet to the hook in the wall. Each click of the ratchet gave me the fine control over the height of the loop that I needed.

Three looked at my work, mistrustful and suspicious, and seemed even more confused by the mirrored arrangement on the other side of the cage.

Three was lying chest down and I applied tape around ankles, wrists and elbows. I had a strong image of Mary as I did it, and that added to my excitement as I helped Three stand up.

'Over there,' I said, pointing at the swaying strap.

I prodded Three a few times to encourage movement, enjoying the awkward hopping to the wall.

I left the strap long enough to loop it around and over the hook that was behind Three's neck.

'What the fuck are you doing?' Three demanded as I pulled the strap up to check it would tighten. I was pleased with the result.

I reached the ratchet, eased the handle up and clicked the slack out of the strap. I paused when it started to tighten around Three's neck. I looked into Three's eyes and drank in the fear. *God that's good.*

I clicked some more, and Three's heels came up off the floor to relieve the growing tension on the windpipe.

I left Three for a moment to double check the camera. I didn't want to miss any of the sublime detail.

A few more clicks and Three was balancing high on tiptoes just as Mary had been. Now I would get to watch the eyes, the muscles shaking and the final desperate collapse.

Three didn't disappoint. It was a performance almost beyond my hopes.

I rushed and released the ratchet as Three started to sway and croak. I lowered Three to the floor and listened to the choking and the wheezing as Three's lungs sucked air back into them.

I didn't want Three to die. Not with the games ahead.

***

'Why didn't you kill me,' Three asked.

The raw bruises on Three's neck were climbing to meet the frying pan's older purples and yellows spreading south.

'Think of it as training.'

Three didn't say anything but frowned with incomprehension.

'You'll thank me later.'

More silence.

'When Number Four arrives, the cage will be crowded. I only have room for one.' I shrugged, *What else could I do?* 'Then we'll play a game. You'll be in your noose and Four will be in theirs.'

I waited for some appreciation but was disappointed when I didn't get any.

'Winner stays on,' I said.

'You're fucking mad!' Three screamed, but a hard jab to the damaged face stopped the noise.

'Don't interrupt. It's a game for you and Four to play.' I put some tape over Three's mouth to stop any further disruptions to my train of thought.

I wanted to see different emotions in both sets of eyes during the game. At some point, the players would work out that it didn't really matter how long they could stay on their tiptoes, as long as they outlasted the other player. I wanted to see hatred for the other player; the collapse of morals and them wishing their opponent would die first. I craved a gladiatorial contest.

I could see that Three had worked the game out.

'That's right,' I said. 'You only have to outlast Number Four. Our little test today will give you an edge. You know what to expect, you know the pain in your calves and toes. You can win.'

'You appreciate the importance of testing, don't you?' I laughed at the irony.

Three nodded but couldn't meet my eyes.

I had things to do so I left and closed the cage door, shaking it to check that it was locked and secure. The clang of metal on metal mingled with my steps as I walked towards the door.

I turned to look at Three.

'Don't worry. There's no need to be shy when you meet Number Four.'

Three's eyebrows rose.

'You've met DC Zoe Jordan lots of times.'

53

DI Clive Lussac

I spent the night in the cell on the narrow bed, but every time I fell asleep the memory of those photos crept up on me, jolting me awake. Sweat glistened on my face as I relived the taste of vomit in my mouth. Every creak of the springs in the thin mattress made me think of Mary hanging on the belt.

I was tired and grumpy when the unsmiling Uniform took me to Interview Room One at 10am. Her certainty of my guilt fuelled her rough shove in my back, and I went stumbling into the table.

I cursed and crumpled into a chair. I dropped my head into my right hand. My thumb found one temple and my little finger the other. They made little circles to ease my head while my other fingers eased my scalp. I felt like shit. I was scared. Would Zoe have found anything? Had she even tried?

After a while, Zoe and Bhatt came in behind me and took the seats across the table from me. My nerves drove the frantic pace of my foot tapping up and down under the table. It was like sitting in the court waiting for the jury.

I scanned their faces, looking for a nod and a smile, but Bhatt's eyes told me before she spoke.

'So, according to the iMe data you're guilty. There's also the forensic evidence of Mary's blood in your bathroom.'

Shit, that's it.

Zoe smiled.

Hope flared in me, but it was extinguished as quickly as a match in the wind as Bhatt continued. 'The CPS will rely on iMe, and a jury will believe it.'

She was right; even to me my story about Suppressors, duplicate signals, and drugs sounded like the sort of thing a desperate fool would come up with.

I sunk back in my chair. It was all over. This is how my life ends: my last days spent in a prison hiding from the people I had sent there.

'But,' Bhatt said.

My head shot up. She had a malicious twinkle in her eye. She was playing with me. 'You're lucky to have Zoe. Tell him.'

As Zoe walked me through her work on the locks and the duplicate entries my hope reignited.

'Told you,' I said.

Zoe pinched her mouth into a tight-lipped smile. She looked grey and drawn. 'You've cost me two nights sleep,' she said. 'Dealing with your arrest and guilt and then last night trying to save you.'

'Thanks, Zoe. I owe you. Did you find anything else?'

'You bet you owe me. And yes, I did.' She paused to suppress a yawn. 'I sent your blood to the lab and begged a favour from a friend to fast track it. I hoped it would take a couple of hours, but it got bumped for a terrorist enquiry. Didn't get it until 3am.'

'And?'

'And it shows traces of some substances that iMe doesn't measure, but that could have put you out for a few hours.'

I had a chance.

'Zoe being with you when the data says you were at home carries a lot of weight. As does her finding two press drones with missing batteries and no data of anyone near them. I talked to the chief constable and the people at the Justice Department.' Bhatt allowed herself a rare smile. 'They agreed that these are special circumstances and there's sufficient doubt. We cut a deal to release you under my guarantee while the investigations continue.'

I hadn't really believed I would be released, but Zoe had saved me. I couldn't find the words to thank her, so I put my hands together like I was praying.

'Our last plan was to go and talk to Art and Esteban again,' I said.

'It still is,' Bhatt said. 'Zoe has been tracking them both.'

Zoe nodded. 'Art is in his country home in Henley, not his Mayfair flat, and Esteban is off-grid again.' She said it with a sigh and a look that implied his guilt.

I had been thinking about Esteban. As much as I liked his lifestyle, he had a Suppressor and all the skills to get around the system he had designed.

'OK. Go to Henley and talk to Art. It will take a while to get there as the traffic's always bad. You can talk to Esteban when he resurfaces,' Bhatt ordered.

It wasn't much of a plan, but it was all we had.

Hope grew in me, but hope can really screw with you.

***

We all stood and lingered for a few moments.

I looked at Zoe. She was tired, nervous, and inexperienced. The last few days must have been tough on her, but here she was, decisive and determined. I heard the door open behind me and spun around. Hope kicked me in the teeth.

Special Investigator Winter burst into the room, full of the smug and righteous arrogance that only a true authoritarian zealot can wear. 'Inspector, you missed your appointment.'

I took a step back to avoid some of his energy, but was stopped by the table.

He seemed pleased that missing the appointment made my situation worse. 'Appointments aren't optional.'

'Not now, Winter,' I groaned and stepped sideways, instinctively trying to find protection behind Bhatt.

Winter raised his hand, his palm facing me. The universal stop command. 'Not so fast. You're mine.'

Winter threw something at Bhatt's HUD – her eye went white as she read it. 'Sorry, Clive. He has the authority.'

Shit, shit, shit.

Winter grabbed me by the wrist and yanked my hand down and then around and up my back. He held the arm lock higher than he needed. He leaned in close to my ear.

'You've impressed me, *Clive*,' he whispered. 'Killing your wife as a way of avoiding your audit shows real dedication.'

Winter shoved me forward and out of the room.

As I reached the doorway, I called back over my shoulder, 'Help me, Zoe!' I tried for brave, full of stiff upper lip, but it sounded weak and pathetic.

Winter laughed. 'You'll need more than her help.'

***

After an hour travelling to the Ministry of Well-being and Health's offices in Knightsbridge, I had been in Winter's interview room for over three hours. He luxuriated in his shirtsleeves and comfortable executive chair enjoying every minute of my discomfort.

I grimaced in my hard chair. I couldn't say much in my defence. It was all true.

'Oscar sold you so many nice things,' Winter said.

'Look, I'll sign anything,' I pleaded, thinking of Zoe. 'I need to get out of here.'

Winter's tut-tut belonged in a pantomime. 'Oh, Inspector. Just because you're a police officer doesn't mean you can stroll out of here whenever you fancy. Freedom Unit abuse is a serious issue. Especially for a man with your record of excess consumption.'

I didn't say anything.

'I'll go easy on you though.'

He had done this the whole time. Say something nice, then pause and twist the knife, so I wasn't surprised when he said, 'I was thinking of a nice six-month trip to a Health Reorientation Camp.'

54

DC Zoe Jordan

What an idiot. I wondered how Clive got himself into these situations?

I couldn't believe it: an FU audit on top of everything else. Why couldn't he live within the rules?

I had tried to get Martin to come in, but he was locked in the hospital by order of his back specialist. None of the members of the crew had completed Self-Defence Level 5 or their certificate in Danger in the Work Place. I was on my own.

For a frustrating hour, I paced around PCU, waiting for the woman from Employee Wellness to find the right forms. EW was meant to help me deal with my job and protect me. She hadn't cared that I had to go and talk to Art on my own. No, all she had cared about was me signing a liability disclaimer – if I died on the job, then it wasn't the police force's fault.

***

The car crawled to a stop as it approached Henley on Remenham Hill. Red brake lights and a long snake of stationary cars filled the road.

'Car… DC Zoe Jordan,' I said in as clear a voice as I could. 'Police traffic override.'

The car processed the command, and in the reflection off the vehicle ahead, I saw my car's exterior lighting turn blue. The others were meant to get out of the way, but the road was too narrow for them to pull out of the way with all the traffic coming in the other direction. My car told the one immediately in front of me to stop, ordered a gap in the traffic coming out of Henley and overtook the car. It took fifteen minutes to get down the hill and over the bridge, one slow overtake followed by another. It drove me mad.

***

Art's home was a white, mock-Tudor place outside somewhere called Lower Assendon. The minor road the car had pulled off of was quiet, lined with hedges and the occasional tree. The house stood alone in the countryside. It was private and secluded.

On the car's screen, I could see Art's signal in a room in his garage behind the house. Good, I thought, that would give me a chance to use the search warrant and look for evidence in the house without having Art for company.

The gloss paint on the door was so shiny I could see myself in it. I grasped the big door handle and pushed the door open.

The hallway was a strange mix of tastes. A modern, long carpet was mixed with antique plastic furniture and pop art. I looked through the first door but only saw a room with a dining table and five chairs.

The next room was Art's study, which was almost identical to his office at iMe. It even had the same horrid fountain. Two doors stood in the far wall. I crossed the room and pushed the first door. It opened into a bare white room with a bed with mirrors on the ceiling and walls. I was wondering why you would have a bedroom off a study when I opened the second door. Now I understood.

The smaller room had a high-backed executive chair and a desk. One wall was made of glass and looked into the bedroom. I turned the display wall on, and the screen drew into nine segments, each one showing a different image of the bedroom. One camera in the ceiling looked straight down onto the bed.

I shivered. *Pervert.* Zane had mentioned Art *casting* girls for the parties. This must be where they took place.

I opened the lid of an old laptop, but it displayed a password prompt. I would have to leave that to the cyber crime guys to crack. I bet they would find lots of interesting files on the laptop. I expected at least one of them to be titled Karina.

***

I couldn't find anything else of immediate interest in the rest of Art's house. I held his laptop under my arm but didn't want to risk Art grabbing it back, so I went back to the car and stowed it safely inside. Now to find Art. I double-checked his signal: still in the room at the back of his garage. *What's he doing in there?*

I had been alright on the drive over, excited even, but now I wasn't too sure. If I called for backup I would have to wait, and Bhatt would be furious at being cross-charged for their time just to hold my hand.

I bit down on my nerves. *Hold yourself together. It's only Art. He's not much taller than me, and I have unarmed combat training. Even if I had never used it.*

'Come on, Zoe. Pull yourself together,' I said out loud. If it came to a fight and I forgot all my training, then a good kick in the balls would have Art coughing and hurting.

I smiled at the image and strode towards the garage – but as I approached, I slowed – my courage fading. The large wooden doors were closed, but the wind was making the half-open pedestrian doorway sway. The hinges creaked as it moved.

I shivered as the wind pushed a black cloud over the sun. The day turned darker, and the wind turned cold without the sun's warmth. I stopped. I was scared again. It felt like a sign of something bad, like I sensed some sort of threat in the garage.

I took in three long breaths. *Superstitious nonsense. How can the weather know something bad is going to happen?* I'd go in and talk to Art. Simple.

It took a real effort to move my feet, but I got them uprooted and headed to the door. I checked Art's signal again: inside and not hiding by the door.

I pulled the door towards me, wincing as the hinges creaked louder.

I stepped inside.

55

Thief

My HUD showed Zoe was in the house, searching upstairs. I guessed she would take a few more minutes before she came into the garage. In the back room, my Mimic was whirring away, creating a false echo to distract Zoe and call her to me.

I slowed my breathing to try and stay calm – waiting for her, but enjoying the time by visualising her battling against her failing muscles and Three.

Zoe's footsteps crunched on the gravel of the drive, the audible commentary to her signal. She stopped at her car. She must have taken something from the house and put it in there. I wasn't worried. I could get it later, and whatever she found wouldn't save her when she was mine.

I heard more footsteps on the drive.

Come on, Zoe, my little fly. Step into my web.

The hinges creaked as Zoe opened the door.

I caught the delicate smell of her perfume.

56

DC Zoe Jordan

I checked inside the pedestrian door, but the room was empty. I breathed out, trying to get my pulse back into a more normal range.

Despite it being colder inside the garage, I could feel the dampness under my arms. I glanced to my right. Through the internal door I glimpsed what looked like a big space where cars used to be kept.

I crept to the door and froze. I could hear someone breathing. It sounded like they were inside the main part of the garage.

There wasn't any signal in the main area showing on my HUD. Art's signal showed in the back room. Just a week ago I would have believed the display without question but now, with Suppressors and duplicate signals, it could mean anything.

I heard a groan from inside the garage. I risked a quick glance. Someone was tied to a chair in the middle of the garage. I took another longer look. I couldn't see anyone else and the victim's hood, and their slumped shoulders and head, made identification impossible.

I almost ran in to help, but something stopped me.

If I believed the HUD, Art was in the back room and his victim in the chair. But Art's signal could be a duplicate. *Shit.* I didn't know what to believe anymore. Art could be sneaking around behind me. Esteban could be the killer and Art could be in the chair.

***

I decided to back out of the garage and loop around to check for someone coming around the building. iMe wasn't helping – it was making me feel vulnerable. I couldn't trust anybody's signal, but they would be able to see me.

This was meant to be simple but now I was feeling like a cornered animal. Part of me wanted to lock myself in the car and call for backup. But what if the victim was killed while I waited? I couldn't live with myself if that happened.

I forced myself to head around the garage with my back to the wall. It felt safer that way, and I would be able to see anyone waiting for me. Halfway around, I got to the window of the room showing Art's signal.

I had to turn my back away from the wall to see into the room. It would leave me exposed for a second or two, but there were fifteen metres of clear ground that an attacker would have to cover before they got to me. I twisted around and looked in through the window, but all I could see was closed curtains. I blew out a long breath of relief.

My back against the wall again, I completed my loop of the garage. All I had done was waste time. The killer could have watched my signal and tracked ahead or behind mine.

I looked at the car. *Should I run to it?* I was fighting the urge when I heard a louder groan.

Think, Zoe, just like Clive said. Use your brain. If I went to the person in the chair, then I would have clear space around me. If it was a trap, then I could defend us both from the centre of the garage.

The clouds cleared and the sun was back. The warmth made me feel a little braver. I was going to go in, but first I was going to swallow my pride.

I touched my ear.

'Thames Valley Control,' came the reply.

'DC Zoe Jordan,' I said. Protocol dictated that I said my name even though they knew it. 'I am on site with a possible hostage. I need backup at my current location.' I had raised my voice so that if the killer were waiting, he would hear it.

'The nearest car is in Marlow. ETA is fifteen minutes,' control said.

'OK, five minutes, thanks.'

'No, fifteen. Repeat. One, five.'

I hung up on them.

Shit, I couldn't wait fifteen minutes.

57

Thief

Zoe was being cautious. I'd hoped she would rush straight in, but she had come to the edge of the door and backed away. I couldn't smell or hear her anymore.

I caught a shuffling movement, a soft scraping on the wood. She was circling the garage. *What a suspicious girl you are.*

After more pauses, the shuffling continued as she completed her lap. Then she was talking, loudly. Asking for backup. Five minutes. But that didn't sound right. If help came from Maidenhead, they had to get over the bridge and that was never quick. The journey from Reading wasn't easy either.

I guessed I had fifteen to twenty minutes. *Plan for ten*, I thought.

58

DC Zoe Jordan

I was still torn. Wait or go, wait or go?

My mind was made up by the terrifying groan from the garage. It sounded bad. I couldn't stand still and let them die.

I edged back towards the garage and into the small first room. I risked another glance.

The garage was still empty except for the person in the chair. Dust sparkled in the sunlight streaming through the rear windows. The signal from the back room hadn't moved.

I took a breath and ran, my back and head down, trying to keep low. I reached the centre of the garage and the back of the person in the chair. I could hear their scared breathing. I couldn't see any wounds or blood. That was a good sign.

Crabbing around the chair, my back to the person, I was prepared if I got rushed by the killer.

I was alone.

I turned to look at the person in the chair and reached to pull their hood off.

59

DI Clive Lussac

'You know,' said Winter, 'a Health Reorientation Camp would transform your outlook on life, Inspector.'

He liked the sound of his own voice and if I didn't reply, he got angry. 'Oh yes?' I said.

'Yes. The long route marches, the nights on the moors, the outdoor survival training. You would learn to appreciate how lucky you are.' He sounded like a travel agent selling the best holiday in the world.

'And if you didn't appreciate it, then there's the aversion therapy to help recalibrate your mind.' Now it sounded like a state-run torture camp. A throwback to when mental health treatment was drugs and electric shock. The image of me strapped to a bench in a straitjacket formed in my mind: I was frothing at the mouth as some sadistic doctor turned the dial, the lights dimming as my body danced and twitched to the electric current.

Winter had stopped speaking and was looking straight into my eyes. 'I see that you understand your situation, Inspector. Finally, we can move on to my real questions.'

Winter's eyes flickered white and black as he read something on his HUD.

'No!' he shouted, and slammed his hand down on the table. A vein on Winter's temple pulsed and his face bloomed red with rage.

'Something wrong?' I asked.

'You're...' he choked, struggling to speak.

My disabled HUD started to show signs of life and my little green Buddy ran across the HUD trailing the banner

'*Access Restored*'. He stopped and jumped up and down, cheering.

Winter's head was the colour of beetroot, and the vein pulsed a wild beat. If he wasn't such an arsehole, I might have worried that the vein would pop.

I didn't understand what was going on until the backlog of messages loaded and I read the most recent one from Bhatt.

Justice Department overruled Well-being and Health – you're released from Winter. Zoe called for backup. Car booked and programmed to Art's home – last location for Zoe. Go.'

I jumped up from the chair, sending it skidding across the floor. Shit, Zoe had gone to talk to Art and needed backup. *What's gone wrong?*

Inspired by Buddy's cheerful gesturing, I raised my hand as if to wave goodbye to Winter, then turned it so that my palm faced me, all my fingers vertical. I dropped all but my middle finger, which stood tall and proud.

Winter managed to go a little darker red, which made me smile, and I took my cue and left.

Halfway down the pampered office corridors of Well-being and Health, the next message from Bhatt stopped me dead.

'Zoe's and Art's signals have both disappeared.'

60

DC Zoe Jordan

My hand touched the hood and I lifted it.

The first thing I saw was a Suppressor, lights blinking showing that it was hiding a signal. Then a taped mouth, scared eyes and hair. I looked into the familiar face, dropped the hood, and gently peeled the tape away.

'What happened?' I asked. 'Are you hurt?'

'No. No. I'm OK.'

I couldn't see blood or any real signs of damage. Nothing life threatening.

'Don't worry,' I said. 'Help's coming. Who attacked you? Are they still here?'

'I think I hurt him. He was swaying and unsteady as he tied me up. Can you look?' I followed the direction of the nod and saw the door to the room with the curtains.

Have I solved the whole thing? The next victim saved. Karina's, Alan's and Mary's killer exposed to the world. I could stand alongside Bhatt. Modest as I took the praise from the press and found Mum's glowing eyes in the crowd.

Or I could wait and let the Uniforms do it.

No way – I'm all over this.

I tore at the tape binding ankles to the chair, but I couldn't separate the handcuffed wrists from the chair's armrest. 'Wait here while I check for him and to find something to cut these cuffs.'

I turned towards the door. As I crossed one of the beams of sunshine from the windows, I cast a long shadow onto the wall. Something was bothering me, something was out of place.

I reached the door and turned the handle.

My pulse hammered in my ears, but I forced myself to open the door wide.

The room was empty apart from cobwebs and a white sports bag with the Barclays logo and the words Health Bank written in blue letters. The bag gaped open and as I bent forward into the room, I could see a big box with lights. Not a Suppressor, it was the wrong shape.

I was wondering if this thing could generate a duplicate signal when I worked out what felt wrong. There wasn't any visible reason for all the groaning.

Why can I hear the clicking of handcuffs opening and clanking to the floor? It wasn't something a victim could do.

Shit.

I turned as fast feet skimmed over the floor, and I saw a distorted shadow flash across the wall.

I kicked out at the shadow but only hit thin air, then I flailed a fist. It found a target and I was rewarded by a grunt, but I felt the sharp explosive pain of something sharp being plunged into my back and the sensation of pressure.

My head felt fuzzy and my legs went bendy, like my bones were somehow melting, one knee folded and then the other. I knelt like I was praying. Perhaps it was a good time to start.

I could hear talking and had to concentrate hard to make it out.

'Number Four, welcome to the games.'

The drugs must be screwing my hearing up.

Hands grasped my shoulders and pulled me back into the garage.

I was on my back, arms and legs stretched out. Hands held my head as it floated away and separated from my body. Something was around my neck – I could feel pressure and warmth.

My eyes were dimming, the world fading.

I saw a face swim in front of me and heard more words.

'It's so exciting.'

The face floated away and came back.

'I'll tell you a secret, Four. I think you'll beat Three.'

They were the final words I heard as I was swept around a dark vortex and down into the black.

61

DI Clive Lussac

It was after four in the afternoon when I left Winter, so I called Zoe from the car. It was an empty gesture, but I had to try even though I knew that no signal meant no calls. What had he done to her?

She could be anywhere now, and all I was doing was rushing to Art's house, the last place Zoe had been, in the hope that it would tell me something. The journey alone would cost me more than an hour and a half, but I didn't know what else to do or where else to go.

The only thing that made sense to me was that Zoe had found some evidence of Karina or Alan at Art's house and the killer had jumped her. Then he must have suppressed her signal and gone off-grid to hide. *Bastard. Wait until I get my hands on him.*

But which him? Art or Esteban? Neither had signals.

The car slowed to 10mph as it approached a postnatal centre with small groups of parents talking outside. *Come on, car. Move!*

I dropped the window to get some air, tapping my impatience on the side of the car as a couple stepped up to the zebra crossing. 'No! Don't stop,' I wailed, but the car's autopilot ignored me and braked to a halt. I kept pushing forward in my seat, willing the car to go. If I could, I would have ploughed straight through them. I heard snippets of the chat as the car waited for the dawdling people.

'Mine's crawling.'

'Mine said her first word.'

I caught the eye of a woman and saw her silent cry for help. It was like she was serving out her one-year mandatory maternity leave, counting down the days left of her sentence. Her suppressed sadness was obvious in her deflated body language. It seemed like she loved her baby but wanted to be somewhere else: back in the boardroom or saving someone's life in surgery. Instead, her days were reduced to these bland exchanges and baby talk.

Maybe I was projecting, but FUs meant that she couldn't hide in the haze of an alcoholic afternoon. Instead, she had to get through the day in frustration and exercise leggings.

I couldn't worry about her. I had Winter, unsolved murders, and Zoe was missing.

Finally. The car moved again. 'Go. Go,' I muttered, spurring it on.

***

Local Uniform had responded to Zoe's call but arrived too late and their car was parked on the drive of Art's home. Its blue lights pulsed a false promise of action and urgency.

'Any sign of Zoe?' I asked one of the Uniforms lolling against his car.

'No. We checked around, but she's not here.'

'Give me the highlights.'

'Looks like a struggle or something in the garage. Perv room in the study,' he said. His moustache twitched as he spoke; it reminded me of a squirrel eating a nut. 'Can we go? Control has something else for us.'

'No, wait while I look around.' I didn't know what I needed yet.

I walked over to the garage.

This place had swallowed Zoe up, but now felt so tranquil. The sun was shining, and birds were singing. Only a brief mechanical wail spoilt the peace and then faded.

I'd watched the last few minutes of Zoe's signal from my car, but gave up: a two-dimensional plan wouldn't tell me as much as walking the actual scene. I mirrored Zoe's signal on my HUD as it did a circuit of the garage, acutely aware that my footfalls could be matching hers.

She had gone into the garage after calling for backup, so I followed her signal through the small room and into the main garage area. The sun streamed in, but the only thing I could see was a dining room chair lying on its side. This was where Zoe had crossed to, spent a few seconds, and then gone to the door on the back wall. I did the same and opened the door that Art's signal had been behind. *Is this where Art waited to attack Zoe? Or was it a duplicate signal?*

Now it was another empty room of dust and cobwebs. I looked at the floor hoping to find some trace of her, but I found nothing to show that this was the spot where Zoe had stood.

The only positive was that I didn't see blood or Zoe hanging from a belt like Mary. I still had hope.

I pressed down hard on the little voice in my head that said that this was my fault. If I hadn't drunk and eaten too much and fought the system, then I could have been with Zoe. I could have saved her.

How could I look Sophia in the eye knowing her daughter had died because of my lack of discipline?

***

In the room off Art's study, I looked through the two-way mirror and into the bedroom. This must be the perv room Squirrel had mentioned. The room where Art judged girls' willingness to attend his parties.

Had Karina been here? The bed was cold and neat. I hoped it meant that Art hadn't *interviewed* Zoe.

After a fruitless search of the rest of the house, I walked back into the daylight and checked the time on my HUD. It was gone half past six. Zoe's signal had already been off for two and a half hours, and I was no closer to finding her.

I dismissed the Uniforms, and Squirrel and his mate left in their car.

I touched my ear and called Bhatt.

'What's the situation there?' she asked.

I ran her through my meagre findings then added, 'The killer must be Art or Esteban. I don't know how to find Esteban, but Art's signal could be encrypted and not completely off. Like for the parties. Can you talk to the chief constable again and find a way to unblock Art's signal?'

'Way ahead of you. I've got a slot with the prime minister.' I could hear her smile in her words. She was well up for this fight.

I stood on the empty drive, the sun cooler now on my back. I couldn't afford to sit here and wait while Zoe's life ticked away.

There must be another way to find her. Bhatt might fail. I thought back to how Zoe had found the data with the locks and how they tested iMe.

I checked for signals again. No Zoe, no Art, and still no Esteban.

62

DI Clive Lussac

I ran across Art's drive and made another call when I got into the car.

'Hello,' Emma Bailey said. Her voice was full of a cold. She seemed annoyed to have been disturbed when she was ill.

'Emma, I need you to trace Art Walker, his signal has gone.'

'I'm off sick. Anyway, you need his approval.'

I was treated to her blowing her nose. It sounded like an explosion through the car's surround-sound system.

'I know that, but you must have to test that the encryption of the signal works, don't you?' I tapped the car's screen to bring up a map of the area.

'Yes.' She sounded hesitant.

'Could you run a *test* to see if his encryption is working correctly now?'

'I don't know, I could get in a lot of trouble for doing that. I'm off sick today. Isn't Manu in the office?'

'Please, Emma. Zoe's life may depend on it.'

'Why? What's happened?'

'I don't have time to explain everything. She's missing.'

A long silence.

'OK, I suppose I can run a test from here. You'll have to say it was for Art's safety if I get caught.'

'Fantastic, Emma. I'll say whatever you need me to. I'll come to you.'

'No need to come here. I'll call you.'

With a test from Emma and Bhatt on the case, I had two chances to find Art.

***

The tyres of the car had just started to turn when I got an alert from iMe Tech Support that told me Esteban was back on-grid. I stopped the car and touched to make another call.

'Hello, Inspector,' Esteban said when he answered.

'Where have you been?'

'Nice to talk to you as well. Good manners cost nothing.'

'I don't have time for that, Esteban,' I said. 'Where have you been?'

'Around. I fancied a drive, so I headed off and followed my nose.'

Had I heard Esteban's Ferrari when I was at Art's house?

'Near Henley?'

'Maybe. I was just driving.'

Esteban's signal showed that he was in a house near Bagshot that wasn't the house he took us to before. 'You're not at home.'

'No, I'm at a friend's.'

I couldn't decide if Esteban was genuine or being evasive.

'Have you seen Zoe or Art Walker today?'

'No.' His answer came after a pause, like he was churning through possibilities before answering.

'Neither of them? They're off-grid, like you.'

Listening to Esteban's evasiveness crystallised my suspicions about him.

I checked the clock again: 18:53. Time was running away from me. My hand hovered over the car's destination input screen. *Who is my killer?*

I decided to track both Esteban and Art. Otherwise, I was taking too much of a risk with Zoe's life.

Esteban first, I decided, and it needed to be done face to face.

Emma could run the test on Art's signal without me and call with the result. No point going to her home if Art was somewhere else. Emma had mentioned Manu as well. We had ignored him.

'OK, Esteban. Stay where you are, I'm coming to you.'

He agreed before I hung up.

Esteban definitely had time to be in Henley, take Zoe to his house, and then go on to his friend's house near Bagshot. I put the address in the car. It was only about twenty-five miles from Art's house in Henley, but it would take me an hour. This could be a complete waste of time, but there was no point staying here. I set off. ETA 8:15pm.

More than four hours since Zoe's signal dropped.

63

Thief

Four was wearing a hood, and I was savouring her being strapped to one of my dining room chairs, the tape nice and tight. At my mercy.

I pushed the table back to allow space to circle her. As I made each loop, her head stayed still, like she was trying to ignore me, but when I paused behind her back, she cringed.

I grew bored. This was no fun to play. I couldn't see into her eyes. I could feel her fear but not immerse myself in it.

I removed her hood. Her hair was all over the place and it added to the wild, hostile look in her eyes. The Suppressor would stop her HUD working so I removed the tape from her mouth.

'You fucker, let me go!' Four screamed, trying to stand. I pushed her down.

Fear was driving her anger. It was glorious, but she needed to learn some manners. I shifted my feet and shoulders, getting the stance my gym trainer had shown me and practised a quick one-two, left-right in the air.

Four watched my hands.

'Is that meant to scare me?' she said.

'No, just loosening up.'

'You're pathetic. You need to let me go before it's too late.'

'Maybe,' I said, and repeated my one-two. This time I was half a pace closer and my hands were lower. Four's head bounced as my left fist landed, not my full force but judged so that she recovered in time to meet the incoming right.

Two solid blows. Some trauma and a little blood spilt from her mouth. Not enough to hurt her chances against Three.

'Have I got your attention? Good.'

Four nodded and a little more blood pooled at the side of her mouth. I could see her tongue touring her mouth, checking for damage and counting her teeth. Her eyes glared at me.

'Just a little taster,' I said. 'Before you go and get all stressy with me, just remember Two. He was horribly rude, and I despise bad manners.'

Four nodded again, the memory written on her face.

'I see you remember Two in his box.'

'Why are you doing this?'

'Why? You sound like Karina.' I bent down close to Four, looking deep into her beautiful eyes. 'Did you like what I did to Mary?'

'No, but let me tell you something,' Four said, and her head bobbed up, encouraging me to come closer. 'You're not as clever as you think,' she whispered, and rocked her head back. Sensing danger, I snatched my head away as Four's forehead jerked forward in a vicious headbutt. The top of her head bounced off my forehead before her fringe whipped at my eyes as our heads flashed past each other. 'Bitch,' I screamed. I could feel the swelling through my hair.

Four stared at me, a defiant smile on her face. I needed to teach her some respect. I danced and weaved. One-two. Head. One-two. Stomach. Back, sides, kidneys. Each controlled blow aimed around the chair. I was breathing hard when I finished.

Four's head lolled forward and she groaned. Subdued for the moment.

Time for a different game.

***

The tip of my knife rested on Four's upper arm. All the love and care I had given the blade made it razor-sharp. A little more pressure and the tip cut through the fibres of her shirt and found skin.

Four gasped and tried to pull away, but the chair held her. I was wary of her head and touched my scalp again.

She watched in silence. I had enjoyed the eleven other small cuts in her shirt that now dribbled with blood. Four had learnt that shouting and swearing had its price.

A little more pressure on the knife. She was stock-still, rigid, staring at it. I watched the tip deform her skin, stretching its surface tension. I held it there, counting to ten, dragging it out. My eyes shut, feeling her breath quiver along the blade, the handle and into my fingers. It was almost climactic when, with a tiny pressure more, Four's skin yielded and the knife penetrated her.

I was rewarded by another dribble of blood and her quiet sobs as she fought the pain.

'You need to stop before it's too late,' she said.

I perched on the front lip of my chair, drinking in the suffering in her eyes as I admired my work. I'd done well but I needed more area to work on. Both her arms had six red lines.

'Are you shy, Four?' I asked.

She lifted her head to ask what I meant. She must have guessed that no answer was going to be good for her, but she spat her defiance at me.

I wiped my face and traced the tip of the blade up her arm and across her shoulder, collarbone to her neck, tracing a long winding route, caressing the material but not cutting it. I stopped below the Suppressor and headed south, following skin until the two sides of her shirt's collar joined.

Four shivered. The blade left a tiny white line in her skin that disappeared as the blood returned.

The knife found the resistance of the cotton holding the first button, a little pressure and it cut through and carried on down. The button fell and bounced away onto the floor.

'Let me go and we can have a fair fight,' Four said.

'I'm not stupid.'

The knife inched its way down to the next button, which I sent the way of its partner. I folded the shirt fabric back and was rewarded with the swell of a breast and some retaining lace.

'Clive will come. We'll bring you down,' Four said. She was a fighter and that didn't bode well for Three's chances in the games.

My problem was that Three vs Four wouldn't last long.

I needed Number Five. There were still a few out there who needed to pay.

Four looked up, and tears pooled in the corner of her eyes. She believed in him – the brave inspector riding to rescue her.

'Your inspector's having a nice chat with an FU audit officer.' I laughed.

I still had a little playtime left before I stole Five.

My eyes snaked down Four's gaping shirt and the unblemished skin that rose and fell with each breath.

64

DI Clive Lussac

Emma called me. She'd beaten Bhatt. She'd found Art's signal – he was heading straight towards her.

I banged the emergency stop on the car's navigation unit, revelling in the tyres' complaints as my weight pressed hard against the seat belts. I wasn't sure what Art was planning or why Emma was important to him. Maybe she was next, but I would be there. Luckily, her house wasn't too far and the display said that I would be there by eight thirty.

My head buzzed with another call. Rob at iMe Tech Support.

'Tell me,' I said.

'I checked for duplicates like you asked,' Rob said. 'You were right. Art had a duplicate signal before Zoe got to his house and then disappeared.'

'Thanks.' I hung up.

That made sense. Art needed his signal to bring Zoe to his house. He must have generated a fake signal, suppressed his real signal and then jumped her before disappearing.

I spent the rest of the journey worrying about Zoe. My mind flashed with the scene where we found Karina's body. I looked at her face, but all I saw was Zoe lying on the leaves. I screwed my eyes tight to crush the thought.

The car pulled into the drive of the house in time for me to see the last light of the day disappearing. I didn't want the car to move in case I needed it again, so I found the appropriate police override on my HUD. The car stayed where I left it like a well-trained dog.

As I approached the door, it opened, and light flooded out. The bright light in the entrance hall turned Emma, who was standing in the doorway, into a silhouette.

'What about Zoe's signal?' I asked.

'No sign. Art's close. Quickly, inside.'

I followed Emma, I felt like a spring being wound and wound and wound. I recognised the signs. Nothing looked wrong on the outside until bang – the spring broke. All over Art.

65

DI Clive Lussac

'Why's he coming here?' I asked.

'I must be next. It must be iMe related.' Emma looked tense and preoccupied. 'Thank you for coming. I'm scared…' She hid her mouth with her hand. 'You don't know what it means to me.'

She turned and headed down the entrance hall into the kitchen. I followed behind.

'I was sorry to hear about your wife.'

She seemed different – not the timid little bird from the office meetings. 'Thanks,' I said. It was too raw still. I didn't want to discuss it with her.

Emma stopped at the other side of the kitchen island, and touched the top of her head again: about the tenth tentative touch on her hairline.

'How did you hurt your head?'

'It's nothing.' She seemed distant, like she was churning something over in her head.

Then the atmosphere changed – our gentle chat replaced by a hard edge as her eyes changed from summer warmth to icy chill. 'Terrible way to go, nailed to a door.'

I took a step back. Specific details about her death hadn't been in the press release.

She looked at me, reading my face. Mary had seen through my every feeling and lie like I was glass. Emma looked like she had the same ability.

I felt exposed and vulnerable. I needed a weapon. I could see some expensive looking knives in a wooden block.

Emma took a pace around the island and I matched it with one of my own, keeping the gap constant, heading for the block of knives.

'I wanted you to know the truth. I wanted you here to play a little game with Zoe.' She sneered at me. 'You're so pathetic. All your blundering around got you nowhere. You had no idea.'

'You can't do anything, my signal's showing that I'm here.' It was a deliberately stupid thing to say. She had killed Mary with duplicates and Suppressors. She could do the same to me, but I was playing to my audience. I had Zoe to save.

My hand touched a drawer handle as I took another step right. I pulled the drawer open hard and it banged against its end stops. I reached in and grabbed the contents and threw them at Emma. *Oh, shit.* Five blue microfibre cleaning cloths fluttered and folded, mocking me in the air and landed on the island.

Emma laughed. 'Wrong drawer,' she said, grabbing a glass of water from the counter and hurling it at me before pulling another drawer open.

The glass flew in the air. It sang past my ear as I ducked down and it crashed against the wall behind me.

As I straightened, I saw Emma's right arm was back, preparing to throw a large wooden meat tenderiser.

The hammer flew towards me, spinning end over end. As it flashed past my ear, I heard the small whooping noise as it rotated like a tiny propeller, then it smashed into the wall.

I heard her running. As she got near, she jumped, using her hands on the edge of the worktop to lift her legs towards my body and smash her shoes into my chest, pushing me off my feet. My arms flapped as I tried to keep my balance, but I went over backwards.

I landed, and a stab of pain flared in my shoulder as it pressed onto a piece of the broken glass. My back felt wet and I hoped it was from the water and not my blood.

Emma was on me, her knees straddling my hips as she started to pummel me – a blur of well-timed pairs of punches, each delivered with feeling. She was focusing on my head, each blow snapping it backwards. Bouncing it against the floor and generating more fog.

I jabbed up at her face, but I couldn't get any real weight behind it. No room for a backswing when you're lying on your back. I raised my left hand, trying to reach her neck and push her back to stem the torrent of blows. It worked. My arms were longer than hers and I managed to land a few more punches.

She shifted her weight, twisting away from my fist. She was reaching behind her for the tenderising hammer. I groaned – it was too far for me to reach. If she got that then it would be game over. I had nothing.

I pushed up hard with my left hand as I dropped my right, waving it around me. All I found was water and tiny fragments of glass; nothing big enough to cause serious damage to her, but glass in the eye would hurt. I picked up a small shard of glass between my fingers and I tried a roundhouse punch.

My fist landed on her head, the glass slicing a cut into my fingers. It did me more damage than her.

She twisted some more. I could see her fingers inching closer to the hammer.

My hand dropped back to the floor and hunted again for something I could hurt her with. Nothing, but I remembered an old self-defence trainer saying anything could be a weapon if it hit somewhere soft and vulnerable. What did I have?

My hand dug in my trouser pocket, reaching for an old business card. I pulled one out and gripped it hard between my thumb and finger so that one corner pointed out.

Emma's right hand was pulling back, high and proud and about to smash my head in with the hammer.

Last chance. I invested all my remaining energy into this one last move. I shoved up as hard as I could, thrusting my card towards her eye, hoping the corner would make contact. It did, followed by my thumbnail, both making inroads into the soft, squishy white of her eye.

She screamed in demented rage and clutched at her face. Her right hand still held the hammer. I wrenched it from her and swung. The metal side of the tenderiser hit her head and smashed into her temple. The crunch of bone and Emma's wail pierced the silence of the room. The momentum of the blow pushed her half off me.

She stayed that way for a moment, frozen in time, and then slid down and collapsed onto the floor, one leg still across my body. I lay panting, waiting for some of the fog in my head to clear.

66

DI Clive Lussac

I shoved Emma's leg off me and pushed myself up onto my elbows. Failing to blank out the screaming pain in my shoulder and the ringing in my head, I checked Emma for a pulse as she lay unconscious. It was there, strong and urgent.

I heard a bang from along the hall. *Zoe.* I shook away an image of her swinging like Mary from a belt. Feet banging on a door. Seconds from death.

I stood up and grabbed the island to stop myself from falling straight back to the floor. I waited for the swirling sensations to pass and staggered back along the entrance hall, bouncing from one wall to the next. My frantic shouts for Zoe echoed through the house.

I stopped at the first door, opened it and looked in on a small study, neat rows of old library books. No Zoe.

I checked behind me for Emma – I could still see one inert foot through the kitchen doorway.

I ran to next door but found only an empty lounge. *Zoe, where are you?*

I burst into the dining room.

Zoe was lying on her back, taped to one of the dining chairs, which must have rocked over backwards. All I could see was her side, but she must have heard the door open because she glanced over her shoulder. She would have been expecting Emma to come back for her as I saw fear pushed away by relief.

I rushed over to her and pulled the tape from her mouth. 'Boss, thank God,' she croaked.

'You OK?' I said.

'Get me out of this fucking chair.'

293

Joy surged through me – she was OK. I shivered when I saw her blood. I grabbed the chair and lifted it back upright.

She was a mess. Her face was bruising – angry red lumps all over. Blood trickled from her nose and her lips were split and swollen.

'I guess I'm not looking my best,' she said.

I could have cried. She still had the strength for humour despite everything she had been through.

'She killed Mary,' she said.

'I know.' An image of Mary on the door flashed in front of me. I tried to wipe it from my mind and looked at Zoe's shirt, which was missing nearly all its buttons. Her skin showed a scattering of small cuts and drying blood.

'Fuck,' I said.

'I was her toy.'

I cringed and tried not to think about the pain of what Emma had done to Zoe.

'Where is she?'

'Unconscious in the kitchen.' I looked around the room and saw a knife and roll of tape on the table. The knife was the missing one from the kitchen block. It was light in my hand and from the way it sliced through the tape holding Zoe to the chair, it must have been incredibly sharp. Zoe flinched away from it when it came near her skin.

'She used this, didn't she?'

She nodded. I finished at her legs, and she was free.

She stood and tottered, testing her legs but they held, and she reached up and removed the Suppressor and threw it on the table. She rubbed at her neck. I could see that each movement hurt.

'That looks like her work,' she said, indicating my face.

I touched my cheek, flinching every time my fingers landed. The bump Alfie had given me was swamped by the new damage. In the aftermath of the fight, every swollen nerve ending was shouting for my attention.

'Yes. *Shit,* her hands were fast.'

Zoe peered at my back. 'You know you've got glass sticking out of you.'

I half jumped with the shock of pain as she touched me. 'Is it bleeding much?'

'No.'

'Leave it in,' I said, nodding at the door. 'Let's get her.'

Emma had seemed so small and quiet that she hadn't really registered as a suspect. I had been too obsessed with Art. I had let my dislike of him run the investigation. My experience and skill had disappeared over the years I had neglected them, but at least we could have a press conference and tell the waiting country that iMe was secure. We could celebrate. Well, as much as iMe and FUs let you.

Zoe pulled herself upright, steeling herself to see Emma again. 'She's going to pay.'

I led the way back down the entrance hall towards the kitchen, opening and closing my fingers around the handle of the knife. Emma would need to come through me to hurt Zoe again.

Emma's foot had been across the doorway, but now all I could see were puddles on the ceramic tiling.

'Wait,' I said, and took two steps forward.

I could feel Zoe right behind me. She wanted to be part of it.

I stopped in the doorway, half expecting to see Emma coming straight at me again, but the room was quiet. A quick loop around the island revealed nothing.

I looked at Zoe then at the block of knives. I groaned.

Two knives were missing.

So was Emma.

67

DI Clive Lussac

'What do you mean she's *gone*?' Bhatt's icy displeasure almost froze my ear.

'She was out cold... I thought Zoe was... She can't have got far, and we need help to search.'

Bhatt put me on hold. I hoped she was negotiating the freeing-up of some more staff. I waited, and I shrugged a *don't know* to Zoe's raised eyebrow question.

Bhatt came back on. 'I'm sending two drones. ETA about eight minutes. They can buzz the area.'

'Anything else?'

'I've got eight Uniforms in four cars coming to you. They can help, but they'll be fifteen minutes.'

I hung up the call and turned to Zoe. 'Drones and backup are coming, but we can't just wait. We need to search.'

Zoe was shaking from the shock. Movement must have opened some of her cuts and little wet red stains decorated her shirt.

'You OK, Zoe?'

She nodded a lie. 'Let's find her.'

'Did you see anyone else here?' I asked.

Zoe shook her head. 'I had a hood on, and it felt like she brought me straight into the dining room after we arrived.' She paused as an idea flashed across her eyes. 'She kept calling me Four and talking about someone called Three. She must have someone else.'

'OK, run a scan.'

She typed and paused. 'No one showing but us. Not that I trust iMe anymore.'

'We need to search the house.'

'I'll go downstairs, you can go up,' Zoe suggested.

She had guts, but that was plain reckless. 'No, we'll go together.'

She started to protest but her heart wasn't in it, and I sensed that it was tinged with some relief.

***

We went room by agonising room. Every door was a potential trap, and every scuffed footfall we made confirming our position.

The ground floor was empty, so we climbed the stairs. As my head peaked over the landing and scanned around, I felt most exposed. It would be the best place for Emma to attack. A well-timed kick to my head would send me sprawling backwards down the stairs and I would take Zoe with me. Two for the price of one, but she wasn't there.

'This is a big house just for Emma,' I said.

'She must have money, but why get such a large house?'

We tracked around the upstairs but found nothing other than immaculate rooms, each one spotless and tidy. Beds were made, and neat towels hung in shiny bathrooms.

Downstairs again, we repeated our tour in case Emma had returned while we were upstairs. We ended in the garage, but that was clean and empty as well.

'Why does she need a garage?' Zoe asked.

Like the majority of people, Emma didn't have a car. There was no need with all the circulating on-demand taxis and most had converted their garage into a usable room.

I scanned around the built-in cabinets. They reflected back the lights in their gloss surfaces. The painted floor shone. I opened a cupboard and looked at the neat rows of small screwdrivers. 'And why have all these tools?'

We'd searched and drawn a blank in the house and garage.

Zoe looked thoughtful. 'Where did she keep Karina and Alan?'

She was right. Nowhere we had seen looked like it had held a reluctant guest.

'Not in the house. Too many absorbent fabrics and carpets. There would have been a mess when she cut Alan up.'

'The garage?' Zoe said.

'Maybe, the floor could be washed clean, but there are too many tools to leave someone locked in there.'

'OK, she must have run,' I said. 'Somewhere safe. But where?'

68

DI Clive Lussac

It was after eleven, and I hadn't slept much last night. The day had been a blur of doubt, Winter and rushing about. I had been fuelled by nerves and now I felt exhausted. Maybe it was the after effects of having a crazy woman battering my head, or the relief of finding Zoe alive.

The investigation had been a shambles and that had to change, but without a signal Emma could be anywhere and the CCTV cameras were useless street decorations. There was no point in wasting time chasing around aimlessly.

My head cocked at a distant buzzing.

'That's the drones,' Zoe said, 'and the backup's nearly here.'

'Program the drones to run a search pattern. Start at the house and get them to circle out. Their thermal imaging cameras should find her in the dark.'

'Not if she's broken into a building.'

'You're right. Send four of the Uniforms to go door to door. Get them to check everyone's gardens and outbuildings.' It felt good to be decisive. 'And get two to search here again.'

In the old days, I would have searched for Emma's car. That wouldn't work now but her friends, family and neighbours might yield something useful. It was a good enough place to start.

'Get the remaining two Uniforms to search online for friends and family and go check them out.'

Zoe nodded as her fingers typed out the instructions.

I jumped up and sat on Emma's kitchen worktop. My heels left small black smears on the shiny doors as they dangled.

If Emma gave us the slip, she was either going to run or go to wherever she kept the victims.

She might head for the coast and find a skipper willing to risk the Channel Blockade. Although the border was tight, protected by a legion of officers and technology, it was designed to stop people getting in, not getting out.

Having been on the receiving end of her fists, I didn't think it was her style to run but I messaged Bhatt and asked her to liaise with Border Protection.

'Where did she keep Karina and Alan?' I asked.

'She must have kept them somewhere close. She'd want to visit,' Zoe said.

'Has she got an accomplice? We've always assumed a single killer, but what if they kept the victims at the other person's place.'

'OK, who? Esteban? Art? Dave?'

'Emma said she'd found Art. I know we won't believe the results anymore, but check for signals.'

I waited while she did.

'No Emma. No Art. No Esteban. Dave's at home.'

Esteban was off-grid again. 'When the two Uniforms searching here are done, send them to Esteban's friend's house in Bagshot.'

Zoe pursed her lips in thought and winced. A fresh spot of blood appeared on the side of her mouth. 'Do you think Emma and Esteban are in it together?'

'I don't know. Bagshot is close...' We were guessing, and I didn't feel that lucky. We needed something else. 'Can you trace Emma's signal over the last year? One plot with all the signals at the same time.'

'Probably.'

Zoe threw her HUD at the wall in Emma's kitchen, and I watched as she hunted through the menus. After some dead ends, she found an option that looked like it would do the job, and her Buddy scampered off with the request.

The wall redrew with a map centred on Emma's home. Each signal from the last year showed as a small dot and Emma's home was a large bright blob in the centre of the map. Lines glowed for each journey Emma had made: infrequent trips were dim, but her commute to work was bold and bright.

Several other bright lines showed the routes of Emma's frequent journeys, but only one really stood out.

'What's there,' I asked, pointing at the bright blob at the end of the line.

Zoe scrolled, zoomed in, then centred the wall on the blob. The map showed a house up a long driveway surrounded by fields and trees. It looked like a perfect location to keep someone. Nice and secluded with no nosey neighbours.

'It's her parents' old home,' Zoe said, as she checked the details of the house. 'She inherited it four years ago.'

It was a possibility, but we needed more before committing. Emma could be at the end of any one of the other lines.

'She might have built some sort of cage to keep people in. If she did, then she would need materials.' *And iMe keeps everything*, I thought. 'Can you search her bank transactions?'

'Sure.'

More menus and clicks and the wall drew with Emma's last year's bank transactions. Zoe filtered out all the food and everyday purchases, but we still had a few pages of data. Nothing recent looked interesting, so Zoe paged through to the older transactions.

'Click on that one,' I said, pointing at a line that read *'Custom Metal Ltd'*.

Zoe did, and the invoice for the payment came up: two lengths of metal chain. The delivery address was Emma's parents' house.

'Looks hopeful,' Zoe said.

I nodded. 'Go further back.'

Zoe selected the previous two years.

The screen redrew with more entries for Custom Metal Ltd and several for building materials, wood, fixings and tools. Lots of orders for electronics. All delivered to the same isolated place.

I replayed our search of Emma's house. We hadn't found any of the materials like that here.

'Boss,' Zoe said. Despite the cuts and bruises, she had gone pale.

The invoice displayed on the wall was for a second-hand butcher's bone saw.

'Alan,' I agreed.

69

Emma Bailey

The weeping from my damaged eye had slowed, but my head still fizzed and sparked.

'Having a bad day?' sneered Three.

I ignored the words and placed the dining room chair in the middle of the cage. I waved at it. 'Just sit down,' I said.

Three was used to the way my mind worked and looked reluctant: suspicious of the chair, the tape and the two kitchen knives I held. Fear glued Three's feet to the floor.

'I have a treat for you.'

Three clearly didn't believe me. Grabbing an arm, I pushed Three into the chair. Three pulled away from me, not wanting to be there.

'I promised you a match against Four, but that's been delayed a while.'

Three slumped in relief, tired after our training session.

'If you beat Four, then you get to play against Five.' I smiled. 'Guess who Five is.'

'No idea,' Three said, sounding hoarse. I guessed that the training had damaged Three's throat and maybe vocal cords.

'Your friend, the inspector.'

'No friend of mine.'

'Four and Five will work it out and be here soon. Then the games can begin.'

'No. They'll catch you. You can't escape now they know it's you.'

I pondered this view of events as I taped Three to the chair.

'I almost forgot. You're in the news. It's everywhere,' I sneered. 'Art Walker, Head of iMe, missing.'

70

DI Clive Lussac

We ran from the house to the car and jumped in. The doors shut, and the heaters started to dispel the cold inside. Zoe programmed the car for Emma's parents' house and as we started to move Bhatt's voice came through on the car's speakers. I told her where we were going.

'I've upset some important people, but I got the result of Art's encryption,' she said.

'Where is he?' I asked.

'His signal isn't encrypted. It's off.'

***

The car crawled through another village at 20mph. The midnight streets were empty of people and traffic, but the car obeyed a rigid set of fixed rules. Programming cars to learn had landed the car manufacturers in court with claims of negligence when the first mistakes ended in injuries. Their lawyers had insisted on 'no learning', so we were stuck at 20mph when we could safely go much faster.

'So fucking slow,' I moaned. 'This is life when rules take away your initiative – when our blame culture crushes people wanting to take responsibility.' I kicked the inside of the car in frustration.

Zoe rolled her eyes at me.

The car's blue exterior lights bounced back at us from the houses' windows as we cleared the village and headed into the countryside.

'Do you think Art is still involved?' Zoe asked.

'I'm not sure,' I said. 'Maybe.' This was a climbdown for me. I had wanted it to be him.

'So why did Emma use his signal?'

'She knew we would question him. It was a good place for a trap.'

Zoe thought for a while. 'So how did she know he wouldn't be there?'

'He's either a partner or a target.'

'Target.'

I had to agree, it made sense. If Alan was killed because of his links to iMe, then Art and Esteban were the logical next targets.

***

We hadn't had to chase anyone in years. It was safer to turn up wherever their signal was. Our car's systems showed a steady 40mph, and it would be another twenty minutes until we arrived.

'The old cars used to tear along, lights on, siren blaring,' I said.

'That must have been exciting,' Zoe said. 'And reckless.'

'Yes and yes. But at least we got there in time to do something other than clean up the mess.'

Zoe scratched her nose but said nothing.

Where else could the conversation go? We were different generations. We were speed versus safety.

'Where's Esteban?' I said.

Zoe was on her HUD and didn't hear me. If we were two people sitting across from each other in a restaurant, not a police car, we would have looked typical. Both sharing the same physical space but separated by the world of the HUD.

'Zoe,' I said louder.

'What?' she said, surprised at my tone.

'Didn't you hear me?'

'What? No,' she said. 'But I found this.'

She threw her HUD display onto the car's screen. She had a menu tree open: '*Car – Police Overrides – Options – Health and Safety – Other – Security – Authorisation Only*'. At the bottom were the words '*Enable Chase Mode*'.

This was more like it. 'Press it,' I commanded. 'Let's burn through the countryside.'

She did, but nothing happened. Then Zoe's Buddy rolled out an '*Authorising… Please Wait*' message banner and stood looking at her arm as if she wore an old-fashioned wristwatch.

Five minutes went by and her Buddy's arm never tired of looking at her watch.

'We're going to be there before the authorisation,' I moaned, but as I said it, her Buddy rolled out another banner, '*Chase Mode authorised by Chief Superintendent Bhatt*'.

Buddy put her banner away and pulled out a file icon that she threw at the screen.

The file was titled, '*Chase Mode Waiver*'. Zoe had lots of things to acknowledge: Yes, chase mode was her free choice; no, the police force hadn't coerced her; yes, she understood the risks. It went on for four pages.

She pressed '*Submit*' and still nothing happened, then her Buddy threw a second file, which was titled '*Second Passenger Chase Mode Waiver*'.

I had to go through all the same questions and after I pressed '*Submit*', her Buddy asked, '*Are you sure?*'

'Yes,' Zoe said.

'*Chase Mode requires double acceptance. Are you really sure?*'

'Yes,' Zoe said a second time, impatience creeping into her voice and the next banner showed the words '*Chase Mode Enabled*'.

The cars lights started flashing alternate red and blue and the speed started to rise. 41. 42. 43... It stopped at 50mph.

No!

'That's it? We're trying to catch a killer!' I said in disgust. 'Fucking technology.'

***

Zoe and I used the rest of the journey to form a basic plan. We examined the layout of the site and the room plans that were all stored centrally. Out of habit, we checked the house and the outbuildings. No signals showed, but that didn't seem to matter now.

The aim was simple – search and rescue. Two people, two search areas: the house and the outbuildings.

'You take the house, I'll do the outbuildings,' Zoe said.

I couldn't risk losing her again. 'No, we'll go in together and stay together.'

She looked upset as she picked at her nails. 'It's slower, and you were all for speed earlier.'

'Yes, but splitting up is reckless.' Somehow, we had flipped sides in the speed versus safety argument. 'My old training manual said partners stick together.'

'I want a face-to-face with Emma when I'm not taped to a chair.' Zoe's sullen eyes bore into me.

'Together. No argument,' I said.

After a minute of cold silence, she replied.

'No argument.'

71

DI Clive Lussac

The car stopped and we jumped out and raced toward the front door of the house. The night was clear, and the nearly full moon cast a silvery light over the house, hedges and drive. It allowed us to see. And be seen.

I checked behind me – Zoe was still there. She ran holding her upper body rigid, like she was feeling her cuts. Her eyes were locked onto the side of the house that led to the outbuildings.

Waving us forward, I approached the door. I heard running feet and snapped my head around preparing for attack, but my brain told me the feet were going away from me.

I understood what Zoe really meant when she said no argument. She wanted some payback time with Emma. She disappeared around the corner of the house and out of sight.

I put my weight on my right foot, preparing to go after her, but the house needed searching and speed did matter. We had a killer to catch. I transferred the weight to my left leg.

I couldn't leave Zoe alone again.

Twice more I shifted my weight back and forwards, trapped in a dance of indecision.

My left foot won. We needed speed. I overrode the lock and headed through the door.

The house wasn't what I had expected. It had been gutted like a donor vehicle stripped for spare parts. Sections of walls were missing, doors removed, floorboards pulled up. I rushed from room to room, surer with each wrecked room that neither Emma or Art were there.

Emma must have used the house to provide materials to build something. It didn't look like she had built anything in the house.

Oh, shit. The outbuildings.

I ran.

***

The closest outbuilding to the house was a small shed which was full of gardening tools rusting gently in the damp air.

The next was larger and I ran across the gap to it, aware of the noise I was making, and pushed against the door. It held fast. I couldn't see a lock, but the old timber hadn't seen paint in years and had warped, twisted and swollen with neglect and rain. I took two steps back and smashed into it. For a moment the door flexed and I thought that I was going to bounce straight back off, but my weight and momentum overpowered the grip of the old wood, and I blundered through.

I was off balance and only just avoided running straight into a pile of metal pipes and their cold, sharp edges. The building was empty of people but full of offcuts of building materials. It was a simple dumping ground, so I left through a well-oiled door in the other end of the building.

I had made so much noise that I didn't try to creep up to the last outbuilding. Zoe was in there.

This time, I tried the handle and was rewarded by its smooth turn. I padded in to avoid running into something else sharp.

This space was much bigger, with lots of workbenches and tools packed against the outside walls. There was a tool for everything and most of them were old enough for Emma to have inherited them. Her newer purchases were much shinier.

The floor showed scrape marks going to the doors, like things had been dragged to a waiting car.

'Could you be any louder, Boss?' Zoe said, as she appeared in the doorway to a room leading off to the side. 'I heard you a mile away.'

'I was worried about you. So…' I felt a little bashful; I was letting my protective feelings for Zoe overpower logic and drive my actions.

'Anyone here?' I asked.

'No. But look at all this stuff.'

I walked over to the door and followed her in.

This room had a stool, huge lights and a U-shaped workbench. The walls were covered with shelves, each holding rows of small containers.

Zoe pulled one open and showed me some electrical components with thin bulb-like bodies painted with stripes and two long legs.

'Resistors,' Zoe said.

She waved her arm to indicate the rest. 'More of the same.'

On the work surface sat a battery of electrical test equipment, soldering irons, circuit boards and wire.

'See this,' she said, and stood aside.

I stared at a mass of wires and circuits built into a shell. It looked very much like a half-finished version of the Suppressor Zoe had been wearing at Emma's.

***

We headed back to the main area of the outbuilding.

'She's been trying for years,' Zoe said, steering me to a corner. 'All her failed attempts.' She waved a hand towards a big pile of discarded electronics. There must have been over a hundred variations of things that looked like Suppressors. She turned to me and said, 'What about the house?'

'The house is a mess,' I said. 'It looks like she ripped stuff out and brought it to the outbuilding. What she didn't have, she bought and got delivered here.'

Some links of a big metal chain lay on the floor, the ends cut through to make the chain itself shorter. I moved one foot and pushed a link with my toe. It was heavier than I thought.

Light caught on tiny twirls of metal on the floor. They reminded me of school metalwork lessons and the beautiful shards you got from cutting and drilling a soft metal like aluminium.

'She made things here and took them somewhere else,' I said.

Zoe nodded. 'I saw the drag marks and thought the same thing.'

I thought back to the screen with all her journeys on and why Emma needed such a big house.

'We're in the wrong place.'

72

Emma Bailey

I winced as I touched the side of my head. The drying blood matted my hair and the swelling was burning and raw. When I peered at my fingers, I saw a mixture of blood and clear liquid. That couldn't be good. *Oh, Five. You'll pay for that.*

My head felt different. Connections had broken and my brain sparked like an electrical short-circuit. It fired random memories at me as the arcing impulses made new links.

My brain flashed white, and I was back stealing from my sister and brother for the first time, but the culprit was so obvious that they went straight into my room. Punches and kicks to make sure I stopped. But I didn't.

'Don't take my Barbie, Emma.' – I didn't.

'Give my birthday money back, Emma.' – I didn't have her money.

'Do you know where Mrs Jenkin's cat has gone, Emma?' – Why would I?

'How did your friend Janey fall down all those stairs, Emma?' – She tripped, honest.

'How did you not see little Ryan when you reversed the car, Emma?' – He ran behind the car chasing a ball.

I had to endure Dr Owen every time I *misbehaved*. Sitting in his office, clenching my knees together and pulling at the hem of my skirt every time his eyes flicked down and lingered. He was a useless, empty man with no morals, but he had power over me. I got more rules and controls from everyone, but it taught me how to hide my treasures in seemingly boring places. About lying and manipulating. I paid close attention in my drama classes. I became talented and inventive.

My brain seemed to vanish for a moment. No thoughts and no control as everything disconnected. An empty void and then it clicked back on, and I was standing over Two. He had corrupted iMe, taken the vision of simplicity and convenience and made it the worst thing ever: a control mechanism.

I rocked back in my chair and closed my damaged eye to the electric throb behind it. I breathed and tried to think of good times. Of Mary. *Oh, Mary.* She had given me the games. My indulgent, overdramatic trap in the garage had gifted me a taste for an unexpected pleasure. The purest form of control was over someone taped to a chair and waiting for the knife to touch flesh again.

The chair and the games were my new favourites.

My vision swam as another bolt of pain seared through my head.

I could run, break for France, but I was a fighter. I wanted revenge. I wanted the games.

Lussac would be my number five, and he could watch Three vs Four. He would want Four to win for sure, but then it would be him vs Four. It would be epic. Would he go for the noble sacrifice or a survival preserving victory? What would Four do against Lussac?

And if Three beat his precious Four, then Lussac would take Four's place and fight for glorious revenge. It was a win-win: either outcome I would relish, record and watch again and again.

I squinted at Three in the cage on the monitors. Time to play.

***

The knife I balanced in my palm was a little too big, but I had left my favourite little one in the dining room and Lussac must have taken it.

'Three, we have some time to kill.' I smiled. 'You know I like games. Let's play a guessing game.'

'What?'

'I'll give you a question, all you have to do is guess the answer.'

Three didn't say anything, but his suspicion glowed in his eyes. They flicked from me to the knife.

'First question: why are you here?'

'Because you're a messed-up psycho bitch!' he croaked.

I touched the tip of the knife against his shirt and let the point rest on his skin. He cringed away.

'That's rude,' I said, but I considered his answer. 'My question was too vague and open to many interpretations. Technically, your answer is correct, although Dr Owen didn't use those words. Well done.'

Three didn't look pleased. I don't think he liked playing with knives. He certainly didn't like *me* playing with knives.

'Next round, and I'll be more specific this time. Question two: what made me choose you?'

Three shook his head.

'Oh, Three,' I said in mock surprise. 'There are so many correct answers. It's a shame to pass.' I shook my head in time with his and it made my head sizzle. I shut my eyes as the pain jolted through.

I rotated the knife through one slow revolution and admired the spot of red that appeared through his shirt. 'Try again.' I eased my weight onto the knife.

He winced in pain and it raised the pitch of his damaged voice. 'Karina,' he said.

I released the pressure on the knife.

'Correct. Karina is one answer. I could have stolen anyone, but I know you encrypted both your signals for some alone time. I saw you watching her at the tech briefings. You were obsessed with her.'

'She *really* wanted to go to meet the celebs,' he smirked. 'But she was special.'

'It hurt you for her to be gone.'

He nodded.

'Really, *you* chose her for me.'

I had found his laptop in the car where Zoe had put it and forced him to unlock it. It rested on the floor by my feet, as I picked it up, I clicked a button. I turned the screen so that he could see it.

'Is that any way to treat someone you love, Three?'

The file I had opened was labelled *Best of Karina*. It was a complete coincidence that I had a file with the same name. Both files had Karina doing everything she was told, but Three's file was full of vile depravity from his study's bedroom. Mine was full of Karina singing and brushing her hair, being my perfect little Barbie.

Despite him getting the answer to the last question right, I pushed the knife in. Three had made Karina a sex object and abused her. That wasn't right. It required punishment.

He screamed and I enjoyed the harsh undertone in the sound.

'Do you see the correlation, Three?' I allowed him space to answer.

He said nothing, but he couldn't look at me. 'I'm only repaying some of the suffering you inflicted on Karina.'

I pushed again. 'And all the others.'

I waited as the scream echoed in the cage.

'Next question. Number three for Number Three,' I said, pleased with my little joke.

Three didn't appreciate it, and I let him subside and moved the knife to a different spot on his arm. 'Why didn't you stop Two?' I said.

I could see that he knew something had changed. This question wasn't one he had to guess the answer to; he knew it, but tried to bluff anyway.

'Doing what?'

'Don't give me that. You know what – taking the purity of iMe and corrupting it. Making it control us.'

He looked at the knife and said, 'I tried, but look at what's been achieved. No more obese Britain. No more crime.'

His scream was longer this time because I pushed a bit harder and a bit deeper.

'You ruined us by taking away our sense of self-responsibility.' Deeper still.

The end of the knife shone a rich red. I wiped it clean on his shirt before moving it.

'You pretended to stop him, but secretly you worked with him. You and Two made yourselves powerful.'

I pushed.

'And rich.'

I twisted.

'Now it's time to pay.'

I engrossed myself in the game for a while. I was levelling the playing field for the games. Four had lots of cuts. Now so did Three.

One of the proximity alarms sounded. I looked at the monitor.

'Oh good. They're back.'

73

DI Clive Lussac

We burst back into Emma's house through the rear door and into her kitchen. The two Uniforms who had been searching the gardens followed us in.

'Any sign of her?' I asked them.

They both shook their heads and dropped their eyes to the floor.

Zoe's bruises had spread, mixing some greens, reds and dark purples into her gold eyeshadow. At least the blood on her shirt was drying. 'You OK?' I asked again.

'I'm fine,' she said with exasperation in her voice, but her eyes told a different story as she worked her HUD. 'Emma's signal's still not showing.' She bent and examined the shiny fronts of the kitchen cabinets where I had sat. 'Emma's here.'

The marks I had made were smeared, as if someone had run a finger mark across them to check the damage.

'There must be something,' I demanded of the Uniforms.

'No sign anywhere,' the taller Uniform said.

'No one in the house. We checked outside. Nothing. Nothing useful from the drones either,' the other agreed.

I shook my head in frustration. 'Shit.'

Zoe was staring into space. 'The garage isn't as deep as the house. I'm going to take a look.'

'Just a sec, Zoe.' I held my hand up to ask her to wait as Bhatt's ID flashed up. I took the call and updated her.

I heard a slight buzz and three rapid clinks as the fluorescent tube-lights in the garage buzzed on.

As I hung up, I turned, but Zoe was gone.

Emma Bailey

I could see on the monitor that Four was on her own in the garage and she was looking straight at the hidden entrance. Perfect.

My heart was racing like I'd run a mile. I found that the chair game did that to me; it flooded my system. Now I needed to focus on getting Four.

I checked the monitor again – she was at the entrance, her head tipped to one side as if she was thinking hard.

Come on Four you can do it. Work it out and come in.

I picked up the spray and shook the can. The contents sloshed around and I could feel that it was nearly full. It would really sting with all her cuts and bruises. I put my mask on to protect mine.

From the cage, the hazy outline of the door to the garage was just visible ahead. I edged along the dark passage towards it, sliding my back along the wall, trying not to make a sound. When Four worked out how to open the door, I would be flooded with light from the garage; picked out like someone caught in a searchlight. Yes, but if I stood next to the door, my back against the wall, facing in, then I would be hidden.

***

The door started to move. *Come to me.* I tensed, waiting to strike.

As the door opened wider, the light from the garage flooded into the passage. An elongated shadow projected onto the floor. The shadow paused and then moved. I could hear slow, wary movements. The shadow's head moved left and right. I couldn't quite see her, but I could hear plenty of rapid breathing. My finger depressed the trigger of the can, moving it to take up the slack in the mechanism.

I jumped out in front of her, grabbing her arm with my spare hand, pulling and spinning her through the door and into the corridor so that she faced me. More panted breaths and a gasp. I smiled, adjusted my aim and pressed the trigger. A perfect mist cone of liquid squirted out of the can nozzle and into her eyes, nose and open mouth. Her scream bounced along the passage.

Four's arms thrashed as she fought the pain. I waited for a fraction of a second, gauging the windmilling arms. I moved but mistimed it, and Four's fist smashed into my head where the hammer had hit. The white shock of it stopped me. Stars burst in my head. Groggy and sick, I hesitated until my vision cleared, then pushed her hard in the chest, my palm flat. It sent her staggering backwards, stumbling over like a rag doll. I closed and disguised the entrance again and went after her.

Four was clawing at her closed eyes, trying to ease the burning. Trying to get the spray out of all those cuts and her mouth.

Her coughs racked her body, and she looked close to hyperventilating. I needed her easier to move, so I edged around her body and knelt by her head. My fingers hooked into that frizzy hair, and I jerked her head up towards me and then slammed it down. She grunted and slowed a little. I lifted her head again, seeing a small red smear on the floor and slammed it down again for luck: mine not hers. She groaned and the thrashing stopped.

I rolled Four onto her front and taped her hands and elbows. Just like I'd done to Mary. I tingled with anticipation.

We can start.

I frogmarched the groggy Four into the cage.

'Zoe,' Three wailed.

Something in the effort of dragging her had shifted something in my head and I had to wait for the patterns of ultra-bright lights in my mind to fade. They left a pulsing ache.

'Don't feel too sorry for her, Three. You'll be competing against her for your life.'

I wanted it to be a fair fight, so I cleaned Four's face and bathed her cuts to get the residue of the spray out. She seemed calmer and blinked her head clear.

Three was already prepared against the left side of the cage and all the straps were ready to lift him into the air. Mentally though, he looked broken, like he wouldn't fight, but when his lungs started to hurt, I was sure that nature would win and it would be game on.

I wanted to see their eyes.

***

It didn't take long for me to get Four in position. She faced Three with her back to the right wall of the cage. My cameras were ready. I wanted to see it live, but if Five found the entrance too soon, then I would have to be happy with the recording.

Four looked around the cage. Her face said that everything now made sense to her. As if all the little pieces of information she had had magically slotted into place.

It wouldn't be a perfectly even start. I couldn't lift and then release them both at exactly the same moment, but Three needed to pay and I really wanted to see Four versus Five, so I started with Three. He was already balancing on tiptoes, battling for his life when I lifted and then released Four.

Any chivalrous thoughts Three may have had were gone from his eyes by the time Four was fighting hard to survive.

I settled in to bask in the glory of the game.

DC Zoe Jordan

I could feel my calf muscles screaming, starting to cramp. I shifted my weight on my feet to try and ease them, but that drew the strap tighter around my neck. I couldn't die like this. There was too much I hadn't done.

My pulse was racing, and my breath ragged. *Breathe. Slow and calm.*

It helped for a second and then my toes started to give way. I winced as I forced them up again and looked across at Art. I could see his legs shaking. He was staring at me. A weird look I couldn't read.

I focused on keeping my weight off my neck.

I had to hang on. Not to beat Art. Just to survive.

But I was losing. My strength was failing. The muscles in my legs howled, and my whole body twitched and shook.

I squeezed every last drop of strength into my legs, but I couldn't hold it. I had to drop my weight.

The strap caught my throat.

74

DI Clive Lussac

I heard a scream.

'Zoe, where are you?' I span away from the Uniforms towards the open doorway.

I was hoping for her normal 'here, Boss,' but was met with silence. I stood as still as possible, playing a living statue, listening hard. It was as quiet as a grave and I hoped that it wasn't a premonition.

'Zoe?'

I tracked back to the garage and stepped inside, but it looked the same – still immaculate with its shiny worktop and cupboard doors, neat tools hung up in a line. No sign of Zoe.

I called over my shoulder to the Uniforms, 'Check the house again and find DC Jordan.'

'Zoe?' I could hear the frantic edge to my voice. I kept stretching my hands, hoping to get the tension out. I needed logical thoughts, not to be lost in a whirl of pointless worry that wouldn't help Zoe.

I shut my eyes to see if I could drag up a mental image from before. *Something doesn't look right; something is different.*

'Footprints,' I said.

The garage floor was concrete sealed with grey paint that had a soft sheen. I got a bit lower and looked along the floor. Small, faint footprints – each one a vague patterned scuff on the gloss.

'Zoe came in by this door. She's got grippy soles and it's damp outside on the grass. They've left a mark.' I was muttering to myself, trying to make my thoughts more solid.

My eyes followed the trail, and my arm tracked the movement between the worktop and a tall double cupboard. Zoe's shoes must have dried, as I couldn't see any footprints leaving. So where did she go?

I started at the worktop, dropping to my haunches and opening a cupboard. It was neat as expected. Different cleaning chemicals ordered by type and size. Everything aligned, labels facing front and at attention.

I went over to the double cupboard and opened it, but was disappointed to find only a mop and bucket. *What am I missing?*

I focused on the back wall of the cupboard. It looked like the top right corner came forward more than the rest, as if the wall was warped. I put my foot on the cupboard floor, trying to steady myself, and I reached into the back with my hand. The floor slid under my foot, and I almost toppled over.

Kneeling down, I put both hands on the base of the cupboard, trying to move it in all directions and was rewarded when the whole floor slid towards me, still supporting the bucket. When it reached the end of its travels, the floor pivoted away in the opposite direction to the door, allowing access to the back of the cupboard.

The mop and bucket swayed on the false floor, but now it was out of the way I could see a faint footprint on the bottom of the cupboard, the toes pointing in.

Shit. Zoe, are you in there?

Emma Bailey

Movement in the monitor caught my eye.

Five was already in the garage but over by the worktop, not the entrance.

I still had time, so I headed back towards the doorway to the garage with one final, longing glance at the game in progress. It was even so far, with both sets of legs pulsing. Their eyes were locked on each other, each willing the other to fail first.

Five would be wary. He would be wondering where Four was. He was going to be careful but also scared. My bet was that he would be looking at head height and ahead of him, not down low and to the side. So, this time I dropped my bum onto my heels, weight balanced and into a comfortable, familiar squat – feet flat on the floor.

Ready or not, Five.

DI Clive Lussac

I reached my trembling hand into the cupboard.

The back wall of the cupboard popped under my push and hinged in, light spilling into a narrow corridor. I felt like a tomb raider entering a catacomb, and that usually didn't end well for the robber.

I was unarmed, and I knew that Emma enjoyed inflicting pain. Fear ate at me. I had to find Zoe, but I needed a weapon.

I stepped back into the garage and scanned the walls for something to use. In a confined space there wouldn't be much room for a tool you had to swing, so I wanted a stabbing tool. Ideally a knife, and I had left Emma's knife in the car. I couldn't see another one here even though lots of shiny metal tools glinted back at me. *What can I use?*

On the far side of the garage some blue handled chisels looked tempting. I chose a narrow one and removed the protective black cap from the blade to test the end. It was as sharp as a razor.

I stepped back towards the cupboard and looked in. *If this is a trap, where would I wait? Right by the door would be best*, I decided, before my eyes adjusted properly.

I took a cautious step into the cupboard, but stayed back from the corridor, trying to build up the courage to step into the unknown. All my senses strained for some hint of Emma about to strike. I thought I caught a slight movement low down.

I tested the weight of the chisel in my hand again and swooped low, bringing my hand back and then forward in a fast arc, aiming low at where I thought I had sensed movement. The chisel bucked as it hit something and then I heard a cry. I pulled back for a second strike, but I was too slow, and Emma leapt forward and ran along the corridor.

Emma Bailey

I stopped outside the cage. The games were still going on, but I could see from their panicked eyes and wavering legs that the end was close.

I looked down at my bicep and the blood oozing from between my fingers. 'Bastard. My arm,' I croaked. I needed to see how bad it was. Relaxing the grip of my hand, I released the pressure on the wound. The chisel's long, clean incision jetted blood in time with my heartbeat. I squeezed the pressure back on, but it didn't stop the flow. I was losing too much blood.

He must have hit an artery.

I stepped into the cage, slamming the door shut. I turned the key to lock the door and threw the key on the floor. It skittered across the surface and bumped into the back wall. I slid down the wall to watch the end of the games.

Lussac would have to watch Four die through the bars.

75

DI Clive Lussac

I started after Emma, my eyes smarting and watering at something in the air. The light further down the passage pulled me forwards and I jogged alongside a trail of fresh red spots of blood. The room at the end of the passage was simple, with a door, monitors and an office chair. As I passed the chair and stepped through the deep doorway into a second room, my iMe shut off. It was like I wore an invisible Suppressor.

The room I had entered was divided in two by a wall of bars. More monitors on my side, Emma on the other side in a cage that looked like some sort of medieval torture chamber. Against the right-hand wall hung... Zoe.

No.

Zoe's swollen, red face looked grotesque. Her eyes pleaded with me. I glanced across the room. There was Art. Zoe and Art were both up on their toes, their legs twitching and spasming as they tried to keep the pressure off the noose around their necks. Like Mary.

'The show must go on.' Emma was slumped in the far corner, holding her arm that was slick with blood. Where her elbow touched the floor, a red puddle spread across the floor. Emma smiled. 'You can't save her.'

I grasped the door in the bars and shook it as hard as I could. The door clanged and rattled against the lock but didn't open. The noise mocked me. A serenade to my uselessness. I still had the chisel, so I pushed the end into the gap between the door and its metal frame. I pulled back, trying to lever the door open. *Crack.* I staggered backwards as the blade of the chisel broke.

Emma's laugh followed me back down the passage. I burst into the garage.

'Uniform!' I bellowed. 'Here. *Now*.' I was answered by the sound of two pairs of size thirteens trampling down the hall and into the garage.

'You.' I pointed at the taller one. 'Call the medics. Get them here now. Then Bhatt.' He nodded.

'You, look for something to get me through metal bars.' The other officer looked confused but must have heard my urgency as he turned to start searching.

I had seen something when I had been in the garage before. I ran over to the cupboard and pulled down a box of split-pins. I could pick the lock.

As I ran back along the passage to the cage, I bent a slight curve into one split-pin to act as a pick and bent the other into an L-shaped lever.

I got to the door to the cage. Zoe's shaking told me I needed to be quick. I lifted the pick, putting it into the lock, trying to feel for the pins. I couldn't feel anything through my shaking hands, so I dropped the lever.

Calm.

I took four breaths and started again.

DC Zoe Jordan

I dug deep, driven by a primal will to survive and found some last strength. I forced my toes back up, but I couldn't hold myself for much longer. My feet collapsed. The shriek from my muscles was nothing compared to the agony of the strap gripping on my throat. Each second closed it more.

Emma's head lolled forward. She slumped into a crooked mess in the growing pool of her blood by the wall.

I shot my eyes back to the door as I heard Clive come back. *Help me.*

He was kneeling by the door fumbling and swearing. Dropping pins and then picking them up again. *Just fucking get on with it.*

He stopped for breath and started fiddling again with the lock.

I couldn't go on. My weight swung on the strap. I gasped for air but found none. I expected my life to flash before me, but instead, I had an image of me lying on Mum's lap. She soothed me, stroking my hair as she had done when I was ill.

DI Clive Lussac

The picks weren't working. I glanced up to see how Zoe was doing but she was gasping for air like a stranded fish.

I looked at the lock again, trying to force myself to think clearly. It was protected on the inside with a thick piece of metal covering the gap between the door and the frame, hiding the metal bolt. It had been installed to keep people in, not out. On my side of the door, I could see the bolt.

I heard feet behind me. One of the Uniforms had come in but stared in open-mouthed shock as he took in the cage, two hanging bodies and the slumped Emma.

He shook himself and held up an ancient blue Makita battery angle grinder. 'This any good?' He blipped the power button and I smiled as the blade spun.

'Perfect,' I said, and took it from him. It was too old to have all the health and safety locks in it. No link to iMe, no link to Well-being and Health. I didn't have safety glasses, gloves, or protective clothing, but the grinder didn't care. It was happy to help.

The blade sang and bucked as it touched the bolt. I corrected my aim and revelled in the noise, the spray of bright yellow sparks and the hard smell of cutting metal. The bolt didn't last long.

I ran to Zoe, grabbing one of the knives by a chair, I sliced at the fabric strap above her head. I eased her to the ground and loosened the strap around her neck. She lay still, with no breath or movement. Shit.

I wanted to stay with her, but I couldn't leave Art to die. I ran over to him and cut him down. He coughed and spluttered as I released the tension around his neck. He croaked, trying to say something. I leant in close so that I could hear.

'Winning,' he said.

I had no idea what he was winning, but I left him wheezing and coughing and went back to Zoe.

I tried mouth to mouth. Nothing. Desperate breaths and pumping on her chest, willing her to live.

Nothing.

76

DI Clive Lussac

My shoulder was almost healed and I wore the fading bruises like yellow make-up. I had stopped for a quick break in the sun but couldn't put it off any longer. I walked back down into the depths of PCU to the evidence store and walked past the ghosts of my life in their cardboard boxes.

All my old cases. I trailed my hand over them as I passed each one, trying to reconnect. Trying to remember the people. The boxes were big, but these days we only needed small ones to hold the physical evidence. All the rest was stored on iMe.

Fraud needed everything we had, so I put the last of the evidence against Doris onto the trolley, then placed Emma's Suppressors and Mimics on top.

**

After dropping most of the boxes at Fraud, I carried the last ones along the corridor of the iMe office. There was something different in the atmosphere, like the fundamental belief in iMe's infallibility had changed.

The assistant let me into the office. I stepped in and up to the desk.

'That's it,' I said, as I pushed the boxes onto the desk.

Art stood and looked inside. He was wearing a soft scarf to hide his neck and his voice still croaked. 'Thank you, Inspector.'

He held his hand out. 'For these,' he said. 'And for saving my life.'

For the first time I sensed warmth and genuine emotion coming from him, but I left his hand hanging like he had left mine at the beginning. We weren't friends – not after all his lies and the abuse we uncovered.

He made out like he was a victim. The bastard must have pulled strings to cover up the evidence and come out of all this squeaky-clean. Nothing stuck to him. Not the parties or the casting room. I couldn't find his laptop in the evidence store, even though it had been in Emma's cage and had been signed into the store. It was like it never happened.

'I'll make sure these Suppressors and Mimics are only used for the good of iMe,' Art said as I left.

Like hell he will.

***

I walked into a room full of women. The late afternoon sun shone through the window and painted the room in a warm yellow glow.

Bhatt was at the end of the bed. Zoe sat propped up, looking much brighter today. Her neck was vivid and raw, but at least she wore a big smile. She had a rash of small plasters on her arms to cover the cuts.

Two nurses were fussing with tubes and charts. Checking and rechecking.

'How are you doing?' I said.

'Better today,' Zoe said in a tight, low whisper.

'No talking,' said one of the nurses. 'She needs to rest her throat.'

We waited in silence as the nurses finished and then Bhatt looked at Zoe and said, 'Are you sure, Zoe?'

Zoe flashed a thumbs up.

'What?' I said. 'Fill me in.' They had agreed on something beforehand. Was Zoe going to transfer out of PCU?

'Your time at PCU has come to an end, Clive,' Bhatt said.

No. After all this time, I couldn't sit at home doing nothing. Was Zoe going to run PCU? *Shit, I know the investigation wasn't perfect but to get the sack?*

'We're setting up a new unit and I want you to head it.' Bhatt smiled, enjoying the deliberate misdirection of my thoughts.

'What unit?'

'We're calling it Off-Grid Crime for the moment. We need it, what with Suppressors, Mimics and the Health Bank bracelets as well.' She paused to let it sink in.

'It's official?' I asked, not sure I could believe her.

'Yes, it was signed off today by the chief constable, the Ministry and iMe.'

I wore a smile that almost burst my face. 'Fantastic. I'll need a team.'

I saw the answer in Bhatt's eyes before she shook her head.

'Just me?' I said.

They would probably lock me in some tiny windowless office all alone.

'Not exactly, you'll be joined by one other officer.'

Zoe tried her best smile but stopped when it hurt. She replaced it with a double thumbs up.

***

I floated along the corridor replaying Bhatt's words. My own department. OK, it was tiny, but it was a start, and being with Zoe all the time made it perfect.

Then the day which I didn't think could get any better, did.

The message came in from Winter. It started full of threat and bluster, but the end was what mattered.

'After discussion with iMe and the Ministry, we have decided to put our active investigation of you on hold for the present time. We will retain a passive monitoring of your intake and should you re-offend then…'

I stopped reading. I had seen all I needed to. Bhatt had come through for me again. I couldn't run my new department from a reorientation camp.

'Delete message.'

My Buddy ran out at the bottom of the screen with the banner that said *'Delete? Are you sure?'* He shrugged with his palms up and waited for my reply.

'Yes,' I said, grinning like Scooby-Doo about to get some snacks.

Buddy nodded, carried out a bin and lifted the lid. The message collapsed on itself and reformed as a sheet of screwed up paper. It flew across my HUD and hit the lip of Buddy's bin, rolled around the top once and then fell in. Buddy closed the lid of the bin with a clang and ran off the screen with the bin and Winter's message.

77

DI Clive Lussac

I was trying to get everything ready. Tonight was our first date together, and I was hosting. The cleaning robot was in boost mode and the poor thing was on its third battery charge. At least the floor looked clean now.

It was the false calm between getting ready and the date beginning. I was an hour early and had time to kill. I couldn't help thinking about Art.

I turned the news on to take my mind off him – I didn't want to be grumpy for the date. The reporter was talking about the sudden rise in popularity of the government and asking if the timing was linked to the latest iMe version upgrade.

Probably just some conspiracy theory, I thought. But then I remembered that I had three new pots of peanut butter, and I hated peanut butter. *What had made me buy those?*

***

In my bedroom, I could hear sounds that must be the corrective work that was apparently necessary to her hair. It had looked good to me, but I had been told that a rogue gust of wind outside my flat had upset the perfection.

In the old days, I would have lit candles, but they were a fire risk and impossible to get anymore, so I had the walls showing images of open fires instead. The sound was turned up high enough to hear the soft crackle of the flames.

The noises from the bedroom stopped, and I stood still, smoothing my new suit and rubbing my new shoes into a higher shine on the backs of my trousers.

Zoe came into the room and smiled. I hadn't realised how much I cared for her until I saw her bleeding and suffering at Emma's home. She still had the bruises on her neck, but at least they were fading now.

'Mum's ready.'

'You sure you're OK with this?' I said. She nodded and lifted her head to look at me. I smiled.

Sophia came out of the bedroom. Whatever had been wrong with her hair was fixed. She was gorgeous. Her hair shone almost as much as her dress, and her smiling eyes held me captive. All I could do was stare.

'Have fun, kids,' Zoe said as she pecked me on the check and then landed another on Sophia.

***

They used to say that the way to a man's heart is through his stomach. These days the saying would have to be amended to the way to a person's heart is through their stomach via a carefully selected nutritious and calorie-controlled eating plan, but that was more of a mouthful than the food it promised.

I'd never known the way to a woman's heart, but I had discovered that rescuing her daughter from certain and horrible death went a long, long way.

Emma had killed Mary and I would carry her loss for the rest of my life – along with the guilt of my new hope.

I shook the thought away and resumed my staring at Sophia.

'What are we eating?' she said.

'Salad to start,' I said, with an embarrassed smile. I knew that I needed to make changes to my life and this was my first concession.

Sophia nodded.

'Then steaks, a bottle of Amarone – 16% alcohol and full of flavour. Then chocolate fondant.' I *had* changed, but not that much. Cooking two steaks was simple, and I had bought the rest already prepared.

She frowned. 'But won't that swamp our FU allowance?'

'We can worry about that later.' I crossed to the kitchen. 'I have a present for you.'

'Really?' She came closer, and then failed to hide her disappointment with the gift as I placed a battered cardboard box on the worktop. I knew that presentation was everything, but I hadn't been able to find a jewellery box in time.

'Open it,' I said.

She prodded the box with a dubious finger, like she thought something would jump out at her. She opened it and held the present in her hand. I could see her mind working: how do I tell him that I hate it?

'It's... nice,' she said, trying to buy some time.

'Trust me, you'll love it.' I took it from her and held her hand. It was cool and soft. Just touching her sent shivers rippling through me.

I put her present on.

'That's a bit tight,' she said.

I passed her a glass of wine.

'Bring up your FU usage page.' I watched her eye and saw her other hand move as she did.

'Take a drink and tell me what happens.'

She did as she was told. 'The alcohol and calories have moved a bit. Like always.'

I pressed her wrist. 'That feels weird,' she said.

'Now take another drink.'

She took a second sip. 'The readings haven't moved,' she said. She took another, larger mouthful. 'Nothing. Where did you get it?' Her smile saddened a little. 'And what about you?'

I held my hand up to stop the questions and reached back into the cupboard. I brought down a second box. It had *'PCU Evidence'* stamped on the side. I opened the box and took out a second bracelet from the Health Bank that had *accidentally* fallen into my pocket when I got the Suppressors and Mimics for Art.

As Doris would have said – I had taken a *fucking liberty.*

With thanks...

To Rax, James, Georgie and my family and friends for all their support.

To Karyn for proving how long she could stand on tiptoe – and the next few days of aching muscles.

To Amanda, my editor at Let's Get Booked.

To Abbie at Pilcrow Proofreading.

To the *TrashFiction* crew for all the support and jokes: Marwa Ayad, Steph Cleary, Esther Eley, Patricia Marques Guerreiro, Nadine Matheson, Luke Morris, Satu Pietila, Amber Raven, Jonathan Richards, Kerry Baptiste.

To my tutors and markers during the City University Crime MA course: Laura Wilson, Claire McGowan, Angela Clarke, Stav Sharez and William Ryan.

Dear Reader,

Thank you for reading Proximity. I hope you found its blend of crime thriller and near future both plausible and thought provoking. Where is your perfect balance of 'free will' versus 'for the greater good'? Where do you see our world going? I would love to hear your views.

If you enjoyed the story, I'd be extremely grateful if you would write a review. Getting feedback from readers is extremely rewarding and also helps persuade others to pick up one of my books for the first time.

For news about the next in the series, please visit me at my website - www.jemtugwell.com or join me on Twitter @JemTugwell.

All the best,

Jem